THE
BLESSED
BONES

BOOKS BY KATHRYN CASEY

The Fallen Girls
Her Final Prayer

THE SARAH ARMSTRONG MYSTERY SERIES
Singularity
Blood Lines
The Killing Storm
The Buried

TRUE CRIME
Evil Beside Her
She Wanted It All
A Warrant to Kill
Die, My Love
Shattered
A Descent Into Hell
Deadly Little Secrets
Murder, I Write
Possessed
Deliver Us
In Plain Sight

Kathryn Casey

THE
BLESSED
BONES

bookouture

Published by Bookouture in 2021

An imprint of Storyfire Ltd.
Carmelite House
50 Victoria Embankment
London EC4Y 0DZ

www.bookouture.com

Written by Kathryn Casey

ISBN: 978-1-80019-370-3
eBook ISBN: 978-1-80019-369-7

For my brothers and sisters-in-law: Mike, Jan, John, Linda, Jim and Kate. For all the good memories; hoping for many more to come.

CHAPTER ONE

The bindings on her arms and legs cut into her skin and prevented her from rolling over. Tied as she was to the bed's metal railings, she had no choice but to lie flat, but to do so made the small of her back ache and the muscles in her sides complain. Periodically, the pains came, rippling through her. Hard. When they did, she prayed they would end. They left her spent and covered in sweat.

How long had she lain like this, helpless and frightened? She thought hours, but it felt like days. Why had this happened to her? Looking back, she'd made mistakes, but at the time…

It had started when she'd trusted the boy. That one night with him had set everything in motion, the turn of events that led to the evening she'd made a tragic decision. *I never should have left with the stranger,* she thought, not for the first time. *I should have known better.*

The drug coursed through her, again sending her body into throbbing spasms, each moment feeling like an eternity. When blessed relief finally came, the agony left her weak and delirious, struggling to focus. In a haze, her memory drifted back to the last time she'd seen her father, that afternoon at the bus depot.

As they stood at the counter, she'd protested: "But I don't want to go. Why do I have to?"

"Be quiet," her father had whispered. "I'll talk to you when I'm done here."

"Why are you doing this?" she'd asked, her voice timid. "Can't I just—"

"No. You can't." A lean, sallow man, he had a mop of brown hair that fell crooked over his forehead. Quickly, he'd returned his attention to the old man behind the counter. "I need a one-way ticket to Denver."

"That'll be sixty-two dollars," the clerk had said.

Petite, small for her age, the teenager's most striking feature was her eyes, a remarkable shade of violet. Her long prairie dress hung limply on her slender body with the exception of around her belly, where a careful observer might have noticed a round bulge. Nervous, her hands were shaking and her stomach had roiled with a bad case of indigestion. At least she'd stopped throwing up. For weeks, she hadn't been able to figure out what was wrong with her. Although frightened, she'd kept her worry to herself, telling no one. Then her father had cornered her, telling her he'd heard about her and the boy from someone who'd seen them together—unchaperoned in the woods. A few hours later, he'd told her that she was taking a trip.

After he purchased the bus ticket, her father shuffled to the side to get out of the way of the others in line. The girl tracked behind, asking, "Aren't you going with me?"

"No, of course not. Why would I do that?"

Her pulse drummed in her ears. "But I don't know anyone in Denver. What will I do there?"

Furrowing his brow, her father shook his head. "I explained this to you."

"Do my mothers know what you're doing?"

She'd asked that question before, and he hadn't answered. He didn't again. Instead, he glared at her. "You know what you did. We can't—"

"But I—" Tears began to flow, and the stomachache she'd been fighting crawled up her throat, making her feel as if she would gag. "What am I supposed to do?"

At that, her father pulled a sheet of paper out of his pocket and handed it to her. "Here, look. There's a shelter in Denver for girls like you, ones who have strayed."

She gulped back sour phlegm. "Father, I—"

"This is not a discussion. This is my wish. Remember what the prophet teaches: A father is to be obeyed."

At that, she wiped her nose with her dress sleeve, but her tears flowed so hard and fast she gave up trying to stop them. "I'll obey you, Father. I promise. Let me come home, and I'll be a good girl. You'll see."

It sent a knife of pain through her when he muttered, "You can never come home. Never."

"Father, I…"

"You made a grave mistake, one that would disgrace our family if others knew. Your mothers and I would become the subject of gossip and ridicule."

"But…"

Her father stared down at her and she recognized the same look he'd had on his face a year earlier when she'd watched him slaughter a pig for Sunday dinner. The girl had raised it from a piglet, poured her love into it, sleeping on a mound of hay beside it when it was sick. She'd pleaded with her father to spare it, but he'd raised the rifle to the pig's head and pulled the trigger. She'd heard the boom and saw the blood and brain tissue spatter across the ground.

"Your bus leaves for Denver in two hours," her father said, with as little emotion as if he'd been dropping her off at school. She began to object, when he hissed, "Do you think I don't have eyes? That I cannot see what has happened to you?"

"No. I—"

"In Denver, hire a taxi to take you to the shelter. Ask the people there for help." Her father had a slight smirk on his face, one she interpreted as contempt for what she'd become. "Tell them that you are with child."

"Father, please," she pleaded, but ignoring the pain in his young daughter's cry, he turned and walked away. The girl waited, hoping he'd return, but eventually shuffled over to a gray plastic chair near the front, one where she could hear the speaker announcing departures. She leaned back in the chair. Eventually, she nodded off.

When she awoke, a man was sitting beside her, in jeans and a black sportscoat. He had the newspaper open. She assessed the clock on the wall, then looked at her ticket. She'd missed her bus. Panicked, unsure what to do, she couldn't stop the tears from again streaming down her cheeks. The man with the newspaper glanced over at her.

"Are you okay?"

Her parents had told her to never talk to strangers, but they weren't there, and she needed someone to confide in. "My father bought me a ticket to Denver. I missed my bus."

"Ah. That is bad luck," the man said. "Why Denver?"

She pulled out the sheet of paper with the name and address of the youth shelter printed on it and showed it to him.

"Why is your father sending you there?"

"I-I was bad, and now I'm having a baby."

The man nodded, as if he understood. "You don't have to go all the way to Denver. I know of a place that's closer, one where they help girls in trouble."

The girl thought about that. The bus was gone, and she didn't know when another would come. The ticket counter had closed for the night, and outside the sky had turned black. She thought of her mothers, her brothers and sisters. Her stomach empty and bitter, she considered how the house smelled with dinner and pictured her mothers clucking in the kitchen as they cleared the plates. She wondered if they'd be upset. If they would miss her.

The man watched her, but when she remained silent, he stood, as if ready to leave. "Good luck."

The girl's gaze traveled across the nearly deserted bus station. Once he left, she'd be alone, except for a scruffy man in a stained raincoat who sat in the corner mumbling to himself. She looked up at the man, wondering what she should do.

Choking back the little voice in her head that whispered not to, she asked, "Mister, would the people at that place you know about, the shelter that's closer, help me?"

The girl had second thoughts when the man smiled at her. Something about the way his lips curled up ever so slightly at the corners made her shiver. "Yes, I'm sure they would," he said. She saw a spark of excitement in his eyes when he asked, "Do you want me to take you there?"

Later, tied to the bed, in the fog of a dream, the girl shook her head and muttered: "No! No! Don't go with him. No!"

That realization came only in hindsight and far too late to save her.

CHAPTER TWO

The day had slipped away. I'd been holed up in the musty room at the back of the station since early morning, seated at a long, library-style table. Above me the yellowed ceiling tiles were stained a sickly brown from a long-forgotten leak. Over the years, water had dripped and eaten away a patch of varnish, leaving a jagged scar on the tabletop's dark wood. Despite the roof's repair, the space felt dank, and it smelled of the aging paperwork it held. Kept under lock and key, the cell-like room had walls lined with metal cabinets. Inside were files, many of which went back decades. After long hours cloistered in this forgotten slice of the Alber police station, I'd come to call it "the Tombs."

On top of the battered table, I'd positioned a dozen stacks of files categorized by types of crimes, all cold cases.

Maybe that wasn't the right way to describe them.

A cold case suggested that these were crimes that had been investigated but remained unsolved. In truth, the matters chronicled in these reports had never been pursued. They were deposited there like corpses buried in unmarked graves. The file cabinets were akin to caskets, never intended to be reopened, their contents destined to molder away.

To comprehend why these cases were abandoned, one had to appreciate the strange milieu of my hometown. Founded more than a hundred years ago in a high valley tucked into the mountains, Alber, Utah, was the home of Elijah's People, a fundamentalist

Mormon sect that practiced polygamy. An insular society, our religion ruled our world. As true believers, we adhered to the strict edicts of our prophets, most recently an octogenarian named Emil Barstow. In town it had always been an open secret that rather than fairly enforcing laws, Alber's police department did the bidding of Barstow and others in the faith's hierarchy. Those in good standing with the prophet could count on not being held accountable for their actions. The police ignored injustices, the suffering of innocent men, women and—all too often—children, at the behest of the men in power.

In the past few years, Alber had changed. Since his conviction for marrying off underage girls to older men, our illustrious prophet resided in a federal prison cell. Foreclosures had lured outsiders in search of bargains, and the wall of secrecy that isolated the town from the secular world had begun to crumble.

Sadly, those changes came too late for nearly all the cases chronicled in the reports on the table before me.

In law enforcement, we are bound by strict rules. Among the most important are statutes of limitations, the finite periods after crimes are committed in which they are eligible for prosecution. In Utah, those statutes limited the prosecutions of nearly all crimes—with only a few exceptions, like murder—to four years. So although the files held accounts of not only run-of-the-mill robberies and vandalism but domestic violence, child abuse, and assaults, if they occurred one day more than four years ago, I couldn't do a thing about them.

That had made my examination of the files maddening. While my heart broke for the victims, my hands were tied.

The unfairness was hard for me to stomach. Especially in this case, the one I held in my hand.

The manila folder had a name written in blue ink on the tab: Danny Benson. I couldn't place Danny, but I knew his family. I may have only taken over as chief of police nine months earlier, but I'd spent the first twenty-four years of my life in Alber. Danny's dad, Clyde, ran a service station on the highway outside town. A big, beefy, roughhouse-looking guy in his fifties, Clyde always had someone's old clunker up on the lift and habitually wore smears of black grease on his uniforms. These days, when I'd had no time for lunch, I popped in and filled my Suburban with gas, then grabbed a Baby Ruth or a Mars Bar out of a bin Clyde kept stocked next to the register.

Not being able to place Danny bothered me.

It was true that with more than four thousand residents, I couldn't know everyone in town, but I thought I should have heard of Danny at some point. I'd not only been born and raised in Alber; I'd taught elementary school here for four years.

Despite my deep roots, my return had been a hard transition.

Alber wasn't the kind of town that welcomed outsiders with open arms, and most of the locals saw me as infinitely worse than a mere interloper. Although I'd grown up as one of Elijah's People, I was an apostate who'd abandoned their beloved beliefs. In the eyes of the faithful, that made me a traitor. I was so mistrusted, so unwanted, that last fall there'd been a series of protests on the streets surrounding the police station. Although the demonstrations eventually ended, the bad feelings never waned. I had a stack of anonymous notes in my desk that warned me against staying. All through the winter they'd arrived, one or two a month. In the beginning they'd been slipped through a crack in the station's front door. Once we installed a surveillance camera, the letters arrived via the mail. All were in pink envelopes and scented with vanilla, marked personal and addressed to me: Chief of Police Clara Jefferies. Whoever she was, the writer didn't mince her words.

LEAVE NOW BEFORE THINGS GET BAD FOR YOU.

Whether or not the majority of townsfolk wanted me around, I'd decided to stay. Maybe part of it was pride. All I knew was that when I left Alber—if I left—it would be on *my* terms. I had no intention of allowing anyone to chase me out, not like last time. And for however long I remained, I would do my best.

That meant I would do what I could for the forgotten victims whose complaints had been buried in the Tombs.

All the folder before me contained was Danny Benson's picture and the one-page report that accompanied it. Nothing else. The photo was of an impish-looking four-year-old with a bowl cut the color of tarnished brass and eyes that pinched in close at the corners above his nose. At least, one of them did. The other eye was nearly swollen shut, black, blue, and had to be painful.

The sixteen-year-old statement was signed by one of Danny's older sisters, Lynlee. At the time, she was twelve. "Dad doesn't hit the rest of us but he goes after Danny," the girl had told the reporting officer. "This time, he got Danny in the eye, but a while back his whole backside was bruised."

I read that line a few more times. Looked at the photo of the kid. And I felt my pulse build from a stroll to a sprint, the anger birthing a hard, undigestible lump in my throat. *Clyde hits Danny a lot,* I mentally paraphrased. *That's what she's saying.*

I turned the sheet over, hoping something would be scrawled on the back, but as in all the other abandoned cases, the boxes that were to be checked as each step of an investigation was concluded and the sections for comments remained empty.

Looking at the date again, I muttered, "Damn, if they'd only looked into this earlier... It's way too late. Way past the cutoff." I started to slip the photo back in the file so I could place it on top of one of the stacks. Then, I hesitated.

For some reason, I couldn't take my eyes off Danny's face. Suddenly I realized why: he reminded me of a kid in Dallas, one

I'd encountered during my ten years as a cop there. That boy had been named Austin.

We'd been called in by protective services regarding a complaint made by a school nurse. Austin had arrived at kindergarten with a black eye and bruises. When the nurse examined him, she found older, faded bruises on his body. The day we rang Austin's doorbell, we had a doctor with us who examined the kid. While he did, Austin's parents swore up and down that their son's injuries had come from a fall down the stairs. The doc ruled the cause undetermined. "I can't say the parents did or didn't do this."

When I asked what had happened, how he got hurt, Austin said, "My daddy didn't hit me."

Having no evidence to move forward, we left. Two days later, Austin's dad rushed him to the emergency room. The kid's mother had beaten him to death.

I stared at Danny's photo again and shook my head. "Nowhere to go with this," I whispered. "It's too late." I'd nearly put the photo down when I reconsidered. I thought about how families tended to be large in Alber and I wondered: *What if Clyde had other children he was mistreating?* That didn't seem far-fetched. And in that instant, I knew that despite the roadblocks, I had to find a way to get justice for Danny, and I had to make sure the Bensons' other children were safe.

But how?

It took a few minutes to get Smith County's district attorney, Jack Hatfield, on the phone. A former first assistant in the office, he'd taken over the top slot a few months earlier. Whispers pegged Hatfield as a straight shooter. So far, I hadn't had a lot of firsthand experiences to judge him by, which was a good thing. We'd had the usual minor offenses in Alber: traffic citations, biting dogs, neighbors squabbling, a few minor thefts. But nothing more serious had happened in the five months since last November's murders at the Johansson bison ranch. I still felt sick every time I thought of that crime scene: two women and two children slaughtered; three victims' bodies underneath a bloody sheet; and in an upstairs bedroom, Laurel Johansson with her throat cut.

That Laurel was the daughter of Jeff Mullins, my lead detective, made the case even more haunting. But it was the gruesomeness of the scene that was imprinted on my mind. The stuff of nightmares, it popped up at times when I was half asleep at night. It came back when I drove through town and saw little kids with dark hair like Sybille and Benjamin. Every day for the rest of my life, I would picture their lifeless bodies on the cold ground.

People shouldn't do bad stuff to kids; it just wasn't right.

I glanced at Danny Benson's photo again and thought of his dad, those big meaty hands of his, and I considered the damage they could do to a four-year-old. "How old is Danny now?" District Attorney Hatfield asked, after I laid out the allegations of abuse in the old file.

I rechecked the birthdate in the file. "He turned twenty last month, in early March."

The DA sounded interested but concerned when he asked, "A lot of times, once they grow up, kids don't want to revisit this old stuff. They've moved on. Does Danny want to press charges?"

Tough question. Hatfield had a point. I'd had child abuse and domestic violence cases where victims refused to cooperate with police. That so many years had passed made it even more doubtful. I had to be honest. I didn't have an inkling of what Danny would want. "Haven't asked him yet. I haven't even talked to him. Before I do—if I do—Mr. Hatfield, I want to know what our options are, if we have any."

Silence, as I assumed the prosecutor was thinking through the case.

"The photo looks pretty bad?"

"It does. And the report suggests this wasn't an isolated incident," I said.

Again Hatfield paused. A moment passed, and he said, "Chief, I'm sorry, but I don't see how we can. It's just too old."

Disappointed, I thought about that. I'd expected the answer but didn't like it. Something had been percolating in my brain, perhaps an unlikely but a possible option. "Well, you know, sometimes this type of recurring physical abuse of a child is tied to sexual abuse."

Hatfield paused, as if considering. "That's true, but there's no indication in the file that—"

"Mr. Hatfield, hear me out. What if I find the kid, get him to talk, and try to find out if there was any sexual abuse. Then the statute of limitations is longer. Right?"

"Well, yes. But there's nothing there that suggests sexual abuse, is there?" Hatfield asked.

"No, but it wouldn't be out of the question. We both know that sometimes they're related."

I heard Hatfield sigh. "Well, it could be, Chief."

"I'm just suggesting that—"

"But you need to be careful," Hatfield cautioned. "You can't nudge him to remember something that didn't happen."

"Of course not," I said, not surprised at his warning but disappointed that he thought he had to say it. With childhood matters, there'd been studies about the dangers of implanting false memories. Cases had been tried, folks convicted, only to find out that there'd been no crime, only untrue recollections that came from suggestions made by unskilled therapists and cops. "I know how to question Danny, to find out what happened without tainting what he remembers. I've worked my share of child sex abuse cases over the years."

"Okay. Good. No offense, Chief, but we have to be careful."

"So you're okay with that? I'll track Danny down and needle around a bit, and if there's a case there, you'll take the charges?" I wanted to be firm that we both understood that I was prepared to take the case all the way to a jury if we had the opportunity.

"Right. Utah's statute of limitations for sexual abuse of a minor is ten years after they reach adulthood. So Danny is well within that time frame," Hatfield advised. "If Clyde sexually abused Danny and he wants to pursue it, we can file charges."

I wondered how Danny would react when I showed up and poked around, dug up what had to be a painful past. But then I looked at the photo and thought about the hell the kid must have lived through. And again, I thought about the other Benson children and worried about what they might be enduring. "Okay. I'll give it a shot. Seems like Clyde shouldn't have gotten away with this. Seems like a guy like this might have done a lot more damage than what shows up in a picture."

"Let me know," Hatfield said, and then he hung up.

Just then our main dispatcher, Kellie, stuck her head in the door. In the past few weeks she'd given herself something of a style makeover. She hadn't said why, but I had happened upon her in the breakroom engaged in a rather friendly conversation with one of our young cops, Bill Conroy. When Kellie had started at the station last fall, she'd showed up in baggy sweaters and jeans. Today she had on a tight pink T-shirt with a sparkly heart on the front, and she wore a pair of skinny black pants that showed off her delicate ankles above a pair of strappy heels.

"You busy, Chief?" she asked.

"Just finishing up. Do you need me?"

"You have two civilians in your office."

"Who?" I asked.

Kellie smiled and said only, "You'll see."

I gave her a questioning glance, but she turned away and I heard her giggle as she rounded the corner.

"Mother doesn't know that we're here," my sister Lily warned me. "You won't tell her, will you?"

Both the girls had jumped up and rushed toward me, wrapped their arms around my waist. Lily had stopped in twice before, a month earlier, skipping the bus ride home after school and walking so our mother wouldn't find out. On those afternoons, she'd filled me in on how our family was doing, told me about siblings I'd never met. This time she'd brought another sister with her, Delilah. They felt like heaven in my arms, like love and warmth and family. This was a pleasure I'd been denied for too much of my life. The two of them squeezed me so hard that the Colt in my holster bit into my hip.

It had been a long time since I'd looked like them in their long prairie dresses, their hair in curls falling from topknots. I glanced down and saw their socked feet strapped into thick sandals. With her dark hair and eyes, her pale complexion, Lily was a near-identical version of me at sixteen. I had only a few old photos of myself, having left everything behind when I fled, but I did have one to compare, and our resemblance was uncanny. In contrast, Delilah had our father's chin, but she'd inherited her mother's auburn hair and blue eyes. While Lily had begun to look more like a woman, at barely thirteen Delilah still had the innocence of a child. When I considered what had happened to her a year earlier, what the outcome could have been, it was remarkable that she appeared to have survived undamaged.

"Will Mother be looking for you?" As glad as I was to see them, I wasn't sure how to answer Lily's question. "I don't want to get you two in trouble, but I don't want Mother to worry either."

Lily shook her head. "It's okay. She thinks we're stopping at the park on the way home. So she isn't expecting us."

I understood how protective my mother was. When you've seen what I have, it's hard not to project the worst. At times, I drive down the streets and see little kids, on bikes all by themselves. I slow down, follow them, probably scare the heck out of them, but I keep on their tails until they get where they're going. I know the names of too many children and teenagers who never showed up after school, women who disappeared off of lonely streets at night. And my sisters not telling our mothers what they were doing? That could be risky. "Lily, like I said last time, it's not good to lie to our mothers. You girls need to make sure someone knows where you are, to keep you safe."

At that, Delilah wrinkled up her freckled nose and gave me a knowing glance. "It's okay, Clara. I told my mom we were visiting you." She said it with just a hint of conspiracy in her voice. "But like Lily said, Mother Ardeth doesn't need to know. Does she?"

The prospect that Delilah's mother knew they'd come to visit me and hadn't tried to stop them surprised me. "Mother Sariah knows you're here? Really?"

"Well, Delilah said she told her, and—" Lily started, giving me a wary glance.

"But she said we can't stay too, too long," Delilah concluded, her voice firm, as if that brought the matter to rest. She looked wired, as if her adrenaline had kicked in with the thought of spending time with her renegade sister, the town's chief of police. Looking at her, I broke into what had to be my first grin of the day. I'd wanted this for so long, any opportunity to reconnect with my family.

Still, I wondered. Mother Sariah had whisked Delilah away from me the last time I'd been brazen enough to drop in at our family's trailer. Could she really be okay with a visit? I gave my younger sister a doubtful glance. "The truth, Delilah. Your mother knows that you're here, and she didn't mind?"

At this, she looked at Lily, looked at me, looked at Lily again. "Well, kind of."

"In what way, kind of?" I pushed.

"I told her we were coming and that she couldn't tell Mother Ardeth, that I was going to see you if she liked it or not," Delilah said, sounding a bit embarrassed but at the same time proud. "I told her that you are my hero, and I needed to see you."

Touched, I took a step back. My family didn't condone children speaking up. Even teenagers were expected to bow to authority. "And Mother Sariah said…"

Delilah looked at Lily again, who took over the explanation. "Mother Sariah said that if we were coming, she was glad to know where we would be, that we weren't sneaking off without telling her."

"But she wasn't happy about it?" I asked.

The girls grudgingly shook their heads. "Not really," Lily said. "But it's okay. We'll probably get some extra chores tonight, but we can handle it."

I didn't argue. I couldn't. After all these months of being home in Alber but still cut out of my family, it felt like a major victory, if not of the war, of a battle. Voicing no more concerns, I raided the vending machine for drinks and snacks and spent the next half hour listening while my visitors talked about school, their teachers, and one of our youngest sisters, Kaylynn, who it appeared at five was developing a devilish sense of defiance and driving Mother Naomi to distraction.

When I had an opening, I asked Lily, "Are you still helping Mother with her herbal potions and only going to school three days a week?"

To my disappointment she said that she was, but she didn't seem to mind. "I'd like to go every day, but I'm keeping up by studying at home at night. And Mother really needs me, Clara." Lily looked troubled, as if a cloud passed overhead that threatened a dangerous storm. "Mother looks kind of sick lately."

I considered how, when I'd last caught a glimpse of our mother at the grocery store a couple of months earlier, she'd appeared to have aged over the winter. Her stoop had become even more pronounced, her hair whiter. Her skin had a tinge of yellow. Only in her mid-fifties, Mother could have passed for decades older. Life hadn't been kind to her, and even in better times many of the women like Mother, those who'd had many children, didn't seem to live to old age. Our family had already lost one mother, Constance, years earlier to cancer.

I wanted to ask more questions, but at that Kellie again poked her blond curls into the office and peered at me. "Chief," she said, "can you come out here a minute?"

I smiled at the girls. "I'll be right back."

I joined Kellie a few steps from the door; I wondered why she hadn't buzzed me, but then realized it must be something she didn't want the girls to hear. Whispering, she bent toward me. "There's a grave," she said, her young brow rippled. "Mostly bones."

"Where?" I asked. My pulse had kicked in as soon as she mentioned a buried body. I'd been looking for a teenage girl off and on since not long after I'd arrived home, someone I suspected had been killed by a serial killer. Since last August, I'd been digging up the forests and fields around Alber, searching for Christina Bradshaw without success. What if someone else had stumbled upon her grave? What were the odds that it would be her?

And if it wasn't her, who was it?

"On the mountainside. Where they're building the ski lift," Kellie explained. "The construction foreman called it in and the sheriff's department got the dispatch. The foreman said they uncovered a human skeleton."

"Any other information? Male? Female? Height? Any details?"

"Just that it's nearly all bone. The guy thinks it's a woman because he can see some of what looks like a dress. Chief Deputy Max Anderson is on his way, and he called and asked me to notify you. He thought it might interest you, because of the Bradshaw girl. He suggested you meet him at the site."

"Good," I said, my pulse racing at the possibility. Perhaps this would be the day the last of the questions about that old case would be answered. Perhaps I could finally put it behind me. One less puzzle to wake me up in the middle of the night, then pick at my brain and keep me from falling back asleep.

"Get the location," I instructed Kellie. "I'll send my sisters on their way then head up there."

"You've got it, Chief."

As she walked away, I stepped back into my office. I didn't want to rush Lily and Delilah off, but I had work to do. They were just finishing their sodas and snacks. When I told them something had come up and I had to leave, they both frowned. "Do you girls want a ride? I'm heading toward the mountain. I can drop you off close to home."

Lily shook her head, adamant. "No, we'd better not. Someone might see us."

"If Mother Ardeth found out…" Delilah started, then raised her eyebrows in terror.

"Sure, I understand," I said, trying not to show the hurt I felt at being rejected by my own mother, so ostracized that my sisters had to hide that they'd seen me. Still, I didn't have time for bruised feelings. I grabbed Danny Benson's file off my desk and followed them out. They dropped their soda cans into the recycle bin, hugged me and turned to leave. As they marched toward the door, I thought of what Lily had said about my mother's condition, how she didn't look well, and I called them back.

"One thing." I focused on Delilah and said, "Would you ask Mother Sariah to get in touch with me? Tell her I have something I need to talk to her about. Okay?"

Delilah scrunched her lips to the side and appeared apprehensive, as if this wasn't a good thing. "Is it bad, like about us coming here, that we're bothering you or something?"

"No!" I closed the distance between us and gathered them to me, grateful for one more embrace. "Absolutely not. Nothing like that. I love to see you. I hope you come again, and that someday I get to meet our other brothers and sisters, to have time, real time together."

"Then what do you want to talk to my mom about?" She appeared uneasy, as if she suspected that I didn't want to be upfront with her and Lily.

I hesitated, unsure. Delilah was right. I didn't want to spell it out. In my experience with my mother, I knew how set in her ways, how unyielding she could be. She wouldn't like what I had to say to Mother Sariah. I had greater odds of success if I could promise Mother Sariah that no one else knew what I asked of her, that there was no way my mother could discover what I planned. But I put on a smile, as happy a face as I could muster, and I assured Delilah, "I just want to say thank you, to tell her how much I enjoyed seeing you two. There's nothing for you to worry about."

That seemed to answer any questions for Lily, who'd been listening quietly. She grabbed our sister's hand. "Come on, Delilah. Clara is busy, and we have to get home before my mom starts asking questions." The girls linked arms and turned to leave, and Lily shot me a final glance over her shoulder.

I waved and kept my position. I had to leave, but I wanted those brief moments to enjoy, watching my sisters walk arm in arm. The door slammed behind them, and I lingered ever so briefly. No matter what else took place this day, something good had happened.

When I turned back to the dispatch desk, Kellie assessed me with sympathy, as if she sensed how hard it had been for me to say goodbye to the girls. I took a deep breath, composed myself, certain Kellie saw more on my face than I'd intended to reveal.

"So we have a grave," I said.

"We have remains. I called it a grave, but I'm not sure exactly what it is. Although I guess so. Sounds like some girl was buried up there. Should I tell them you're on your way?"

"Absolutely, but first, where's Mullins?" I'd scanned the office and all of my crew's desks were empty. This time of day, that's the way they were supposed to be, everyone out on patrol or taking care of business.

"He's taking a report," Kellie said. "Sylvie Barr called nine-one-one upset because the Reingolds' cows broke through the fence and laid down to sun on the road. She couldn't get out of her driveway to pick up the kids after school. Mr. Barr wasn't home, and Sylvie's sister-wife had to push one cow to get it to move. It kicked her. "

"Is she hurt?"

"Not bad. But Sylvie was fuming."

"I bet." I thought of Sylvie Barr's staunch manner and carefully coifed hairdos and considered that she wasn't known in town for having an even temper. "Well, let's not disturb Detective Mullins, then. I think he probably has enough to deal with. Who else is around? I have something I need to have checked on."

"No one, really," Kellie said. "They're all on patrol. One officer is helping the crossing guard over at the school. They've had a problem with folks not heeding the stop sign. Do you want me to bump one of the others for you?"

I considered the options. "No. But when Stef gets back to the station, tell her to call me," I said, referring to Stephanie Jonas, who'd moved up from dispatcher to rookie cop over the past months. She was finishing an associate's degree in forensic sciences at the community college in Pine City. Two days a week I gave her afternoons off to wrap up her classes. "I have something for her to do."

"Sure, Chief," Kellie said.

"And give her this folder." I handed Kellie the Danny Benson paperwork.

"Got it." With that, Kellie handed me a map she'd printed of the location where the construction crew had unearthed the remains. "The medical examiner and CSI folks have been dispatched?" I assumed they had but wanted to be certain.

"Doc Wiley and Lieutenant Mueller and his team are on their way. And Deputy Chief Anderson will meet you there."

I sized up the map and made a mental note of the best roads to take, then turned to leave. As I did, I considered where my route up the mountain would take me: past a place I'd avoided since my return to Alber, one that held the most painful of memories.

CHAPTER THREE

As Max slid into the squad, he glanced at the backseat and realized that he'd forgotten to throw his canvas bag in the trunk. The sight of it brought a smile as he recalled the days before. He and Clara had met at the mountain cabin his friend loaned them off and on. Max thought briefly that someone might see the duffle and wonder where he'd been, and he considered stowing it in the trunk. Then he decided he didn't care. He wasn't the one who was keeping it secret. *How much longer,* he wondered, *before we let everyone know that we're together?*

He'd brought it up over dinner that first evening at the cabin. She'd simmered a thick marinara and poured it over pasta and Italian sausage. It surprised him that Clara was a good cook; it wasn't something he would have expected. She'd been blunt about the fact that she'd never been much of a housekeeper. When Clara hadn't responded to his suggestion that they stop being so secretive, he'd added, "I'd like to talk to Brooke about us. I'm worried that she'll find out somehow, from someone else."

At that, Clara twirled a long strand of pasta on her fork and, to his deep disappointment, shook her head. Max couldn't understand why. He knew that Brooke, his nine-year-old daughter, adored Clara. And from everything Max saw, he felt sure that Clara returned Brooke's affection. When they were together, Clara chuckled like a teenager. The two of them had taken to pulling practical jokes on him, like the day they hid his tennis shoes when he and Clara were going on a run; Max had spent half an hour searching and found them on the second-floor balcony.

A couple of times, Clara had even stepped in for Max's sister, Alice, who cared for Brooke while he worked. On a day when Alice had a sick kid of her own to watch over, Clara picked Brooke up from school and took her to physical therapy. Max had arrived home to find the two of them on the living room floor, Clara guiding Brooke's exercises, designed to build her upper-body strength and help her get in and out of her wheelchair.

Still, even in front of Brooke—especially in front of her—Clara insisted that she and Max act like friends, nothing more.

"Why are we hiding?" he had asked that evening at the cabin over dinner.

"Because folks will gossip. They already consider me an outcast. I don't want them tittering about my personal life."

"Why would they titter? We're both single. We're free to do as we please, aren't we?"

"Not necessarily in Alber." Clara had sighed, appearing troubled.

"I know, but—" Max abruptly stopped talking. Anything he said, he worried, might sound selfish. He knew her situation in town hadn't been good. She'd tried to act as if the previous fall's protests didn't worry her, but he knew otherwise. He'd seen the discord in her family firsthand, the pain it caused Clara that her mothers kept her at arm's length. And she'd confided enough so that he had no doubt that the marriage her father and mother had forced her into—the one that left her fleeing for her life—had been a nightmare. But while he empathized with her situation, he'd hoped that they could move past it.

Worry lines creased Max's brow as Clara shook her head again, this time as if trying to dislodge a bad memory. Her voice had sounded raspy, strong emotions tearing at the edges. "Max, people talk. People in Alber can be judgmental and…"

Clara hesitated, and Max finished her sentence. "Cruel."

Clara had nodded, then put her head down and stabbed a piece of sausage and cut off a thin slice. She'd stopped the fork halfway to her mouth and heaved a sigh. "I hadn't wanted to say anything, but I'm still getting those notes. The ones telling me to leave."

Looking at Clara, he could see how that troubled her. It worried him, too, but it did no good to admit that. It would only make her more anxious. Max chewed on a forkful of pasta and again thought of the protesters, the tension in Alber, the candles flickering the night they surrounded the police station and the hateful signs they carried. He thought of the notes she'd shown him a few months earlier, with their veiled threats. "I think it'll probably go away," he'd said, only half believing his own words. "They've been coming for a long time now, and no one has done anything. Whoever is sending them will eventually give up."

"How can you be sure?" she'd asked, and he didn't have an answer. He had no way of being certain, or of knowing who the person was, although he'd been investigating without telling her. A week earlier, Max had talked a clerk at the Pine City post office into letting him view surveillance tapes. He hadn't told Clara, but he thought he saw someone mail an envelope like those that contained the notes. From the pink stationery and the vanilla scent, they'd presumed it would be a woman, and it was, but she didn't look as he'd expected. He and Clara had talked of it often, and they'd felt certain it was a local, someone from Alber, one of the followers of Elijah's People. But instead of a prairie dress, this woman wore jeans and tennis shoes, a hoodie that she'd let fall over her forehead then tied up to her chin, and sunglasses. He couldn't see enough of her face to identify her.

"Are you still submitting them to the crime lab for fingerprinting?"

"Not the last few," Clara admitted. "Whoever is behind this is careful. No prints on the ones I did send. I saw no reason to keep it up."

"It wouldn't hurt to try. Maybe they'll slip up." Clara nodded rather half-heartedly and returned to her pasta, and he'd felt unsure that she'd follow through. From the beginning, he thought she'd had rather a strange reaction to the notes, as if they were somehow destined to come and couldn't be stopped. No matter what he said to her, he'd been unable to change her mind. All he could do was be reassuring. "Whoever is sending them will have to give up, because you're not leaving. You've come home, and you're staying."

Clara didn't respond beyond a shrug.

Although he didn't say it, Max had thought: *Clara, you can't leave again. Not ever.*

The two of them fit together in so many ways. He felt comfortable with her, safe. They shared a history. Considering her past, that she'd been married off as a teenager to a man old enough to be her grandfather, he couldn't have blamed her if she'd been disinterested, even cold with him at times. But it turned out that while she'd never experienced physical love before their first night together, Clara craved the closeness, the excitement they shared when their bodies joined. Those hours when they held each other and talked in whispers came as close to being one person as two can ever be, left him breathless.

"Clara, I think if people saw us together, understood that we're… well… dating… I mean, that we're…" Max had stuttered, trying to decide how to say this without scaring her off. He feared that any talk of commitment might end the relationship. "Don't you think folks would be happy for us? The ones who really count, at least?"

Her lips pursed, she'd admitted, "I don't know, Max."

He'd been wondering for the past few weeks if she was holding back, waiting for him to spell out his feelings. Maybe that would make a difference. As he'd torn off a hunk of bread, he'd decided that perhaps this was the right moment. Max put down his knife and left the bread unbuttered. "Clara," he'd said, and she'd peered at him. He wasn't sure how to read her face. "I… Well, the truth is that I…"

Clara's face blanched, and Max had felt his heart thump. He couldn't finish the sentence, not with her staring at him that way, as if this wasn't a discussion she wanted to have.

"Max, it's not that I don't care for you. I do. But I need to take this one day at a time. I can't promise more."

Max had felt a pain so sharp that he thought it might be a bit of his heart breaking. He'd wanted to push her to understand, at least nudge her to see that they shouldn't miss this opportunity, but instead he held back.

Recalling that emotional conversation as he drove toward the mountains, Max felt that pain anew. He squashed it down and thought about the bones that had been found. He thought of all those mornings and weekends, cool fall and winter evenings when Clara had dug up fields around Alber looking for Christina Bradshaw. Was it her? When he first heard about the discovery, Max had wondered if the construction workers had stumbled upon a Native American burial ground. That theory evaporated when the caller said the remains were partly covered by fabric, what appeared to have once been a prairie dress. That meant it was most likely a woman from Alber or one of the other polygamous towns scattered around the mountains.

As he considered the possibilities, Max approached the halfway mark, where he'd turn off the highway onto a narrow road, barely two lanes with no shoulders. Another route had better access, but it would have taken longer. In the far distance, Max saw his destination: the scars on the mountainside, the four wide rows of trees that had been toppled, where a consortium of investors headed by a Salt Lake company were constructing a ski lift and clearing three runs.

In the silent car, the dispatcher on duty at the sheriff's office broke in on the radio. "Chief Deputy, we have a caller for you. Can we patch him through?"

"Who is it?" Max slowed down behind a pickup pulling a travel trailer. A tourist, he decided. From spring through fall they camped out in the woods. The trailer wide, the pickup veered toward the center, blocking both lanes. Max thought about switching on his siren to get past, but he decided to wait. This wasn't a scene where he had to hurry: no active shooter; no one in immediate danger; no fleeing suspect. Based on the condition of her body, whatever had happened to the woman in the grave, she'd met her fate long ago.

"The caller is the construction foreman. A guy named Jerry Cummings," the dispatcher said. "He's the same guy who called nine-one-one."

"Tell him I'm on my way. We can talk when I get there," Max said. The pickup pulled to the right, and Max assumed the driver was making room. But when he tried to pass, the trailer swayed, and Max had to pull back. The entire rig didn't look particularly steady, not stable enough to take a chance on passing.

"Chief Deputy, I explained that you'll be there soon. But Mr. Cummings is insisting that he needs to talk to you. He says it's important. What do you want me to tell him?"

Max sighed. "Put him through."

With that, an unfamiliar voice, one that sounded stressed and tired, filled the squad. Max understood. Finding human remains tended to upend anyone's day. "Chief Deputy Anderson? That you?"

"Yes, Mr. Cummings," Max said, his patience wearing ever thinner as the pickup slowed and tried to pull over again, but this time a car came barreling in the opposite direction, blocking him from passing if he'd wanted to. Max tapped the brakes to bring his speed down and the squad car barely crawled. "What can I do for you? I'll be there in fifteen minutes. Less if we get off the phone."

"I wanted to make sure you were on your way. We've got a situation up here."

"I've heard about the skeleton. That's why I'm coming. Is it something else?" *A waste of time,* Max thought.

"That's the big thing, of course," the construction foreman said. "But I'm calling because there's a guy up here, and he's asking a lot of questions and wants to see the body. So far, we've been keeping him back, but I'm not sure I can for much longer. What should we do?"

Max wondered if the others could have beat him to the scene. "If it's Doc Wiley, the medical examiner, or if Lieutenant Mueller's there with the Smith County Sheriff's crime scene unit, you can let them in. They know not to disturb the scene until I get there. Is that who you're talking about?"

"No, it's some guy named Ash Crawford," the foreman whispered into the phone, lowering his voice, presumably so those around him wouldn't hear. "Big tall guy, I'd guess in his sixties. He says you know him. That true?"

"US Marshal Ash Crawford?" Max asked, surprised. "What's he doing up there?"

"This guy's a US Marshal? He's some kind of a big-shot cop?" Sounding plainly put out, Cummings' voice rose, indignant. "Hell, if he'd shown me some ID, I wouldn't have been concerned. I wouldn't have called you. All this guy said when I told him that you were on your way was that he knows you."

"Well, I'll be," Max murmured.

"What do you want me to tell him? Is it okay if he takes a gander at the bones?"

"Shucks, I... Well..." Max wondered why Crawford hadn't flashed his badge. What was he doing on a scene so far from Salt Lake City? As top cop in the marshal's office, Crawford oversaw the entire state, but for the past decade or more he'd mainly functioned as an administrator. He sent his assistants out in the field. And showing up where a body had been found? That made no sense either. The US Marshals had defined responsibilities; they provided judicial security, searched for fugitives, and administered the federal government's witness protection program. Max had never known them to interfere in criminal investigations.

The whole thing seemed strange.

The pickup ahead of him veered off onto a slender dirt road that led to a campground, and Max pressed down harder on the gas pedal and picked up speed. "Ask him to wait for me," he told Cummings. "I'll be there in ten minutes... less. I can see the lodge up ahead now."

CHAPTER FOUR

There's this thing that happens to a cop when she thinks that a long investigation may be coming to an end. Some of it is physical, a tingle of nervous expectation. But most of it is mental, a mix of conflicting emotions: a mild euphoria at the prospect that the work she's done may have been worth it mingled with the worry that all might not come to pass.

As I drove in my black Suburban, "Alber PD" stenciled on the side along with "CALL 911" and the department's seal, a checklist flicked through my mind. I considered everything I'd done to get to this point. Ever since I'd learned that Christina Bradshaw might not have left her family voluntarily, I'd believed that she'd fallen victim to a killer. The monster I had in mind buried his victims, hence all the holes I'd dug in the fields and woods outside of Alber looking for her remains. I'd lost count of the number of times I'd gotten my shovel out, but I guessed at least two dozen over the previous eight months.

None of it mattered. All that counted was that we might have found her. If we had, I hoped to have enough evidence to investigate and finally answer all the questions about her disappearance. As important, Christina's family could say goodbye. Sadly, I'd learned that the families of murder victims rarely get true closure. What happened to their loved one imprints on their lives and changes them forever; yet there is some peace that comes with knowing. To have a missing child, a vanished husband or wife, that is an agony that never ends. If those were Christina's bones waiting for me on the mountainside, at least her family would have a funeral, a grave with a headstone, the hope that their loved one would never be forgotten.

Those feelings mingled with thoughts of Max waiting up the mountain for me. It worried me that I so looked forward to seeing him. We'd worked a handful of cases together since I'd returned. I enjoyed that as much as our dinners, his long phone calls at bedtime to talk before we fell asleep, even our weekends away. On the job, I watched his mind work, saw his responses. Even when we argued about cases I respected him. I'd never been this close to anyone before. At times, it felt as if our minds meshed. I blushed thinking about the physical intimacy, the thrill of being so close, bonding so tightly with a man. I liked that his hands felt rough running over my skin, the musk of his aftershave, the way he cupped my cheek when he kissed me.

I touched that same spot on my face. Warm. And I felt my body respond to the memory.

A bit of traffic ahead, I considered flicking on my siren and lights to speed up the drive to the scene. My hand paused on the way to the switch as my radio crackled into life.

"Chief, it's Stef," my rookie said, her voice booming through the SUV. "Kellie said you have a job for me?"

"I do. Did she give you the file?"

"Open in front of me on my desk. This kid's old man did a real job on that eye. How come they never prosecuted him? I can't find any charges, not even any investigation notes against Clyde Benson in the computer."

"This is one of the files from the Tombs." That answered everything. I didn't need to say more. Stef had been the one who first unlocked the secret room for me, so she well understood that this was a case that had been abandoned.

"Got it," she said. "Looking at the date, this is way old. Way past when we could go after this human trash for doing this. What am I doing with the folder?"

"I have an angle. May not work, but I want to give it a try. I need you to find Danny for me. I want to talk to him."

"Just find him? You want me to ask him some questions? I'd like to get this old man of his in an eight-by-eight room with bars across the front. Looks like that's where he belongs. And to think we buy our gas from this POS."

Needless to say, Stef was still in her honeymoon phase, where she thought she could take on the world. I've always liked that about a good rookie. But it could be dangerous. They need supervision and guidance so it doesn't become hubris, and she didn't have the background to interview Danny. She could taint the investigation, as District Attorney Hatfield had worried.

"Just find Danny for me, Stef. Don't talk to the kid. Don't approach him. Get contact info and give it to me. This is delicate. I'll take over once you have a location for him."

"Got it." I wasn't surprised that she sounded disappointed; I knew she ached to get into the fray. But she confirmed, "Will do, Chief."

"Thanks."

"I heard about the remains. You think that could be the Bradshaw girl?"

"Not sure. I'll call in and let Kellie know when I have more info."

"What's your ten-twenty-six?"

"I'm twenty minutes out." I was a mile away from the turnoff from the highway on to the narrow back road leading to the construction site where they were building the ski runs.

It was then that I reminded myself where this route was taking me. I'd been so excited about the possibility of recovering Christina's remains that I'd forgotten. Immediately, I tried to block it from my mind. *No time for this now,* I cautioned myself. *Keep your focus.*

As I drove, I promised myself I would keep my eyes straight ahead. But once I mounted the crest of a small rise, I couldn't resist the urge—it felt almost physical—to look over to my right. There it stood, just as I remembered it: a palatial structure covered with gray stucco, the windows bordered with dark green shutters. Three stories high, the house had four chimneys and balconies on each floor. The sister-wives' pristine cottages with their bric-a-brac fronts spread out on one side. As I passed, a dozen or more of the ranch's championship Arabians grazed in the pasture bordering the road. The arch over the closed gate was topped with the name of this sprawling compound: SECOND COMING RANCH. I involuntarily shuddered. Tense fingers strained my upper back, my neck and shoulders, and squeezed the muscles across my chest.

The compound looked as I remembered it: like a fortress.

Since my return, I'd known that one day I'd confront this. I'd dreaded it, but I hadn't anticipated such a strong physical reaction. I averted my eyes, stared straight ahead at the road and willed myself not to look at it.

"Listen, Stef, I've got to go." I heard it in my voice, the residue of old fear.

"You okay, Chief?" she asked, apparently picking up on the change. "You sound kind of strange. Is something going on?"

I cleared my throat and took a swig out of the plastic water bottle in the cup holder. Despite my best efforts, I couldn't keep from again turning to catch a glimpse of the house. I felt as drawn to it as I was repulsed by it. A wave of anxiety coursed through me; memories flooded my mind, and his rumbling voice rang in my ears. "Clara, you are a waste of a woman."

In the field where the horses foraged, a tractor hauled hay. In years past, tending the livestock had always been one of his favorite pastimes. *That couldn't be him,* I thought. *He's too old. But maybe—*

"Chief!" Stef interrupted my thoughts. "Are you okay?"

"Yes." My voice sounded hollow in my ears, fighting the other voices, the ones out of my past that sent shivers through my soul.

"I'm okay, just distracted, looking for the cutoff to the access road for the ski lodge."

"You need directions?"

"No. I see it now. Up ahead. I'm making the turn in a few minutes."

"You're sure that you're okay?"

I must have sounded truly off for Stef to be so concerned. "Yes. I'm fine. Bump the chief deputy and tell him that I'll be there in fifteen minutes or less."

"Will do." And the radio silenced.

The Second Coming disappeared behind me, but the flashbacks continued: the massive table in a dining room big enough to be a banquet hall, the women buzzing around feeding the children, tending to the men, while our husband shouted orders.

A horn blared, and in the rearview mirror I glimpsed the CSU trailer, the crew letting me know they were following me to the scene. I took the narrow road that led to where the ski lodge was taking shape just below the mountain's slope. I thought of the trees that had been cut down to make room for the building, the lift, the runs. Some were a hundred years old or more, and they were felled like twigs then scavenged for their wood. Probably taken to the lumber mill my father ran until his death, the one my brother Aaron now owned. I thought of myself as a teenager in my dresses, and the day my father put my young, smooth hand in the cold palm of a man entering the final decades of his life.

"That's old news. This is who I am now. A cop. A police chief," I muttered, glancing again in the mirror and seeing the crime scene unit make the turn behind me. *I am not that girl anymore. I am not the young woman who ran in fear. I am no longer powerless. And I have no reason to be afraid.*

CHAPTER FIVE

I hadn't been on the construction site before, although I'd heard rumors about the grand plans. The millions being invested to turn the mountainside into a resort was the talk of Alber. While some folks lauded the prosperity it could bring, the descendants of the original settlers, members of Elijah's People, balked at the prospect of even more outsiders flooding their town. Up close, the lodge didn't look particularly impressive, although I'd heard that it would have a hundred guest rooms.

The front of the building, a primitive, rough timber structure, resembled the Ponderosa from *Bonanza,* that sixties western where Ben Cartwright raised his three sons. When I was a kid our father and mothers monitored what we watched. We had one TV in the house, but it wasn't used for anything but videos. Many were church-related, recordings of the prophet's talks to the faithful. Two evenings a week, we sat in the living room on the big couches and watched what the church hierarchy billed as "inspirational messages." One I remember was a long, confused missive, extolling the virtue of living the Divine Principle, plural marriage, and chastising the mainstream Mormon church for "abandoning" what the prophet described as "God's plan for his people."

The only other entertainment available to us—although I'm not sure the prophet's ramblings qualified as such—were television series that were old even then: in addition to *Bonanza, Little House on the Prairie, Daddy Knows Best, Lost in Space* and the like.

Our parents purchased the DVDs through a shop in Pine City, where they made a business of selling to families in Alber and the other polygamous towns. Part of their customer service involved blocking out anything the least bit suggestive, including any display of affection. That meant we'd be watching and suddenly the screen would go black. Any scenes where the mother and father entered a bedroom disappeared. Later, I thought how odd this was, considering that we lived in a house where we saw our father circulate between our mothers' bedrooms at night and where one or another of our mothers was usually pregnant.

The lodge was a timber and white mortar construction, with high-pitched roofs and a wide front porch. Attached to the main building at the rear was a separate structure that looked like a dorm, which I assumed must have contained the majority of the guest rooms.

I didn't see Max's car in the parking lot, just what appeared to be the construction workers' rides, so I kept driving toward the mountain and took a track toward the back where they'd cut down the trees. When I swung behind the building, I found his squad and the medical examiner's van. A new purchase by the county, it enabled Doc Wiley to transport bodies on his own, not wait for a hearse. Before, if the funeral home had a conflict, it could take hours to remove a corpse from a scene. As soon as I came to a stop, the CSU trailer pulled in alongside me. Lieutenant Mueller and the others rushed out, and I followed them toward a group clustered fifty feet away. I spotted Doc Wiley's silver hair, but he stood out anyway in his lab coat, bow tie, khakis and galoshes. When I saw Max, I couldn't resist the reminder of our weekend together, the comfort of his body against mine in the night.

"What have we got?" I asked, shaking the memory away as I joined the group. I didn't recognize most of them—predominantly men and only a couple of women, their clothes covered in mud. I assumed they were the construction workers.

Max shot me the briefest of glances, the slightest of smiles, and my nerves pricked in response, then he was all business. "Chief Jefferies, I have someone I want you to meet."

Max wasn't a short man, a full six feet, but the guy standing beside him had to be nearly half a foot taller, with another six inches or so added onto that for the rise of his tan cowboy hat. He looked to be in his mid-sixties, had silver hair that matched a mustache that dripped down on both sides to his chin.

I stuck out my hand. "This is?"

The man gave my hand a shake but didn't respond, and Max took over the introduction: "Clara, meet US Marshal Ash Crawford. He runs the agency's Salt Lake office."

I wasn't sure how to react. What I felt was surprise. I'd worked with the marshals in Dallas on an escaped convict case. We'd chased the guy all the way to Texarkana and arrested him over a plate of steak and eggs in a Waffle House. The only other case I'd worked with them involved a district court judge who took bribes. I'd never known the marshals to show any interest in an investigation into a criminal case.

"Good to meet you, Chief," Crawford said as he shook my hand, his voice as deep as a croaking frog.

"Same here, Marshal," I said. "So what are you doing here?"

Crawford gave Max a slanted glance, like they were part of some boys' club I wasn't invited to join. Maybe I was being overly sensitive. Over the years, I'd found some guys in law enforcement, especially the senior ones, weren't particularly welcoming to women. But I could have been jumping to conclusions. I mean, I didn't know the guy. All he said was, "Whoa, Max, she gets right to the point, doesn't she?"

"One of those things I find refreshing about her," Max responded, perhaps to cut him off.

Personally, I thought the conversation felt like a distraction. "That didn't answer my question," I pointed out. "Why are you here?"

At first, the guy didn't reply. He chewed a bit on the inside of his cheek and his eyes turned to impatient slits. Eventually, he gave me a slow smile. "I'll explain once we've taken a look at the scene. Mind going ahead? They've been holding me back for the last hour, waiting for the two of you to arrive."

Max and I exchanged a glance, mine suspicious. I didn't particularly trust Ash Crawford, although I couldn't have explained why. But Max nodded. He knew Crawford, so I didn't object. "Okay," I said. "Let's go."

That decided, the construction foreman, a skinny guy with a straggly beard named Jerry Cummings, walked us up the mountainside about two hundred feet. Cummings kept swallowing hard, nerves I guessed. He had thinning hair and puffy eyes, a lower jaw that folded into an overbite. Not long into the walk, I realized that I probably needed to start running again. The slant was dramatic and my thighs burned with the effort. Lieutenant Mueller trudged behind me followed by a few of his crime scene techs. As we got closer, Mueller looked worried. "How much farther? We need to stop a distance back from the gravesite," he said. "All these people are going to make a mess. I don't want the scene trampled. There could be tire marks or footprints."

Cummings shot Mueller an over-the-shoulder glance. "I'm sorry, Lieutenant. My men have been working all around here for months. There's gonna be lots of footprints, but probably none will have anything to do with the body. We're building a ski lift, you know."

Mueller groaned, but the truth was that he was being overly optimistic even thinking there'd be prints. Those bones had most likely been buried for a long time. I did have concerns, however. "Okay, but have your folks stay back. They don't need to put any more footprints on the ground around here. And we all need to watch for anything that could be evidence, something as small as a cigarette butt, a piece of fabric, anything that could be used as a weapon, anything out of place," I ordered, glancing at Cummings. Everyone else knew the drill, but this wasn't his area of expertise. "Be careful. If you see anything at all, tell Lieutenant Mueller or one of his men. Don't touch it."

Behind me, Mueller whispered, "Thank you, Chief."

On the way, we passed two areas that had been excavated, both with cement poured—foundations, Cummings explained. Eventually the piers would rise up to hold the ski lift. A short walk, another few minutes, and we were clustered around a rectangular hole. We stood about ten feet back on all sides. A half dozen shovels lay strewn about, I assumed because the workers panicked and dropped them. The entire skeleton wasn't completely exposed, just the upper half. Max, Mueller, Crawford, Doc and I edged forward, while the others hung back.

A foot below the disturbed rocky surface lay the nearly skeletonized remains in a stained prairie dress, resembling a grotesque Halloween decoration. Yet that ghoulish holiday had passed six months earlier. This was April, and we were in the mud season, when the rains came often and the mountain snow was melting.

All I could see was the skull, the neck bones, and one arm, sticking out from beneath a torn sleeve. In places, thin ropes of muscle and sinew stretched across the bones, swathing them in a thick, leather-like layer. But the muscle that had once connected the head to the body had withered away, and the skull lay loose, like she'd been decapitated. From previous cases, I understood that was unlikely. Rather, the heavy skull became dislodged after the muscles that held it to the neck rotted away. Something else *was* odd, however; the top of the skull had a hole in it big enough for a golf ball to roll through. The chunk of skull that had broken off lay on the ground a couple of feet from the body.

Doc squeezed his eyes nearly shut, his face flushed, and he appeared as perturbed as if someone had left the door open on one of the lab refrigerators overnight, letting a body warm. "How did that skull break? What'd you use to uncover her? A forklift?" he asked Cummings, who had the good sense to look embarrassed.

Max bent forward and examined the bones. "Doesn't look like that's an old skull fracture, does it?"

"No, it does not," Doc complained. "Fresh, I'd say."

At that, Doc pulled on gloves, then picked up the chunk of skull and turned it to display the rough, broken edge. Unlike the rest of the visible areas of the skull which the earth had tarnished a dark brown, the fracture remained a creamy off-white. "If they'd found the skull this way, the edges would be stained from being buried in the earth over a long period of time. That the broken area is clean and unstained is a big tip-off that this damage is recent."

Max looked warily at Cummings, who turned toward me and objected, I guessed because I was the only one who hadn't already expressed an opinion. "Chief, we're building a ski lift here, you know? That's not delicate work. We break into the ground, dig out the dirt and move on. So, yeah, we were using equipment and not being particularly careful. We're not up here looking for bodies."

Doc appeared ready to lose it with Cummings. The ME's mouth clamped down, scrunching his upper lip. From my point of view, Cummings had a point, and it made no sense to argue with him; we needed his cooperation. I changed the subject. "How did you find her? Explain what happened."

Cummings began a lengthy, rather convoluted account of their method for clearing the land, how they had to sink the foundations to a particular point to adhere to the engineer's specifications.

Out of the corner of my eye, I saw Mueller whispering to his crew. They responded by splintering off in various directions, I assumed to hunt for evidence. One guy stayed behind, the photographer, who snapped photos of the remains.

All the while, Doc scowled at me. He didn't look happy that I'd interrupted, so he made a show of shaking his head to be sure we all understood he was displeased, then bent down to get a closer look.

Across from Doc, Ash Crawford folded his long body and knelt on one knee. Crawford swayed forward. I was about to caution him against touching anything, when he stopped his hand inches above the skeleton's chest, covered by shreds of a filthy, stained dress that appeared it may have once been some shade of purple. The bones and remaining tissue barely made bumps underneath the rotting fabric. Crawford held his hand palm down, as if hoping to raise the woman from the dead. Then he took his hat off, held it in his hand, and his head dropped, as reverent as if he prayed in a church pew.

Apparently oblivious, Doc kept busy, examining the body from different angles, but the rest of us stared at Crawford. Max shot me a curious glance, just as Cummings began to wrap his story up: "We'd only gotten down eight, ten inches or so when someone hit something hard and it cracked. That was the skull. We were about to have a heart attack, but we kept digging. I wanted to make sure we had what we thought we did. When we dug a little deeper, we unearthed more bones and I called nine-one-one."

At that, Doc's head shot up. "Where are they?" Cummings didn't respond, and Doc explained, "Where'd you put the damn bones you dug up?"

The construction foreman took a deep breath, as if trying to swallow what wouldn't have been a pleasant response. "I have what we found in a box in my truck. I didn't want anything to get lost. I was trying to be careful."

"We'll need it all," Doc said, openly suspicious. "You need to get it."

"Of course," Cummings responded, but then Max put his hand on the guy's shoulder.

"Listen, why don't you and I go to your truck. I'll get one of the forensic techs to help us, and we can bag the bones for Doc while I ask a few more questions." Cummings agreed, and the two men turned to leave.

As they sauntered off, Doc shouted at another of the crime scene guys. "Get a body bag out of my van, will ya?"

"I'll get it," Crawford offered, and he stood and towered over me.

"I'll walk you there," I offered. "We can get out of Doc's way."

Crawford shot me a disapproving glance. We were both seasoned cops. He knew as well as I did that this wasn't an act of kindness. I'd picked up on something, and I wanted to talk.

"Sure, Chief," he said.

The guy had long legs, big steps, and a kind of crooked gait, and I had to move fast to keep up. We headed toward Doc's black van with "SMITH COUNTY MEDICAL EXAMINER" on the side. One door was open, and Crawford stuck his head in and started scouting around. "They're up there on the shelf," I said, pointing at a stack of black vinyl body bags.

Crawford grabbed the one on the top and held it against his chest. I thought he might start back up the slope, but instead he turned to me. One eye closed and the other stared at me, suspicious. "You gonna tell me what's bothering you, or you just want me to start talking?"

I gave him a strained look, the kind investigators use to let folks know they aren't all that confident they'll be getting the straight story. "You can start talking. But if I'm not hearing what I need, I'll take over with questions."

A bob of the head, and he said, "I'm not a US Marshal anymore. Retired about a year ago."

"I didn't think you were still on the job. I didn't see a badge, and you let Max introduce you. You didn't identify yourself as a marshal."

"Good catch," he said with a half snicker.

"So why are you here?"

A short huff, like he was thinking about how to answer, and Crawford's deep voice turned to gravel. "It's really nothing sinister. I recently settled in the area, on a ranch a way down the mountain. I heard you'd found a body. Got interested. Thought I'd look around."

Cops get pretty good at knowing when folks aren't telling us everything. Watching him, the way he avoided looking directly at me, my suspicions mounted. I felt certain that there was a lot more to this. "How did you hear?"

"I was talking to someone when she heard that a call about a body had come in over the radio. One of the dispatchers I've kept in touch with. I'd been telling her I wanted to help out some, find cold cases to work, keep my hand in the game, and this was close to the ranch, and I—"

Enough with the camouflage. Something wasn't right. "Why'd you react like that? Getting down close to the body. For a few minutes, you looked like you were praying over it."

Crawford let loose a snort, irritated, implying that I'd gotten it wrong. I wasn't buying it. I felt pretty sure that I'd struck a nerve. None of this felt normal.

"I was just giving the victim a little respect, like she deserves." He smiled at me and crescent grooves folded from each side of his nose around his mouth. For being so tall, he didn't have much padding on him.

"I'm not sure what's going on here," I started, determined to get to the bottom of it. "But that didn't look like a cop's usual reaction to found remains. What you did? That looked a lot more emotional." He said nothing, just slimmed his eyes down and glared at me.

"Chief, I'm not sure what you're suggesting. Why would you—" he started, then stopped dead, mid-sentence.

I pushed harder. "I need the truth. Because none of this is coming across to me as two cops talking about a case."

His eyes flicked an acknowledgment, and I thought he might talk. I felt like I could see the wheels turning, the Rolodex inside his brain skimming through index cards of possible scenarios he could spin, excuses to explain his odd behavior. His lips parted, he paused, and I waited, returning his gaze, not taking my eyes off his. "Well, I—"

At that moment, Doc shouted down to us. "Clara, come here."

I glanced up the slope, and saw he was still crouched down. The pile of dirt around the bones had grown, and it appeared that Doc had been pushing it away, uncovering more of the skeleton.

"Can it wait a few minutes? We're discussing something," I shouted back.

Doc sounded irritated that I'd asked. "No. You need to see this."

Crawford shadowed me on my right as I hurried the short distance back. He still held the body bag, but as we approached Doc didn't appear as interested in it as when he'd sent us to retrieve it. Instead, he was laser-focused on the grave. The CSI unit's cameraman snapped shots of the scene, head to foot, while Doc pointed down at the remains, part skeleton, part mummified. "Look at this, right here."

When he'd uncovered the body, Doc had made a pile of loose fabric from the dress on a sheet of brown evidence paper. Although the dress was in bad shape, stained and torn on the top, its lower half, waist down, nearly in shreds, it took me a moment to decide what Doc wanted me to look at. Then it stood out. I couldn't understand how I'd missed it: a second skull, a small one. I knelt to get closer. The eye sockets and forehead looked too large for the size of the skull. Some of it remained covered in tissue, but on a patch of bare bone I noticed suture lines and I saw an indentation that I thought might be the soft spot on the top where it would have expanded to accommodate growth. My eyes trailed down from the toothless jaws, and I made out the outlines of bird-bone-size legs and arms, ending in miniature hands that formed fists. The diminutive body was curled into a fetal position.

I felt Crawford hovering beside me, his breathing as labored as if he'd stopped running mid-sprint, when I whispered, "A baby?"

"Yup." Doc nodded.

"She was pregnant when she died?" Crawford appeared shaken.

Doc had a curious look when he explained, "Looks like it. And based on the size of the skull, I'd guess that the baby had to be close to full-term."

CHAPTER SIX

She screamed as a wave of pain coursed through her. They still came infrequently, but harder. Writhing on the bed, she tried to remember what her mothers had done during childbirth. She'd seen only snatches, once when she'd brought in towels for the midwife. She thought that they'd sat up slightly to ease the pressure on their backs, but she couldn't do that, not tied to the railings as she was.

"Momma," she whispered.

"Did you say something?" the woman asked.

The girl opened her eyes just enough to see her fiddling with the gauge on the IV. As the pain began to ebb, she caught her breath and whispered, "Why are you doing this to me?"

"Me? Doing this to you? I'm not responsible for your condition. You did that on your own." The girl heard a soft laugh as the woman shuffled out.

Alone again, her thoughts trailed back to the man at the bus station and then to where he'd taken her. Memories flooded through her, as she recalled that place and those she'd met there.

It had seemed to the girl that everything changed from her first moments at the home. Even her name. That first evening, Nurse Gantt, the head nurse who also acted as the midwife, looked at her and announced, "Your eyes are the same shade as the violets in my garden. I'm going to call you 'Violet.'" The name stuck, and the staff, even the other girls referred to her that way. Violet hadn't objected. After all that had happened, she decided it was better to forget who she'd been before she arrived at the home, because she'd never be that girl again.

The home had a living room with a television, and on one evening Violet remembered four teenage girls gathered around watching *The Bachelor,* oohing and aahing at the screen. All wore jeans and big T-shirts, most with pithy sayings on the front: Rock Hard; Sweet As Candy. Under their shirts, their baby bumps bulged. On the TV, the bachelor presented a rose, and one girl grabbed another's hand, cooing, "Isn't it romantic?"

On a table off to the side, Violet played checkers with her friend Samantha. Both girls had discarded the belts from their prairie dresses to make room for their spreading girths. Samantha was younger, only fourteen, but the two girls had become inseparable. They had shared experience, both coming from polygamous towns nestled in the mountains.

"Your turn," Samantha had said.

Violet had reached over the board but then stopped and chuckled.

"Why'd you do that?"

"My baby is tickling me," she said, her voice light.

Just then, the aide walked in the room and made a beeline for them. The name tag on her blue scrubs read "Miss Lori." A plump woman with long blond hair piled loosely on top of her head, Lori had a round face and thin creases around her lips and eyes.

"Violet, it's time for your vitamins," Miss Lori cooed as she handed the girl one of the small white paper pill cups she carried on an aluminum tray.

All the girls in the home liked Lori, who hummed old songs as she brought them their meds along with a morning and an afternoon snack. In the quiet moments, Lori talked to them about their pregnancies, comparing them to her own. Sometimes, in the evenings, she hung around after her shift, watched TV and told them stories about her family.

As Violet gulped down her pills, Lori whispered to Samantha and pointed at a red checker. "You can jump two with that, munchkin!"

"Cheating!" Violet screamed.

Lori and Samantha hooted at her.

At the TV, one of the Gentile girls stood. Near term, she held the small of her back with her hand as if to brace it. "You prairie dressers better stop yapping. We can't hear!"

In response, Nurse Gantt's voice boomed from the hallway: "Girls, be quiet! You hear?"

A thick-necked, heavy-set woman, she had the manner of a high-school gym teacher ordering her class to run one more lap around the football field. As she shuffled in, she ordered, "None of that noise. We've got a girl upstairs ready to deliver any day now. She might be sleeping."

Wary, Violet fell silent when Nurse Gantt glanced at her. The teenager didn't like the woman. Perhaps because the man who'd dropped her off had warned that Nurse Gantt could be tough. "Do what she tells you," he'd urged. "You don't want her mad at you."

"What're you looking at?" Nurse Gantt asked, her lips screwed into a tight scowl.

"Nothing, ma'am," Violet answered.

With that, Nurse Gantt lumbered over to the table and snapped at Lori, "If these two have had their pills, it's time to move on."

Lori dropped her head, nodded, and didn't object, just obediently plopped a pill cup for Samantha on the table and padded over to the Gentile girls. As soon as Lori left, Nurse Gantt placed her hand on Samantha's swollen abdomen. "Has the baby been kicking today?"

Samantha gulped the pills down and nodded, but Violet thought that her friend's smile looked weak around the edges, like it was half of a frown.

"Yes, ma'am," Samantha said.

"You're getting closer. Pretty soon you'll be taken upstairs."

Violet shifted in her chair. A lot of things about the home bothered her. They didn't have telephones, except for the ones the staff carried in their pockets. And no visitors ever came. Violet especially didn't like that the girls were moved to the third floor the month before they delivered. Once they left the main two floors, no one was allowed to visit them and they seemed to disappear.

Despite what the man had told her about not riling up the head nurse, the thought of losing her friend scared Violet even more. "Nurse Gantt, why does Samantha have to stay upstairs at the end?"

"Because that's the way we do it here," Nurse Gantt said, her mood instantly darkening.

Across the table, Samantha squirmed, trying to get comfortable. She'd told Violet that the baby's father was her older brother. He'd been sneaking into her room at night since she'd been a little kid. When her parents found out, they were mad at Samantha, not their oldest son. Violet thought that wasn't right, but then she considered her own situation; her baby's father had gone on with his life while she'd been banished from her family. None of it had seemed fair.

At times, the two friends talked about their babies, how they'd wished they could keep them. But both had signed the home's admittance form, agreeing that their infants would be put up for adoption. One thing Violet knew for sure: she didn't want to be separated from her only friend. "Nurse Gantt, Samantha could stay in my room with me. I could help take care of her."

At that, Nurse Gantt hunched down and stared at her, eye to eye. Nervous, the teenager slipped her trembling hands under the table. A tremor rippled through her as Nurse Gantt clipped out each word: "You will do as you're told."

"But I—"

Nurse Gantt's eyes widened. "Violet, you don't want to get on my bad side, do you?"

The girl bit her lip and shook her head. "No ma'am."

Her voice rough, the woman growled, "Then follow orders."

CHAPTER SEVEN

Lieutenant Mueller and Doc Wiley debated how to handle the bodies. Neither one had ever transported a nearly skeletonized corpse of a pregnant woman before. The bones were fragile, and Doc worried that lifting them together could jostle them enough to cause damage. At one point, he examined the corpses and thought he might be able to lift the infant from its mother. Perhaps that way they would be more stable. But enough mummified muscle remained, anchoring the infant inside the mother, that Doc ultimately judged such an approach unwise. "We'll move them as they are," he finally announced.

"You sure?" Mueller prodded, not for the first time. "Could be trouble down the road, that we mixed remains, don't you think?"

"We didn't mix anything. They're already mixed," Doc scoffed. "The baby's still inside the mother."

Lieutenant Mueller pulled on his lower lip, thinking about that. "Seems to me, one body per bag. So two bags."

Doc glared at him. "Seems to me this is my area of expertise, not yours."

I'd spent a good bit of time with Doc since I'd returned to Alber. With his bow ties and lab coats, I'd always thought of him as a grandfatherly sort. Maybe part of it was that going on eleven years ago, he'd been the one who treated my bruised body days before I fled. That day he'd also put a splint on my right arm, to mend a fractured bone.

Mother had poultices for bruises and broken bones, ones she made by mashing comfrey leaves in hot water, then rolling the mixture inside of cheesecloth. Under other circumstances, I would have gone to her when hurt. But I'd tried to talk to her and to Father before, to tell them of the nightmare my marriage had become. I tried to explain how late at night, when I slept, I'd wake to find my husband sitting in a chair, a mixture of lust and hatred in his eyes.

"Clara, I'm here." His next words had turned my blood cold: "And you are my wife."

Our encounters never went well. As the years passed, I understood that if I apologized, he grew angry. If I kept quiet, he fumed. If I cried, a blood rage came over him. I cowered below him, his hand above me in a fist, one that came down hard against my chest, my shoulder, my abdomen.

Seven years into the marriage, I had nowhere to turn. Then came the night that he'd grabbed my arm and twisted it, snapping the bone like a twig.

In his office that day, Doc had looked over his wire-rimmed glasses at me. "Clara, you didn't do this in a fall." He'd sat on the exam table beside me and focused so intently on me that I'd felt as if he could see my soul. "Who did this to you?"

With my prairie dress sleeves pulled down, no one could see the damage, but when Doc held my broken arm in his hand, I had no way to deny it. I knew that he knew. And I was afraid.

"I can't—"

"You can," he had stopped me. "We'll call the police. We'll stop this."

As much pain as I was in that day, as much as my body ached and my arm hurt, I'd smiled at his naivety. *He should know better,* I'd thought. *He should know that no one in Alber, not the police, not even my own parents will protect me.*

Perhaps he did know. Because the next thing he'd said to me was: "If you can't be safe where you are, you have to leave."

Two days later, I fled Alber with only the clothes I wore and a few small pieces of jewelry to pawn. My friend Hannah had plotted my escape. Without her, I truly believed that I would have died.

Returning to Alber after ten years on the outside hadn't been my idea, but so far I'd stayed.

What I'd learned in the past eight months working cases with Doc was that he had a temper. I got a glimpse of it on the day he told me to flee if I wasn't safe. It was there again when I'd helped him take down the slain body of a young girl left to rot hanging in a barn, and when I'd told him who'd murdered the women and children at the Johansson bison farm.

Yet I'd never seen him quite as riled up as he appeared staring down at the remains of the mother and her infant. The sad visage had touched him, and he was angry. We'd removed remains often enough since my return that I automatically went to the shoulders, and Doc to the feet, while Max and Mueller met at the center.

Doc's lips curled, and I heard pain in his voice when he explained: "There's not much holding them together, but I want to keep them as they are if we can. So we're going to scoop our arms underneath and move them in one smooth motion into the bag. Okay?"

None of us answered verbally, just nodded as we pulled on gloves.

The woman's damaged cranium had already been placed in another bag along with its dislodged piece and miscellaneous other bones the construction workers had found. So I inserted my hands under her shoulders. Doc put an arm beneath each of her legs, and Max and Mueller took her hips and back, trying to get below her dress, although there was little to save. The earth, her bodily fluids as they'd drained, had dissolved most of it away.

"One, two, three, go," Doc said, and we lifted, as carefully as we could. She felt so light in my hands, a feather, little more, and I thought of the life cut short, the child that never took a first gulp of air, the loneliness of death and the loss of two lives.

In seconds we had the body laid out inside of the black vinyl bag. A few bones had stayed in the hole, and Doc took out a brush, swept around them, worked the dirt off and released them, then put them beside the skeleton. I stared down at the headless figure, the tiny baby tucked inside of her.

Max sidled up next to me. "Do you think it's Christina Bradshaw?"

"No one said anything about her being pregnant, but maybe they didn't know," I said.

I felt Crawford over my shoulder. I'd forgotten he was there while we worked on the body. He'd stayed in the background, watching, observing.

I took a deep breath as Doc zipped up the body bag. I did my best to look calm, not to let my emotions show, but I felt a deep rage taking over with the certainty that something had gone very wrong and another woman, and this time her infant, had paid the price.

"Let's get a couple of techs in here," Lieutenant Mueller called out, and a few of his officers moved forward, ready to get to work. "We need to sift through this dirt, see if we've got any more bones, any evidence that was buried with the bodies."

Once the others had taken over inspecting the grave in which the remains were found, Doc said, "Make sure the techs take soil samples. It will help to know the acidity level when we try to figure out how long they've been out here. I'm going to take them to the morgue, do some preliminary work."

"You think you'll be able to get DNA?" I asked.

"Probably," Doc said. "I'll do an exam, and then we'll send all of it to the bone lab at the state, have them try to pull DNA from both the mother and baby."

"The baby's DNA will give us the father, assuming we can find a match," Max pointed out.

"If you can get DNA at all," Crawford interrupted. We all gave him a look, and he grimaced. "A good friend of mine, a guy I've known for decades, runs the state lab. We've talked about this a lot, how hard it is to retrieve DNA from old bones."

I thought about that. DNA was our best shot at identifying the dead woman, but there were others. "How about getting the skull reconstructed so we can see a face? That woman in Salt Lake City does that using clay."

"No. Takes too long," Crawford said. This time, the rest of us looked at each other, wondering about this man who'd insinuated himself into this case. "My friend at the lab has a computer program. He told me all about it. They do CAT scans of skulls and then use a computer program to build the face. It just takes a day or two."

"Good for them," Doc said. "But when we've tried to get help like that from the lab, the door is slow to open. We have to get in line, and it takes months, if we're lucky. If we're not lucky, it can take a year."

At that, Crawford grinned. "Not if I'm the one who asks for you. Like I said, the guy in charge of the entire lab is my friend."

I looked at him and sighed. All this sounded good, very good, but I didn't trust him. Something seemed off. While I liked the idea of cutting through the red tape, I wondered why Crawford was so invested in this particular case.

Max, however, jumped at the offer. "You really think so, Ash? That would be great, to be able to turn this around that quick. What would we have to do?"

"I'll deliver her to the lab myself," Crawford said. "And I'll call in some favors. We'll get it done."

"Why?" I asked. He didn't answer, and I said it again, spelling it out: "Why are you showing so much interest in *this* case? Why are you calling in favors for *us*?"

Crawford shook his head, as if confused. "I have friends in the right places. Why wouldn't I help?"

For a moment, no one talked, then Doc gave me a perplexed look. "Clara, what does it matter? We need the help, don't we?"

At that, I realized that Doc and Max didn't understand. "Mr. Crawford can't transport the remains for us. We can't let him do that."

"Why not?" Doc asked.

"A police officer or an evidence tech needs to do that. And Mr. Crawford's not a cop," I explained.

Max started, "But Ash is a—"

"Not anymore," I said. "It's no longer Marshal Crawford. It's Mr. Crawford. He's retired."

Max appeared stunned. "Retired? Then why are you here, Ash?"

Crawford sighed, looked from one of us to the other as if exasperated that we'd questioned him. "Like I said, to do what I can to help. Like Doc Wiley said, why does it matter? I have connections. Why not let me use them to help you solve your case?"

Then the silver-haired man in his tall hat bent down next to the black vinyl body bag. He slipped his arms under it and gathered it up. His expression was as it had been earlier, displaying reverence and deep pain.

Something occurred to me, and I asked, "Do you know who she is?"

Ash Crawford glanced at me as if stunned. "No. Don't be ridiculous. How could I know that? In this condition, who could even guess?"

CHAPTER EIGHT

"I'll see you at the morgue, Doc," I said, as I turned to walk toward my Suburban. Mueller's men were still working the scene, searching the woods for evidence. So far, no luck. All we had were the two bodies, the baby tucked into the mother. I was hoping that would change, that whoever buried them left something useful behind. Meanwhile, Max had Ash Crawford corralled near his pickup truck, I figured asking him questions.

"No reason for you to go to the morgue. I'll just do an initial examination. There won't be an autopsy tonight, Clara," Doc replied. "It's getting late."

"You sure?" I asked. Max and I had planned our usual dinner out that evening with his daughter, Brooke. We did this a few times a month at a pizza joint in Pine City. Brooke routinely ordered a deep dish with pineapple and Canadian bacon. I suspected she did that because she enjoyed having it all to herself, taking home three-quarters of it for lunches for the following days. Max and I easily finished off a thin crust with Italian sausage and mushrooms. None of that seemed to matter, however, with what we'd just found.

"I'll start in the morning," Doc said. "I want to read up a bit tonight on how to examine the body, to remove the mummified tissue to get a better look at the bones. And there should be some information on fetal development and skull circumference which will help confirm how far along the infant was at the time of death."

Doc's day job was as one of only a couple of internists in the area, who treated the flu every winter and poison ivy infections in the summers. His work as the county medical examiner was a sideline. When he hit a tough case, he researched first, which I appreciated. There would be no way to reconstruct the remains, get them back to their original condition, if he botched an autopsy by handling it the wrong way. So, as eager as I was to get results, I didn't argue.

"Okay. Morning, then. I'll be at the morgue by seven?"

"Should work," Doc answered as he slammed the van's back doors shut. He moseyed over to the driver's side door. Doc's not a big guy, and he used an inside handle to pull himself up into the driver's seat, then peered down at me through the open door, unhappy. "Clara, that Crawford guy's trying to help."

"Yeah, but—"

"Let him," Doc ordered.

"Well, Doc, maybe you didn't hear me. He's retired, not officially a cop anymore, and—"

"I don't give a you-know-what," Doc said, cutting me off. "It's frustrating as hell working out here in the sticks, no resources, no money, budgets so tight they strangle an investigation."

I glanced over, saw Max and Crawford had stopped talking and the former marshal was heading toward his car. Considering what Doc had just said, I opened my mouth, flipped through possible responses, and closed it. Doc was right, of course. I'd been scraping for money to replace a squad car that had a couple hundred thousand miles on the odometer and to buy equipment to open the forensic unit I planned to have Stef head up when she became certified. I'd asked the mayor and city council three times for funding. Each request was denied.

"Let the man do what he can for us," Doc insisted. "Don't look for problems when maybe we've finally gotten a break."

Again, I paused, considered, then nodded.

"Okay then," he said. "We're agreed."

After Doc pulled out with his precious cargo in the back of the van, Ash Crawford followed him toward the road in his pickup.

Mueller was off working the scene with his techs, and Max and I were alone for the first time.

"So what did Crawford tell you?" I asked.

"Pretty much the same he'd said earlier, that he lives in the area and wanted to help." Max had a frown that twisted his left cheek. "I guess that could be it. But I have the impression that you think he was acting a little odd."

"Yes, I do," I confirmed. Max shook his head, perplexed, and I thought about what I'd promised Doc. Despite that, I needed answers, so I suggested, "How about we call the Salt Lake marshal's office, see what they can tell us?"

Max gave his head a bob, agreeing, then said, "I know someone else who works there. Let's sit in my car, and we'll put him on speaker."

In his Smith County Sheriff's squad car, Max scrolled through his list of contacts. "I can't remember the guy's name or how I filed it," he said, but then, "Oh, here it is."

The receptionist answered, and before long we had one of the deputy US Marshals who worked in the office on the line. Max filled him in on the rough background, then finished by asking, "So, my question to you is, what's up with Crawford? Why did he leave?"

At first, dead air. Then the guy's voice took on a noncommittal tone, as if we'd asked him what brand of canned chicken soup he preferred. "Marshal Crawford reached retirement age. Nothing else that I know of."

"That's it?" Max asked.

"Yup. He was eligible, and he simply took retirement."

"Nothing at all unusual?" Max asked.

For a moment silence hung around us, then the guy said, "Nothing."

"But he's—" I started.

"A great investigator," the man said. "One of the best I've ever worked with."

"I don't know. It seems odd. This isn't the type of case the marshal's office usually takes on," Max pointed out. "Crawford is inserting himself into the investigation, and Chief Jefferies and I need to understand why."

A long sigh came over the car's speaker.

"Max, my guess is that Ash is simply at his wit's end in retirement. He's an active guy who's lived an eventful life. It's gotta be boring as hell up on some tiny horse ranch in a Podunk county. No offense intended."

"None taken," Max answered. "But there must be more, don't you think? I mean, he's acting like this is personal. Like the girl, the body we found, has some kind of special meaning to him."

Another pause, then the guy said, "Ash has always been pretty hands-on, and he's always had a soft spot for the victims. I wouldn't assume anything beyond that he's a cop who wasn't completely ready to hang up his badge and wants to help."

"I hear what you're saying, but he seems overly invested in the case," I said, spelling it out.

Again, the guy was silent, then he dropped his voice low, maybe trying to keep others from hearing. "Okay. But you didn't hear this from me. Ash has a lot of friends in the office, and I don't need them upset with me."

"Sure," Max agreed.

"The only odd thing was that the final year he was here, Ash changed. He got morose, depressed, and he started acting differently."

"Different in what way?" I pushed.

"Ash started talking about how the violence in our society had to stop. You're right that we don't handle murder cases and such in our office. He sounded regretful about that, like he'd chosen the wrong path and wished he'd done more work on violent crimes."

"Any insight into what changed him?" Max wanted to know.

The guy kind of stuttered. "Well, no, no, not really. The consensus in the office was that Ash was getting older, and some things seemed more important to him as he aged."

In the squad, Max shot me a glance. I gave him a noncommittal half-shrug. If pressed, I'd admit I still had suspicions. It wasn't the answer I wanted to hear. I'd hoped for something clearer, some justification for Crawford's actions. But I thought about what Doc had said, that Crawford wanted to help and we'd be fools not to welcome it, and I shrugged yet again.

"That's it?" Max asked the guy.

"That's all I know."

"Okay, thanks," Max said. "If you think of anything else, you'll fill us in, right?"

"You've got it," the guy agreed.

After we hung up, Max and I sat in his squad car, silent. Thinking. "Maybe we are reading too much into this," he suggested. "Why wouldn't Crawford want to keep involved a little? He probably just does want to help."

Although unsure, I nodded. "Maybe so, but something about this doesn't seem right to me." Quiet surrounded us as we mentally parsed through the afternoon's events. I thought about Crawford with his hand suspended over the bones while still in the grave. "Max, I can't shake the feeling there's more to Crawford's interest in this case. That somehow it's personal to him."

"How is that possible? We don't even know who the victim is. That body is so badly decomposed, Crawford would have to be psychic to figure it out." Max tied his lips into a nub and gave me a sideways glance. "On the other side, we could sure use his connections. Without them, those remains will sit at the lab for a long time while we try to get DNA and a facial reconstruction."

Like Doc's advice, Max's words rang true. In rural Smith County, we had no right to turn away assistance that could help solve a case, answer questions, identify a victim, and perhaps bring a family peace. Despite my misgivings, I had to agree. "I know you're right. Without someone to push it, this case could take years. But I'm going to keep my eye on him."

"Sure. Absolutely. But let's not just assume the worst, okay?"

I thought about objecting, but again, he had a point.

"Autopsy tomorrow then," Max said. "Should Brooke and I meet you at the pizza place?" Max looked disappointed before I spoke a word. I guessed he could see on my face that I was going to back out. "Oh, Clara, really, can't it wait until tomorrow? There's no autopsy tonight. Nothing to do. The woman and baby have been dead for a long time, and we have no evidence to follow up on."

"All true, but I'm going to head back to the office and comb through the reports of missing persons, see if any mention a pregnant woman. There are a few things I can do tonight to get a jump on tomorrow."

"Clara, no, let's—"

"Max, I don't want to wait on this. I need to see what we have, find out if there's a case that's a good fit before I head over to talk to Christina Bradshaw's family. They're going to hear about this and wonder if it's her. I want to have some answers to give them."

Max wasn't happy. I understood. Brooke would be disappointed. I was, too. The two of us had become pals, and I enjoyed pizza night as much as she and Max did. But we had a woman, a baby. We didn't know how she'd died, but by the way she'd been buried, I was pretty sure it wouldn't turn out to be natural causes. My bet was that we were looking at a murder case. "Now I'm regretting calling you in on this," Max said, but at the same time his lips curled into a slow smile, and he looked a bit proud, certainly not truly upset.

"Admit it, Max." When he shot me a questioning glance, I explained, "If I wasn't offering to do this, you'd be up half the night doing it yourself."

I didn't need any confirmation, and he didn't give any. Instead, as I prepared to get out of his squad car, he gave me a look I'd come to recognize, one that wasn't focused on the case or Brooke, only the two of us. I hesitated, and he reached for me, pulled me to him. Our lips met. I couldn't breathe, my heart thudding inside my chest. I reminded myself again to be calm, to keep a distance. I'd lost control years earlier, and it had turned out very wrong. As much as I trusted Max, I couldn't risk having anything like that ever happen to me again. So I pulled away.

"I'll get in touch if I find any possible matches in the files," I whispered, my voice raspy and soft. Refusing to be quieted, my pulse pounded as I reached for the door.

"Call me later, one way or the other," Max said, eyes steady on mine. I had a hard time concentrating when he looked at me like that. "After eight thirty, Brooke will be in bed. You can fill me in on what you found out. After we talk about the case, maybe, for a little while, we can talk about us."

"Max, I…"

Max's expression turned serious. "Clara, I want your voice to be the last thing I hear tonight."

I took a deep breath. I couldn't bring myself to admit it, but I wanted that, too. "Sure. Of course."

I stood with my hand on the open car door. Max watched me, and his eyes filled with such affection that if anyone had happened upon us, they would have instantly known our secret. I traced his familiar face with my eyes, considered the turn of his cheek and the slight dimple in his chin. But then the image of the Second Coming Ranch rushed through me, and I remembered that in a few minutes I would have to drive past it again as I returned to

Alber. I flinched as the old man's voice assaulted me, aged and harsh, cruel and terrifying.

"Clara, are you okay?" Max asked, his brow creased with worry. "The way you're looking at me, it's as if I've frightened you. Did I say or do something wrong?"

"No, of course not, it's just…" This wasn't the place, the time. He wouldn't understand. I couldn't explain. "I'll call later. We'll talk."

CHAPTER NINE

The road to the construction site disappearing behind me, Stef came on my radio. "Chief, you there?"

The sky was darkening, and I followed Max's brake lights as we approached the turnoff on to the highway. I thought about highways in Dallas, where I'd trained as a cop: six, eight, a dozen lanes, some more, bordered by skyscrapers downtown, in the burbs, shopping centers, and outside the city gas stations and rest stops. In Smith County our highways were four lanes of asphalt with a stripe down the center, farmland on either side, cattle grazing and no need to pass because I hardly ever encountered another car.

"I'm here, Stef. What's up? Did you find Danny Benson?"

We hit the intersection and Max took a left to Pine City, to head home for pizza with Brooke. I hung right. Up ahead, the Second Coming leered back at me. I briefly considered stopping. I wondered if my sister-wives had heard of my return last August. As isolated as Alber was, the ranch was even more insular. Rarely did the wives leave the compound. The children were all homeschooled through ninth grade. From the beginning I'd been an anomaly. My father had used his stature in the community to pressure my husband to allow me to go to college. It cost nothing, since I'd earned scholarships. My husband had grudgingly agreed. But later, when I got the teaching job in Alber, he'd confiscated all my paychecks, then told me that allowing me to get my degree had been his biggest error in judgment.

"Women should be home, cooking, cleaning, working the ranch and having babies." His sneer had exposed chipped, yellowed teeth. His rheumy eyes sank deep into their sockets, giving his head the outline of a skull.

"Chief, here's the deal," Stef explained, bringing me back to the present. "I ran all the checks on Danny Benson. There's no birth certificate for the kid. Maybe this is a sham? The kid doesn't exist?"

As I saw the Second Coming ahead, the headlights on a truck approached from the opposite direction. "Well, in Alber, that's not unusual," I explained, fighting to ignore the distractions and keep my focus on the phone call. Stef wasn't from a polygamous community. Her family had moved to the area just a couple of years earlier, bought a goat ranch outside town in an auction. She lived there with her parents. She had one dad and one mom, which, for our area, was still fairly unusual. "Danny would have been delivered by a midwife, and they often don't fill out paperwork. It's entirely probable that he wouldn't have a birth certificate, did you check—"

"School records? Yup. Nothing there either."

"Could be that the Bensons homeschool, too." I considered, not for the first time, how the secrecy of polygamous families made them so much harder to investigate. "Danny should be twenty now. Done with his studies by a long shot. If he's working, then there's the chance that he has a Social Security card. But some folks don't get one. He could be working off the books, doing day labor or something, but it's worth a shot. Or maybe he was forced out of Alber."

"A lost boy, like Chief Deputy Anderson?"

"Yes, like Max," I said. "I explained to you how the system works. How the church hierarchy forces out the boys they don't want to keep. Makes their parents abandon them. Maybe that explains what happened to Danny."

"Well, that makes sense, but it's going to be tough to find him then, right?"

The pickup drew closer as I approached the Second Coming on my left. I took a deep breath. At the driveway into the ranch, the truck crawled to a near stop. Someone must have hit a button, because the wrought-iron gate slowly opened. My eyes were drawn to the truck's cabin. Two men were inside. Even in the shadows, I recognized them both, and the sight of them sent a shiver through me, like jumping into a winter lake.

"How do I find Danny if he's a lost boy?" Stef asked.

I kept my eyes on the truck, the men, and the driver glanced over at me. I couldn't see him well in the dark, but I knew the outline of that face. Long ago, a terrible night had imprinted it on my memory. While my sister-wives led a sheltered life, the men in the family had always kept abreast of everything that happened in Alber. I had no doubt that they recognized me in my official car, the insignia on the side—how could they not?

"Chief? You there?"

"Yeah, Stef, sorry. Listen, find the sister. What's her name? The one who signed the report."

"Lynlee?"

"Yes, Lynlee. She should be in her late twenties now. Probably married. See if you can find her. Once you track her down, we can ask her about Danny. They may have kept in touch. She was protective of him at one point."

"Okay, got it," Stef said. "You heading back to the station or calling it a day?"

"On my way in. I have some research to do."

"See you then, Chief."

The phone cut out. Behind me the truck had entered the gate and in the rearview mirror I saw it heading toward the fortress-like ranch house. *Later*, I thought. *Don't think about them. Not now. You have work to do.*

I kept driving, slowed my breathing, whispered to myself that this too would pass. Then, ten minutes down the road, on another lonely stretch of highway, I saw the gas station with "BENSON'S BODY SHOP" on the sign. For a brief moment, I thought about Danny's battered face in the photo out of the Tombs. Although it was growing late, Clyde's car was still there and the "OPEN" sign was lit. I considered stopping and asking him about his son, demanding answers. But that wouldn't help my investigation. So, I drove past. Before I questioned Clyde, I needed to know where the kid was. I needed to know what we were looking at, and whether we had any hope of moving forward. Sixteen years had passed since the report was taken and buried. Maybe I didn't have a case at all.

Coming up on seven, the police station's lot was unusually full. I noticed a couple of squads parked in a far corner under a tree. One had Stef's number on the back, the other Officer Bill Conroy's. He was just starting his twelve hours on night shift, but he should have been out driving the town, patrolling, not hanging around the office. I didn't see the night dispatcher's ride—a beat-up VW bus—but Kellie's car remained where it had been parked all day.

Walking in the back door, I saw no one but heard voices, murmurs. I paused, then came around the corner slowly. A big kid in his twenties, Conroy had thin lips and a pallid complexion. Kellie stood behind him rubbing his shoulders, and Conroy was sitting in her chair, his head back, moaning softly in appreciation. His sandy-brown hair was mussed. A light on the phone console blinked red.

"Someone on hold?" I said, deadpan.

Kellie jumped and brought her hand up to her chest so that it covered that sparkly heart on her shirt. "Oh, Chief, you frightened me."

"Yeah," Conroy said. While Kellie looked surprised, my young officer flushed with embarrassment. Rightly so, I'd say. I had no issue with the two of them getting close, but not on my time.

"Aren't you supposed to be gone by now, Kellie?" I asked.

"Gladys is running late," she said. "One of her kids had a ball game, and her husband couldn't take him."

"She's been late a lot recently," I said, and Kellie and Conroy didn't comment. Our night dispatcher, Gladys Malcolm, had nine kids. When I hired her, she said her sister-wives—Gladys had quite a few of them—would pitch-hit at home. It rarely seemed to work that way.

"When will Gladys be in?"

"Pretty soon," Kellie said.

This time instead of just asking, I pointed at the phone with the blinking light. "Who's on hold?"

"Oh, gee, Chief. I was going to call you about her," she said, "It's—"

Just then, the station's door swung open and a woman shuffled inside.

"It's her on the phone," Kellie said, her face blanching as if a poltergeist had floated through the door. Instead of talking to me, she turned to the newcomer. "I'm so sorry. I forgot to get back with you."

The previous fall, Christina's older sister and I had talked often. A tall woman with a rawboned face, Jessica seemed to habitually smell of fresh-cut hay and the ranch she lived on with her sister-wives a bit of a drive outside of Alber. I figured she'd been working in the fields all day, maybe with the livestock. I rather appreciated that about her. She wore her prairie dresses with a proud bearing, but she hadn't bowed to the pressure to hide who she was. I'd always thought she had something of a hard glint in her clear blue eyes.

"Clara, you didn't call me," Jessica said, plainly displeased. "And my parents heard that there's a body. A woman. Is it Christina?"

"Let's go in my office," I suggested. Without objecting, Jessica fell in behind me. I turned to lead her when I had another thought, and swiveled back to Conroy. "Time to start that patrol, Officer Conroy. Don't you think?"

"Yes, Chief," he said, jolting out of his chair and running his hands over his hair to calm his disheveled mop. "Absolutely."

Moments later, seated across from me in my office, Jessica had a grasp on the button tab on the front of her dress, as if she needed something to hold onto. "Is it Christina?" she asked again. "Did you find my sister?"

I considered how to answer. I didn't want to give her false hope, and I didn't want to shut her down either. But folks often don't react well to a cop simply saying they don't know, even if it's the truth. That they're going to have to wait for answers. I, however, didn't see that I had a choice. "Jessica, it may or may not be Christina. I have no way of knowing. The autopsy is tomorrow. We'll need to wait for DNA, for the lab work to come in. It may take a while."

"How long?" she asked. "My family… all of us… well… we're pretty upset about this. We need to know soon."

"I understand. If she were my sister…" I started, then I thought of the sister I had lost the previous year and how I would feel if it could be Sadie's remains found buried on the mountainside. I'd want answers, too. And I'd want them without delay. I thought of Ash Crawford and wondered if I did need to be grateful. "Jessica, we're putting a rush on this. I can't give you an exact time frame, but I'm thinking, if we're lucky, we'll have a reconstruction of the face for you to look at, if not the DNA, later this week."

"That's a long time to wait when we're wondering like this," she said, not truly complaining but more acknowledging the toll it would take. "Is there any way you can hurry it up?"

"That is hurrying it up. We have someone talking to the lab for us, to move it to the top of the list. These types of cases, where we don't have an ID, take time." I hesitated before saying more. I didn't want to sound like I was blaming Jessica's family, but there was no way around it. With so many of the folks in our town not believing in traditional medicine, not seeing dentists or doctors, we didn't have the usual tools. "If we had dental records, we could move faster. Since Christina hadn't been to a dentist, we—"

"I know. You've said this before." A scowl ribboned her forehead, but I knew it wasn't directed at me, rather at the reality of the situation. "There's no other evidence, jewelry or something I could look at?"

"No. No jewelry. Nothing like that. Jessica, the body we found…"

"Yes?" Her eyes narrowed; she was concerned, I knew, about why I'd stopped.

"The woman was pregnant, quite far along."

"Pregnant?" She was quiet for a moment, then said, "I guess, I mean, Christina's been gone long enough. That could have happened. But you have nothing to use to identify her? Nothing to show me?"

I thought about the photos on my phone, ones I'd taken at the scene. I only had one thing she might be able to identify, but the photos weren't pretty. "Just what's left of a dress. But are you sure you want to see it? The condition of the body… the remains… they'd been out there for a long time. Buried. There's not a lot left to…"

Jessica's head dropped, and she squeezed her eyes shut. I almost wished I hadn't said anything. But then, if it was Christina we'd found, eventually Jessica would have to be told about the state of her sister's body. When Jessica again locked her eyes on mine, her determination had taken control. "Show me."

I flicked through the photos of the skeleton on my phone, checking for the least grisly. I found one, a shot of the dress from the collar down to the waist, the only visible bone an inch or two of neck and one skeletal wrist. The tendons had contracted as they'd dried, and the hand was clenched in a fist. "Okay," I said. "This was how she was found, in this dress."

I handed my phone to her, and Jessica stared at the photo. Before I realized what she was doing, she'd thumbed to the next and the next. As the gruesome images flicked past, photos of stained bone, muscle, tissue and strands of skin cured a leathery amber, Jessica's face registered the unfolding horror. Still, she kept going. I wanted to grab the phone from her, but I knew from other cases that my impulse was wrong. Folks react to these situations in odd ways. Some don't want to see or know anything. Others need to see everything, all the photos and evidence, to hear all the answers to their questions, no matter how painful.

I waited, quiet, gauging the impact, and before long the hand that held the phone shook ever so slightly as she returned it to me.

"I'm sorry. I know that must have been upsetting for you."

Jessica cleared her throat. "It was my choice. I needed…"

I gave her a moment, long enough to regain some composure. "Anything look familiar?"

A sad headshake, a long pause, her chest heaving ever so slightly as if she were trying to catch her breath. "I wish we'd taken her to a damn dentist," Jessica murmured. "If that's her…"

"I know," I said, meaning it. "You can't decide whether to hope it is or isn't her. Either way, it's not good."

Jessica clenched her mouth tight and gave me a slight nod. "You'll let me know as soon as you can?"

"Absolutely."

Before she walked out my office door, she stopped, her eyes solid on mine: "Thank you."

Once Jessica left, I sat down in my desk chair. I logged on to my computer and NCIC, the FBI's National Crime Information Center database, then started a search for missing women in Utah. There'd been some strands of brown hair still clinging to the skull, so I added that to the filters. I didn't know the race for sure, so I left that blank, but I noted that she was pregnant.

At that moment, as the database churned through tens of thousands of entries, Stef popped her head in. "Is it Christina? Jessica's sister? I saw she was here. Did you call to notify her?"

"We don't know who it is yet. We probably won't for at least a couple of days, maybe much longer, so we can't speculate," I said. "But what about you? Did you find Danny's sister?"

Stef puckered her lips. "Another odd situation." She slumped into the chair across the desk and explained, "No records of a Lynlee Benson to be found. Not anywhere. I looked and looked."

"Social Security, driver's license, school, bank, phone records…"

"Nowhere," Stef insisted. "She's not a lost boy. It's not like Danny. Shouldn't we have some records on her?"

I took a deep breath and thought it through. Sometimes in polygamous households the women were hidden—usually we found some small mention in a record somewhere, but not always. "Maybe not. Let me think about this."

"You want me to put out feelers?"

I knew Stef wanted to help, that she had the urge to run with this, but I kept thinking about what DA Hatfield had said, that we needed to proceed cautiously. I thought of Hannah Jessop, my friend, and that she'd been such a good source since I'd returned home. Hannah had converted the rambling mansion in the center of town where our jailed prophet, Emil Barstow, had lived with his many wives and scores of children, into a women's shelter called Heaven's Mercy. It was where I rented an upstairs bedroom. I thought about how Max had been urging me to put down roots by renting a small house. There were some available in town. I couldn't quite get there. I no longer had one foot in town and one on the highway back to Dallas, but leasing a house? That felt like a step toward commitment.

I shut my laptop. "I'll go to the shelter and talk to Hannah," I told Stef. "Maybe we can figure out who knows the family. She may be able to refer us to someone to talk to about Lynlee and Danny."

"I could do that," Stef said, but I shook the suggestion off.

"Hannah's a friend, and I'm heading to the shelter for the night anyway. I'll do it."

Disappointed, Stef slipped out of the chair and quickly out the door. As soon as she was gone, I grabbed my bag to leave, but Gladys walked in. A pudgy woman, our night dispatcher had her graying brown hair pinned in a French twist that rose to an impressive pompadour and swept over her forehead, nearly covering one eye. When I'd interviewed her for the job, Gladys had insisted that we were related on my mother's side, that we shared a great-great-grandfather. That didn't strike me as a particularly remarkable coincidence, since I was pretty sure that with so few fathers for so many wives, most of the town was related, if family trees were carried back far enough. Gladys did, however, look a bit like my mother. They had the same dark eyebrows that arched into pyramids when they were displeased.

"You're here?" I remarked.

"Sorry I ran late, Chief," she said. In the beginning Gladys had tried to call me Clara. I'd made a point of stressing that wasn't appropriate, even if we were somehow vaguely family. "The good news is that my son's team won the game. Looks like they'll be in the championships later this week."

"Good for him. But you need to keep your home life from interfering with work."

"I don't think Kellie minded," Gladys said with a conspiratorial glance. "She was beaming when she walked out, said something about a date with our young Conroy."

"Well, still, I need you here, working, and on time." She gave me a noncommittal look, but nodded, so I wasn't quite sure she'd latched on to the fact that I wasn't making a suggestion but issuing an order. I was getting ready to push the matter when my cell phone rang. Gladys used the call as cover for her swift departure.

"Clara?" the woman on the phone said.

I recognized the voice. "Mother Sariah, yes." I thought back to earlier that afternoon, when I'd asked Delilah to have her call. "Thanks for getting back to me. I wanted to talk to you about—"

"Clara, your mother's in the hospital in Pine City," Mother Sariah blurted out. "You need to come. Quick. Mother Naomi and I, we're not sure what happened, but there's something very wrong."

CHAPTER TEN

Doc Wiley wasn't in the morgue but in my mother's hospital room in the ICU when I arrived. Mother Sariah looked as if she'd run out half dressed. Her auburn hair, so like Delilah's, was mussed and falling out of a topknot, and she wore an old apron over her long dress as she ran to greet me. "Clara, thank you. Thank you so much for coming," she said, her eyes wild. "Ardeth, your mother, well, she collapsed at the trailer, flat down on the floor. We didn't know what to do."

I couldn't see Mother, just the delicate mold of her thin body lying stone-still under a blanket as Doc bent over her, looking into her eyes with a small penlight, assessing the response of her pupils, I guessed. I crept up beside him. Nearly as pale as the white pillowcase beneath her, Mother had a slender tube delivering oxygen at the base of her nose.

"What's wrong with her, Doc?"

He glanced over his shoulder at me, and I saw the worry in his eyes. "I'm not sure. I think something neurological."

"No theories?" I thought of all Mother had been through the past few years. Father's death, last summer's search for one of my sisters, the death of another, the financial turmoil of trying to keep the family together. I wondered how my return had added to her stress, my attempts to work myself back into the family. The last time I'd talked to her, she'd ordered me to leave the family double-wide—the battered old trailer that overflowed with my three mothers and more than a dozen of my siblings. That day she'd talked of how hard their plight had become, and I'd offered to help, to subsidize the family financially. She'd turned me away, not willing to take even such sorely needed help from an errant daughter.

"I'm thinking it could be a stroke," Doc said. "We aren't sure yet, but the signs are there. I ordered blood work. We should know soon."

"Unconscious?"

"We put her under. Her brain is swelling, and we have her on meds to try to stop it. We'll wake her when the danger passes."

Mother's long salt-and-pepper hair was spread out across the pillow, her face placid, expressionless. She appeared asleep. Behind her an IV on a pole dripped, a long clear tube draped across her arm feeding into a vein on the back of her hand. The equipment monitoring her vitals beeped and her blood pressure, at least to my lay eyes, looked elevated: 160 over 92. I pointed at it. "Doc, isn't that pretty high?"

He grimaced. "We're working on bringing it down."

At that moment, the third of my mothers, Naomi—soft brown hair and wire-rimmed glasses—ambled in carrying two white paper cups of water from the cooler beside the nurses' station. She handed one to Sariah and scowled when she saw me. I wasn't surprised. I'd attempted to talk to her off and on since last year's bison farm murders. My investigation had gotten in the way of her planned marriage, one that would have brought her prestige and money. Each time I'd approached her, she rebuffed me. It turned out that Mother Naomi, despite her tendency to praise the Lord at every turn and light up at the mention of the divine, hadn't fully embraced the teachings that said the only way to gain God's forgiveness was to forgive others.

I shot Mother Naomi a concerned glance, then turned back to my mother on the bed, slipped my hand over hers. I shouldn't have been surprised at the coldness of her skin, like a marble sculpture, but I was. I remembered holding Mother's hand as a child, the warmth of my small hand inside hers, the security I'd once found there.

"It's good that you've come, Clara," Mother Sariah said. "I need to talk to you. There's a matter to discuss."

I nodded at her, but I felt unsure what to do. I placed my other hand on top of Mother's, hoping my two hands could warm hers, as if that would somehow save her. Doc peered over his glasses at me. "Clara, it's okay. I'm watching over Ardeth," he whispered. "You can talk to Sariah. We'll call you if anything happens."

"Clara?" I felt Mother Sariah's hand on my sleeve. "Please, can we talk?"

"I'll stay here with Ardeth as well," Mother Naomi said. "Clara, go with Sariah."

Numb, I let go of Mother's hand.

In a small family waiting area, Mother Sariah motioned for me to sit on a plastic-covered couch. "Tell me again what happened," I said.

She winced at the memory. "We're not exactly sure." Then she repeated what she had said earlier, fleshed out a bit, mentioning that Mother had just finished cleaning up after dinner with the older girls, while Lily and Delilah helped Sariah dress the toddlers in their pajamas. Mother Naomi had the younger children at the outhouse behind the trailer, to get them ready for bed.

"Was Mother angry, emotional, upset about anything?" I asked.

"She'd been fretting over the bills all day, working herself into a frenzy trying to figure out what she could pay and what she couldn't. She worried that they'd turn off the electricity, but we'd run up a bill at the grocery store, too. We were short this month. The quilted skirts I make are selling well, but with so many of the local families gone from Alber, Ardeth's poultices aren't as popular as they once were. Of course, Naomi doesn't harvest honey from her bees over the winter, and she sold out months ago. But Naomi and I told Ardeth that it would be okay. That we'd manage. We couldn't quiet her. On top of that, Ardeth hasn't been sleeping well. Naomi and I had cautioned her that she was wearing herself out, but you know your mother, Clara. Ardeth is hard on others, but she's harder on herself."

How true, I thought. I remembered a time when I was in junior high. Mother had decided to sew all of us girls—I had eight sisters at that time—matching Christmas dresses. She'd put her potion money aside and bought bolts of silky fabric. The prophet frowned on wearing the color red, said it was reserved for God, so Mother chose a bright green. For more than a week, she worked all day at the big house we then lived in, cleaning and cooking, then sewed all night. When she finally fell asleep, the last dress finished, she woke during the night and tripped, hit her head on the corner of a nightstand and opened up a cut that required stitches. She still had the scar above her right eyebrow. Nothing stopped Mother. Except, thinking of her in the hospital bed, perhaps something finally had.

"I'm glad Delilah mentioned that I wanted to talk to you," I said. "But we don't need to do this now. Not with what's happened with Mother."

"You wanted to talk to me? The girls hadn't told me. About what?"

Maybe Lily and Delilah hadn't had time to tell her yet. "Nothing important. What did you want? You tell me."

"Well." Mother Sariah cleared her throat, visibly ill at ease.

Whatever this was, she didn't want to say it. I guessed at what she might want to say and thought that I would make it easier for her. "If you're going to tell me to stay away from Delilah and Lily, well, I do think that—"

"No! No! That's not it."

"What, then?"

"I wanted to talk to you about…" she started, then paused. I waited, and finally she took a deep breath and said, "Money. We need money."

"For the electricity?"

"Yes, that would help, but for the hospital bill," she said. "We have no health insurance. No way to pay, Clara. We're... well, we're barely keeping everyone fed."

I sat back on the couch, and the plastic cover rustled. "This is rather ironic. I'd asked Delilah to ask you to call me because I want to help the family financially. So there's no reason to be embarrassed." Relief spread across Sariah's face, and before my eyes she began to relax.

"You want to help us?"

"Yes. I offered last fall, talked to Mother about setting up a monthly stipend to cover some of the household expenses. She turned me down. Actually, she said she would never take money from an apostate."

Mother Sariah wore a pained expression as she reached out and put her hand over mine. "Oh, Clara, I am sorry that she treated you so harshly. Ardeth can come across as severe, I know. It isn't that she doesn't love you. It's—"

"You don't have to explain. I asked to talk to you because I thought we might be able to work something out between the two of us."

Sariah's blue eyes glistened, and she dropped her head. I thought that perhaps I'd upset her, but her lips spread into a slight smile. "Thank you. Mother Naomi and I, we didn't know what we would do. We have so little since your father died. And Ardeth, she tries, but we can't..."

I leaned toward her, gathered her in my arms, and she finally allowed the tears to flow. "I know. It's okay. I have some money. I can help. I want to help."

"Aaron has said that he will try to help more, too," she said, referring to my oldest brother, the one who'd inherited the sawmill when my father died. "Aaron gives us a check each month to help with the bills, and he'll give more. But the sawmill isn't turning much of a profit lately, and he has two wives and seven children to support. We are too many with too little to live on."

"Okay, it's okay." I tried to reassure her as I held her. As a teenager, Mother Sariah had held me like this, comforted me when life took its toll. "We'll work it out."

"We will," Sariah agreed. "Thank you."

"But mother can't know," I cautioned. Sariah sat back, appearing ready to argue, but I didn't allow it. "If she found out, she'd refuse my help. And we can't have that. She needs the care. I can afford to pay, and I will."

Naomi and Sariah departed for home not long after our talk, returning to the family's trailer that bordered the cornfield below our town's landmark, Samuel's Peak. They needed to make sure that the older ones had gotten the younger ones to bed. The children had school in the morning.

An hour or so after they left, Doc returned to Mother's room and explained that the test results had come in. As he'd suspected, she'd had a stroke. "The good news is that she's stable now. There shouldn't be any issues tonight," he assured me. "Her blood pressure hasn't quite returned to the normal range, but it's close."

"That's good to hear." I'd been thinking about how proud Mother was, and about the substantial harm a stroke could do, impairing limbs, speech, the ability to think. "Do you know how much damage has been done?"

"No, we won't know until she wakes. But Ardeth is a strong woman, and I'm hopeful it won't be severe. Clara, please try not to worry. Go home. Get some sleep. There's no reason for you to stay through the night. Your mother has been given enough medication to ensure that she'll sleep. The nurses will notify you if her condition changes."

"I'll head home soon. And I'll see you in the morning."
Doc appeared taken aback, not sure what I was talking about,
so I explained, "At the autopsy, the pregnant woman from the
mountain?"

"Oh, of course. Such a day this has been. I'd nearly forgotten."

Not long after Doc's departure, my phone vibrated. It was Max.
I texted: *Can't talk tonight. Busy. No news on the case.*

Another vibration: *You okay? Everything all right?*

I sat back in the chair and considered calling him. I thought
about how good it would be to hear his voice. Max had a way of
calming me, of making it seem like everything would eventually
work out. When I was with him, when he touched me, for a short
time I felt whole. But I didn't want to disturb Mother, and I wasn't
ready to leave her side.

I'll explain tomorrow.

I hit send, then sat staring at my mother in the bed, as still
and pale as a china doll. I took her hand again, and tears collected
in my eyes. I bent toward her and kissed her cheek. I thought of
the mother I'd loved as a child, the one I'd been so angry with as
a young woman, the one I'd yearned for since my return, who'd
banished me and kept me at arm's length.

Moments passed. As worried as I was about Mother, other
thoughts intruded, and my mind circled back to my plans to
spend the evening working on the case. I pulled a chair close to
the bed and opened my laptop. A few clicks of the keys and I was
logged back on to NCIC. I entered the same terms I had at the
office earlier: MISSING; UTAH; WOMAN; BROWN HAIR;
PREGNANT.

As the website churned away, I considered how, not far down
the highway in Alber, families were turning off their lights for
the night. I thought of Naomi and Sariah, of my brothers and

sisters asleep in the worn-out trailer, barely enough room to all fit. I thought of the big house I'd grown up in, how comfortable we'd been, all I'd had as a girl that my family had lost, and how desperate they were without Father to support them.

A row of potential matches flashed on the computer screen, and I searched for leads on the bones found in the shallow grave. I read accounts of missing women from Salt Lake, St. George, Orem, Sandy, Ogden, and small towns across Utah. One pregnant woman had disappeared, and I thought that perhaps I'd found a match. Thankfully, she'd been found safe, wandering the streets of Provo. While relieved for that woman and her family, I felt a deep sadness that there wasn't a similar, happy resolution for the mother and her sweet baby whose remains awaited autopsy in the morgue.

As the clock clicked toward midnight, the hospital lights dimmed, including those inside the room. Determined to use the time, I stayed on the computer. I'd barely begun combing through the listings when my eyelids grew heavy. It had been a long day, but I fought to keep them open, scanned one profile, clicked on the next, then considered yet another. None of them seemed to be a good match, but I kept searching. At some point, I must have drifted off. I surrendered to a restless sleep, one filled with dreams of my mother, much younger, when I was just a child: my mother seated, her back rigid, beside my father during worship services; my mother stirring soup over the stove in our old house; leading me through my homework at the kitchen table.

When I awoke, it was with a start. The room had filled with daylight.

Morning.

CHAPTER ELEVEN

"Clara, why didn't you go home last night?" Doc and Ash Crawford were waiting for me when I walked into the morgue a few
minutes after seven. I'd taken the elevator down from Mother's
room without pausing to do more than wash my face and hands
and comb my dark hair back into its usual bun at the nape of my
neck. No time for breakfast.

The remains we'd dug up the day before lay in front of them
on an autopsy table, much of the bone poking out between amber
shards of mummified tissue pulled so tight in places that sections
of her skeleton appeared shrink-wrapped. I inspected the swelling
around her middle, the baby's shriveled body protruding from its
mother's abdomen. Doc had placed the damaged skull and the
chunk knocked out of it above the woman's shoulders. He had it
propped up with small wooden blocks, making it easy to see the
broken edges. I again considered the difference in the color, the
lack of staining that confirmed it was a new fracture. The edges
of the break, too, suggested it was post-mortem. Live bone more
often breaks in spirals, while after-death breaks are smoother, like
a china plate dropped on a tile floor.

I hadn't noticed out in the mountain air, but in the autopsy
suite the remains gave off the stench of rotting meat. The smell
made my empty stomach lurch.

"Max isn't here?" I asked, disappointment creeping into my
voice. I still felt uneasy, worried about Mother, uncomfortable
around Crawford, who I didn't trust.

"Max had to swing by the sheriff's office for a meeting. He said he'd check in with you for an update later," Doc said. "By the way, I looked in on your mom earlier. You were sound asleep. Her condition doesn't appear to have changed. No evidence of more strokes, which is good. As I said, you could have gone home to bed. I told you she was stable for the night."

"Yes, I remember that." I felt wrinkled and worn. My uniform's starched collar stuck to me, and I wondered if I'd drooled on it during the night. However uncomfortable, I'd managed a few hours of sleep.

"I'm sorry to hear about your mother, Chief Jefferies." Crawford had such a deep voice that he sounded as if he'd just downed half a bottle of whiskey and smoked a carton of cigarettes. "If there's anything I can do…"

"Thanks, but Doc is taking good care of her."

"Actually, I've called in a neurologist who is going to work at stabilizing that brain swelling we discussed," Doc explained. "He'll be here late this morning. Once he assesses her, I'll call and brief you."

"Good." I considered asking more questions, but with Crawford at my side, it didn't seem like the time. Although I did want to make sure those caring for my mother investigated every possibility. "Doc, Mother appears to have lost a significant amount of weight. I'm worried that she may have other issues that predate this stroke."

His face screwed up in thought. "I'm glad you mentioned that. Not having seen your mother in years, I didn't realize."

"I thought that perhaps some other tests might be useful."

"Of course," he said. "Wait just a minute. I'll get on the computer and put in orders."

At that, Doc padded over to his office and closed the door. Through a window, I saw him sit at his computer.

"Are you and your mother close?" Crawford asked, and I turned and looked at him. It seemed an odd question, perhaps inappropriate since we didn't know each other well, and I was about to point that out when he mumbled, "I shouldn't have asked. I was just… well, my own parents died years ago, and I…"

"Yes, well, let's talk about the case," I said, redirecting him back to the autopsy table.

"We're taking the skeletons for a CT scan this morning," Crawford said, peering down at the bones on the table. "Afterward, Doc will take tissue samples to send for tox screening, clean their bones and look for evidence of sharp- or blunt-force trauma."

I considered what Crawford had laid out. "The tox screen will take a while to get back, and in her condition, so much deterioration, it may not be reliable."

"Yes, of course. You're right. But it may show something helpful." As he had the day before, he peered down at her with incredible sadness.

I watched him, waited, couldn't shake the feeling that something was wrong, and I said, "You know, I have the oddest feeling that there's more going on than you're admitting."

Crawford's lips curled up slightly at the corners, but I wasn't buying it. A faint flush spread upward from his shirt collar. "That's absurd. I just—"

"Why are you so invested in this case?" If eyes truly could burn holes, mine would have set him aflame.

His response, a nervous chuckle, implied that I'd made a ridiculous suggestion, yet the flush had darkened, and so had his eyes. "This young woman, whoever she is, deserves justice. That's all. Is that so hard for you to understand?"

Of course I understood strong emotions. I felt them too. I wanted to find the person responsible as much as he did. But I couldn't shake my suspicions. So I didn't respond. Instead, I stared at him, didn't make a sound. This worked with a lot of folks. Most people try to fill emptiness because the dead air troubles them.

As a seasoned investigator, Crawford, of course, was wise to my tactic. While he squirmed slightly, he resisted any urge to talk.

When he kept quiet, I took over again. "I am wondering if you have information you're not sharing. Not if you have a crystal ball, but rather prior knowledge. Does this case remind you of another one? Maybe something you've worked on?"

Crawford's eyes narrowed and he shook his head, that slight smile still there, but fuming. "No. We don't handle these types of cases at the US Marshal's office, Chief. You know that."

I did know, but there had to be some reason. "Why, then? Do you think this is someone you know?"

Crawford let loose a short huff, as if insulted. "If I knew who this was, if I could ID this body for you, I promise you that I would!" Dropping any pretense of finding me amusing, he seethed. "I will say this one more time: I don't know who she is."

"And you're here because?"

"I want to help." He shook his head at me, as if I were the most preposterous person. "Why is that impossible for you to believe? If you suddenly stopped being a cop, wouldn't you feel a loss? Wouldn't you still want to do what you're good at? Have a purpose?"

We glared at one another. He hadn't said anything wrong. Not a single word. But rather than settle my concerns, Crawford's responses had amplified them.

Doc's voice cut through the tension. "I've ordered everything for your mother, Clara, the whole shebang," he called out as he sauntered back in. I watched Crawford, who smiled. Relieved, I thought, that we'd been interrupted.

"Thanks, Doc. I'm sure Mother hasn't had a check-up with a real doctor in…" I considered the options, that my family, like most of Alber's citizens, rarely went to Gentile doctors and instead relied on Mother's herbal remedies. "Probably never, actually."

"No, thank *you*, Clara. I should have done that last night. But now we'll get to the bottom of *this*," Doc said, nodding to the body as he hit a lever on the autopsy table that released brakes on all four wheels. "Help me push her to the CT suite. Let's get this case moving."

As the tech worked the machine, the images on the screen were haunting. Crawford and I huddled behind Doc as the CT captured cross-sectional images of the woman's skull and flashed the outlines of the bone in white on the dark screen. Doc had the tech examine the skull without the chunk first, then the chunk by itself. Then Doc used a fast-drying epoxy to bind them and scanned the repaired skull. Once he finished, he handed a disc with the images on it to Crawford. "You think this will work for the computer's facial reconstruction program?" Doc asked. "Do you need anything else?"

"This'll work," Crawford replied. It appeared that he'd set aside our argument. All of his attention was focused on the CT screen. "I'll take off and email this to my friend at the state lab. Get him started. He's waiting on it."

"We appreciate that, don't we, Clara?" Doc prodded, and I gave the retired marshal a shrug in half agreement.

"I know the chief is rooting for me," Crawford said with a somewhat sardonic-looking grin. With that, he was gone.

Once alone, Doc and I arranged the remainder of the skeleton on the scan bed, and the process started anew. "I wish you'd be friendlier with Marshal Crawford," Doc mumbled as he stared at the screen. "He's being of service."

"Doc, I don't trust him. I can't explain why not, but I'm not buying this boy scout routine of his."

Doc gave me an exasperated over-the-shoulder glance, an irritated one. "Clara, we both know that we need the help. We can't afford to turn away offers like Marshal Crawford's. Last time I tried to get the state lab to do something cutting-edge like this for me, my case went to the bottom of the queue. It took months to get a report back."

With Crawford gone and Doc lecturing me, I'd begun to wonder why I was digging in my heels. Maybe it didn't matter why Ash Crawford wanted to help, only that he *could* help. After all, we had a dead woman and child, most likely a murderer to find.

"Okay, Doc. You've made your point. I still don't like it, but I'll do my best to work with Crawford, to speed this up. Now, tell me what you've found. Are you getting any ideas about height, race, age?"

"Yes, look here." Doc pointed out the ends of the thigh bones, then traced the upper right arm bone down to the elbow.

Unsure what I was supposed to be looking at, I asked, "What should I be seeing?"

"The growth plates aren't closed in the long bones. And the ribs where they meet her breastbone? Rounded. Smooth."

"What does that mean?"

"That this woman is young."

Doc went into a bit of a mini-lecture on how leg and arm bones grow and how the plates close by age twenty-five or so. He talked about how ribs wear and sharpen with age. Our Lady of the Mountain, he said, wasn't truly a lady at all: rather a teenager.

"How young?" I asked.

Doc screwed his lips up and considered. "This is just an estimate, of course, but somewhere between fourteen and seventeen years old."

"That's young to be pregnant," I remarked, and Doc agreed. "What about race? Height?"

"Give me a minute." Using a scale on the CT scanner, Doc measured the humerus. "Her height is approximately five times the length of the bone. So I'd say she was somewhere around five feet two inches. Again, that's a rough estimate." Silence, while he brought up images of the skull yet again, turned them on the screen to look at it from all angles.

"Look here, Clara," he said. "Based on the shape of the eye sockets, the narrow nose aperture, she's likely Caucasian. I can't be certain without DNA analysis, of course, but the balance of probability tips that way, especially considering her prairie dress and the demographics of the area."

I'd been taking notes, and I looked down at the pad. "So our victim is likely a white teenage girl, somewhere around fourteen to seventeen, approximately five feet two inches tall with long brown hair. Based on her prairie dress, she's most likely from a polygamous town. Is all of that correct?"

Doc considered for a moment, then nodded. "That's my best guess."

"Anything else we can figure out here?"

"Once we're done, you can help me load her up and bring her back to the lab," Doc said. "I'll get her back on the autopsy table and gather the samples to send to the lab. I should be able to get mitochondrial DNA from her teeth, grind off some pulp. I read about that last night. Decided to do it here instead of sending her to the lab."

"Any way to figure out how long she's been dead? Buried?" I needed some kind of a timeline to use to narrow the cases down when I considered possible matches. Was I looking for a teenager who disappeared decades, years, or months ago?

Doc's brow creased and he took a deep, staggered breath. "I've been thinking about that, and I'd guess that she's been out there for at least a year. Based on the acidity of the soil, the condition of the body, the discoloration of the exposed bones and the mummification of the remaining tissue. That some of the dress has survived, not deteriorated away, I don't think longer than five years. But I'll request a test to gauge the nitrogen level in the bones to be sure. That'll give us more information."

"What about the baby?" I asked.

Doc inspected the images taken by the CT. For a while, silence, then he said, "It's a boy."

"Oh." It felt like those three words had knocked the air out of me. I thought of ultrasounds where mothers and fathers waited in high expectation to hear the three words that revealed the sex of their much-anticipated offspring. "How far along was the pregnancy?"

Doc looked at the infant's skull again, lined up a ruler to measure and computed a formula on a pad of paper. "The circumference of the skull is about thirty-two centimeters. What I speculated on the scene was right. This child is somewhere around full-term."

"Great. That helps." I was doing a mental inventory of what I knew about Christina Bradshaw. None of what Doc had said ruled her out. She was fifteen when she disappeared, slight build, just a bit over five feet tall. Maybe it was her. Could she have lived longer than we believed, long enough to carry a baby nearly to birth?

Doc frowned. The case bothered him. It bothered me, too. I thought of Ash Crawford again. Could it be that he was just as affected by the girl's death as we were? Was it as simple as that?

"Wish I had more," Doc said.

"No indication of how she died?"

"No. I'll have to get a good look at the bones and wait on the toxicology. Maybe something will show up."

"This is a good start." I slipped my notebook into my bag and grabbed my cell. "Call me if you have any more thoughts on the case, if you see anything to indicate manner or cause of death."

"Sure, Clara, of course. And I'll let you know about your mother's test results, what the neurologist has to say."

"That works, Doc. Thanks." Halfway to the door, he called out to me.

"Clara!" I glanced back and Doc gave me a stern look. "I know you cops don't always play well together. That police officers can be protective about cases. Not welcome interference from other agencies."

I knew where this was going.

"Let Crawford open doors for us, so we can get to the bottom of this," Doc ordered. "This may be your case and Max's that Crawford has forced his way into, but it's really not about you. It's about a dead girl and her unborn baby."

CHAPTER TWELVE

The other woman, the sister-wife, slipped a sliver of ice into the girl's parched mouth. She sucked it down. "Not so fast, Violet. Let it melt," the woman whispered. "Let it moisten your mouth."

"Why can't I have anything to drink?" she asked.

The woman shrugged. "I don't know. I do what I'm told. She said only the ice."

Violet gazed up at the strange woman. Between contractions, the girl's body ached but at least the pain lessened. "Please, untie me. I can't escape in this condition. I can't even walk."

The woman's frown squeezed her eyes nearly shut. "No. You don't know what they're like. What he would do to me."

"Please, I…" before she could finish the sentence, the woman had wandered off, leaving her alone again with only her thoughts. Exhausted, she closed her eyes. Soon the dreams continued, memories of that place and what had happened there. Violet pictured one particular day, the one when she'd discovered the hidden staircase.

By then, Samantha had been moved upstairs to the birthing rooms. Violet had wanted to visit her, but the only way up was a rickety elevator, one kept locked. Nurse Gantt wore the key on a chain around her neck. As painful as it was, Violet had slowly given up hope of ever seeing her friend again. Then, that afternoon, someone left the storeroom door ajar. Violet peeked in and saw stairs. After she glanced around to make sure no one was watching, she climbed the steep steps. The third-floor door opened on to a deserted hallway. The girl paused, unsure what to do. She couldn't tell which of the hallway's three doors led to Samantha's room. If Violet stumbled into the wrong one, whoever was inside could report her. If they did, she'd be in trouble.

As she hid behind the staircase door and pondered what to do, another door swung open, and Nurse Gantt walked out. Violet watched through barely a slit in the staircase door.

"Oh, we can't allow that," Nurse Gantt said, talking to whoever was inside the room. "You know the rules. Visitors aren't allowed."

The girl inside the room responded, saying something Violet couldn't quite make out. Was it Samantha?

"No, not even Violet," Nurse Gantt responded, her voice projecting weariness at the question. "When I say, 'No visitors,' I mean: *no visitors!*"

That has to be Samantha's room, Violet thought.

Glowering, the nurse slammed the door shut and sashayed down the hall to the elevator, her ample hips rocking back and forth in her too-tight surgical scrubs. Once inside, she pressed the button, and the cranky old thing groaned as it lumbered out of sight.

When Violet slipped inside the room, Samantha sat up in bed. She wore a faded gray cotton gown that tied in the back. It barely stretched over her distended belly.

"Oh, I missed you so much!" Samantha cried out.

Violet placed her finger across her lips and shushed her friend, then the girls hugged. Samantha felt good in her arms, but Violet thought her friend looked pale and unwell. "Why are you in bed? Are you okay?"

"I guess. But I sleep a lot. They won't let me get out of bed. I get in trouble if I do."

"Oh." Violet thought back to when her mothers were pregnant, how they'd cooked and cleaned. She didn't understand why

Samantha was so confined. "Is something wrong with your baby that you have to be in bed?"

"I don't think so."

"Are they being nice to you?"

"I feel like a prisoner," Samantha said, as she ran her hands over her baby bump, caressing it. "I don't really want to give up my baby. Do you?"

Violet shook her head, then she'd wrapped her arms around Samantha and held her as she'd wept.

CHAPTER THIRTEEN

"So, you're still worried about Ash?" Max asked, his voice blaring over the SUV's speakers.

"Max, I can't get past this. I think he's hiding something."

This was a time when Max apparently didn't share my concerns. "Clara, I've never heard anything about Ash Crawford that wasn't positive. Always that he's a good cop. Are you sure you're not reading too much into his reactions? Body language isn't… I mean, folks don't always act the way we think they should."

"No, they don't. And I don't have any evidence."

I'd already filled Max in on Mother's condition, that I'd spent the night at her bedside. In the car, I turned onto the main road leading to Alber, on my way to the shelter, to take a shower and change into a clean uniform.

"Well, I don't know what to do about this. It's not that I don't believe you, but there's nothing solid. And maybe I don't see it as the problem you do. After all, Ash is helping, and maybe you should—"

"Relax and be grateful, like Doc says." I finished the sentence for him. "I caught an earful from him this morning, all about not looking a gift horse in the mouth."

Max chuckled, and I thought of the sparkle in his eyes when he laughed. I shook my head and refocused. The shelter loomed ahead. I needed to clean up and get to the office.

"When will the autopsy be done?" Max asked.

"This afternoon. I'll call and you can meet me at the morgue for the results, okay?"

"Sure. The way that woman died, the baby... Something we do agree on: she wouldn't have been buried like that unless someone was trying to cover up something very wrong."

I hung up and parked in my usual spot. At the shelter's door, I stepped back to make way for a cluster of women and children, each talking over the other. One, a woman who'd only moved in the day before, smiled and nodded at me, but the rest eyed me and kept walking. A dozen steps down the walk, the others whispered to the newcomer, and when they finished, she flashed a suspicious glance my way. I felt certain that based on what her friends had told her, in the future, she'd be less friendly.

The encounter left me saddened. As much as I told myself I didn't need friends or to be accepted, I considered yet again that I must be a masochist to remain in Alber working for folks who would prefer I took the highway out of town and kept driving. Not only that, I lived with them. A lot of them.

Women came and went from the shelter, many with their children beside them, as they fled violence, like I once had. Or they ran out of money and stayed a while as a transition before moving on, most heading to other polygamous towns in the area, Salt Lake or a big city where they thought they could find shelter and work. The women quickly bonded, brought together by their hardships. I had a lot in common with them. But because of the way I'd left, my disavowal of polygamy and the faith, I would always be an outsider.

As I walked into the parlor, I considered that Max might be right; I might be happier if I found another place to live. There were a bunch of houses on the market, including the one I'd grown up in. I'd heard that the mainstream Mormon family who'd bought it at the foreclosure auction had decided that they didn't belong in a polygamous town where the locals weren't particularly welcoming to outsiders.

"Hannah!" I shouted, when I saw her bustling through the living room heading toward a wing of bedrooms.

"Oh, Clara, you're home. Where have you been? I was going to report you missing to the police, but you are the police." At that, Hannah Jessop, the woman who'd founded the shelter and kept it running, laughed as if she'd just told the funniest joke. She whispered in my ear, "I thought you and Max would drive back yesterday. You stayed over an extra day at the cabin? This must be getting very serious."

I almost didn't correct her; it appeared that the prospect made her happy. But I have this thing about telling the truth.

"We drove from the cabin directly to work yesterday morning. I was…" I hesitated, and my friend cast me a curious glance. We'd been tight years ago and had grown even closer since my return. If the rest of Alber viewed me as an interloper, Hannah considered me a good friend. "I spent the night with Mother. She's in the hospital. A stroke."

"Oh, Clara." She grabbed me and held me, and at first, I started to pull back, but then, it felt so warm, so good, that I leaned into her and rested my head on her shoulder.

"I stayed in her hospital room overnight. Doc is bringing in a neurologist to consult this afternoon."

Hannah understood the realities of my family life, and she asked, "Ardeth didn't send you away?"

"She was unconscious." I pulled back, looked at Hannah, and I couldn't help myself, I released a short laugh. She looked just a touch taken aback. "Oh, Hannah, think about it. It is funny. Poor Mother. If she'd only known I was the one at her bedside, she would have fought through the meds they had her on to stand up, point at the door, and order me out."

At that, Hannah shot me what looked to be the unhappiest smile I'd ever seen, as she again pulled me toward her and held me tighter. "She'll be okay, Clara. Ardeth isn't that old. I bet she'll recover well."

I cleared my throat to try to dislodge the lump that blocked me from speaking. Then I remembered what I'd wanted to talk to her about: Danny Benson, the kid with the black eye in the folder out of the Tombs. "Hannah, do you know the Benson family? Clyde and his wives, the one who owns the service station outside of town."

Hannah let go of me and pulled a few steps away, curious. "Not well. But we have a niece of his here. Do you need information on the family? Should I get her?"

With so much intermarriage between the families, I'd expected as much. It seemed that Hannah, who could have done a family tree for the whole town out of memory, nearly always knew someone who knew someone when I needed a lead. "Yes, if you could. I'll go upstairs and change. It won't take me long. Say fifteen minutes."

I showered, changed into clean clothes, and grabbed my bag, not taking time to button the long sleeves on my uniform shirt. At the foot of the steps, Hannah waited with a young woman, maybe mid-thirties, faded brown hair and eyes that looked older than they should at that age. Her nose jutted a bit to the left, as if it may have healed wrong after being broken.

"This is Krystee. She's Clyde Benson's niece," Hannah said. "Krystee, this is my very good friend Clara Jefferies, the police chief in Alber. She wants to ask you a few questions about your Uncle Clyde."

Krystee bobbed her head. Although she'd agreed to talk to me, her sullen look made it clear that she wasn't happy about it.

"You two can use the parlor," Hannah suggested. "I think it's empty."

We seated ourselves in a corner in two overstuffed chairs that had been donated by a Salt Lake ward house. I leaned toward Krystee. "I'm looking for Danny."

"Danny?"

"Danny Benson. He's your Uncle Clyde's son. Should be about twenty years old. Do you know where he's living? How I can find him?"

Krystee sat as far back as possible in the chair, extending the distance between us. "I don't think you can. I mean…"

"I have to find him, Krystee. It's important."

I pulled down my left sleeve and fumbled with the button on the cuff. I noticed Krystee focusing on the three-inch eagle tattoo on the inside of my right forearm. Women in Alber never had their arms uncovered around others—it was considered immodest. They certainly didn't have brightly colored tattoos. Watching Krystee stare at it, I wondered how long the news would take to spread through the shelter and out into the town—another example of my brazen behavior.

Drawing her attention back where I needed it, I said, "Krystee, I asked about Danny. I need to talk to him."

If her expression had initially been noncommittal, maybe a touch inquisitive, the sight of my eagle had turned her dour. "That's not possible."

"Why not?"

"Danny is gone. He left years ago. When he was a kid. I barely remember him. He couldn't have been more than kindergarten age. He and one of his older sisters ran off together."

As soon as she said it, I knew, but I asked to be sure. "Which of the older girls?"

"Lynlee. She and Danny, they were close, and one summer, I don't remember the year but Danny was just a little kid… they both disappeared. Lynlee was young, too. But Uncle Clyde said that she'd run away with Danny. Taken him and left."

I thanked Krystee, and she wandered off. As I got ready to leave, I saw Hannah again, this time shepherding a clutch of the younger children into the dining room for studies. The kids were chattering and jostling one another. Hannah stopped to give me another hug before I walked out the door and asked, "Was that helpful?"

"It was." I thought for just a moment, then asked, "One more thing, have you heard anything about any girls missing from town, maybe accompanied by rumors that they were pregnant?"

Hannah stood back, curious. "Why?"

"Just a question. We're working on something, and—"

Hannah's voice rose at least two octaves. "Those bones they found yesterday, up near the lodge, it was a girl, and she was pregnant?"

I took a deep breath. "I can't answer a lot of questions yet."

Hannah didn't hide her disappointment. I would have liked to tell her more, but this wasn't technically my case. Max had called me in because of the Bradshaw girl. It wasn't my call to decide what information to release. And although I trusted Hannah, anyone could slip and say something she shouldn't. A comment made to the wrong person could ruin an investigation.

"Hannah, I'm sorry. That's all I can tell you."

At that, she nodded. "Okay. I understand. No. I don't know of any missing girls. But I will ask around."

In the Suburban on my way to the station, I realized that I'd missed a call while I was in the shower. Doc had left a message to say he'd finished cleaning the bones and wanted me at the morgue to go over the autopsy. I thought about Danny and Lynlee and considered what to do.

"Doc, I have a stop to make on my way," I explained, when I got him on the phone.

"Okay. Max will be here soon, but we'll wait for you. And I notified Marshal Crawford."

"Ex-marshal Crawford. He's not a cop. He's retired. I'm not sure why you'd—"

"He asked me to let him know when I had some results, and I did." Doc sounded defensive, and I knew that he'd grown tired of my stubbornness.

It did no good to argue with him. I sighed and moved on. "Just tell me about Mother."

"Oh, all right." I gave him a minute to settle down. "Ardeth's stroke was a significant one. We're keeping her in the drug-induced coma, and the neurologist has changed her therapy to better ease the brain swelling. He's doing more blood work, trying to figure out what caused it."

One word had caught my attention—"significant"—and I realized that I'd stopped watching the road. I wasn't sure when, but I didn't remember leaving Alber and turning onto the highway. I pulled over to the shoulder, flipped on the flashers and put the SUV in park next to the ditch. "Go on."

"We believe the meds will ease the situation in the next twenty-four hours. Once it's safe, we'll gradually wake her. At that point, we'll assess any damage. Maybe, if she's lucky, she'll come out of this relatively intact."

This time I focused on "relatively intact."

"You have any predictions, Doc? Will it affect her speech? Her ability to walk? I noticed one hand seems to be locked in a tight fist. Is that from the stroke?"

My heart caught in my throat when he answered, "I don't know, Clara. These are things I can't predict. Your mother is truly in God's hands."

CHAPTER FOURTEEN

Clyde Benson was dispensing premium into a black sedan when I pulled up to the garage. The first thing anyone describing Clyde would note is that he was a big man—massive arms and legs, tall, powerfully built. He had a blond monk's fringe and big ears, bulgy eyes and round cheeks. "Time to fill 'er up, Chief?"

"Hey Clyde," I said with a smile. "Sure. Let's do it. I'll wait until you're finished with your other customer. No hurry."

The body shop had a gravel parking lot, with the only cement the platform the pumps were built on. The overhead doors were open on both bays, and Clyde had an old Chevy on the lift, maybe just an oil change but the thing looked like it could have used a complete rebuild and a paint job. In addition to new fenders and bumpers, Clyde did all manner of engine repairs. Off to the side, four clunkers rusted, weeds growing up around them. The building needed a new coat of paint, too, along with the sign on the pole with the name on it; the "B" in "Benson's" had faded off.

A few minutes passed, the sedan sped out of the station and on down the highway. Clyde pulled out an oily rag tucked into the pocket of his gray-striped coveralls and wiped his hands. The rest of the nation had gone to self-serve but at Benson's Body Shop, Clyde still gave great customer service. A grin on his face, he strolled over and stuck the nozzle into my Suburban's tank, then squeezed to get the gas flowing. "I filled up a few days ago, so probably won't need a lot. But I was driving by and decided to stop."

"Always good to see you, Chief."

In the past, I'd kept it all business with Clyde. But this time I hadn't come for the gas. Stef had come up dry looking for Danny and Lynlee, and I intended to do a little prospecting for information. "So, how's the family, Clyde? Well, I hope?"

"Good, Chief."

"The wives?" I would have mentioned them by name, but I couldn't remember them. I couldn't remember having ever met any of the women.

"Fine, no complaints," he said, chomping on what I assumed had to be a plug of chewing tobacco. "Nice of you to ask."

I'd heard Clyde had moved, but I wasn't sure where. Before I'd fled, he'd lived in a spread on the highway near the edge of town. "Where are you living now, Clyde?"

He gave me a strange look. "Up the mountain, Chief. Bought a farmhouse. Old place was too small."

I would have liked to ask more, but he looked suspicious, and I didn't want to alarm him. I thought of his old house. When I used to drive by, he always had a sway-backed bay grazing in the front pasture. "That horse of yours still around?"

"Daisy?" I nodded, and he continued. "Yeah, the old girl's still kicking. She's getting up there in years. The kids love her, so we keep feeding her."

That was the opportunity I'd been waiting for, a natural opening to ask about his family. "You know, we've never talked about your kids, Clyde. Remind me. How many do you have?"

"Eight." He put one hand on his hip and his chest expanded, the proud dad. "Five boys. Three girls."

"How wonderful. I bet you're really proud of them." I came close to gushing. "What are their names? How old?"

I'd poured it on, and Clyde appeared pleased at my interest. "Oh, now, you're not going to hold it over me if I get an age wrong, are you?"

"Nah. With eight, I think a year or two off on one isn't a big deal, is it?" I laughed, keeping it light, doing my best to act friendly.

"All right, then." At that, he pulled the spout out of the Suburban and inserted it back into the pump. That done, he held out his fists and put the first finger out. With each child, he extended another finger. He listed all eight, ages twenty-two to six. But he didn't mention Lynlee or Danny.

"That's a great family," I said, making sure I gave him my friendliest smile.

His grin spread ear to ear, and I knew he was eating up the attention. "Yeah, they're pretty wonderful. Jewels in a father's crown, you know."

I thought of the proverb and how it actually referred to grandchildren, but I let it go. I waited, hoping Clyde would say more about the family. But his smile faded some, and it appeared that he'd tired of the conversation. "You want I should put it on your account, like usual?"

"Sure. That's easiest. Say, does your family homeschool?"

At that, he turned his head just a bit to the side and gave me an inquisitive glance. That wasn't a question he'd expected. "Nah, well, sometimes the wives have, off and on. But most of the time, the kids go to the school in town. Why do you ask?"

I'd wanted that bit of information, but I needed to pin it down. "You know, I taught for a while. I think I remember one of your kids. Let me think about this."

I stood there, silent, as if contemplating what child of Clyde's I might remember. He glanced at his watch as he continued to gnaw on that wad of tobacco. He had that Chevy on the lift to get to. I was trying his patience. On purpose. I wanted him to talk to get rid of me. It worked, and he asked, "When were you there teaching? Maybe I can tell you which kid you might have had in class."

"I started fifteen years ago, taught kindergarten. Then, you know, I left town going on eleven years ago. Were you sending your kids to school in town while I was there?"

"Well, I think so," he said, sticking his right index finger in his ear and scratching. "I am sure we sent the older kids to the school. But I can't think of one who would have been in kindergarten around that time, though. Not sure who you might have taught."

At that, he turned to leave, but I followed him. "Clyde, I think I'll buy one of those candy bars out of your dollar box."

"Have at it. Leave the money by the register."

"You bet." I tracked behind him into the station. The place was old but well kept, and I'd always assumed that one or both of his wives cleaned a few times a week to keep it that way. I'd walked in with him because I'd remembered that there were family photos in small frames around the place. Clyde shuffled past me, and I picked up one that looked like it might have been an older picture. The glass was dusty, and I wiped it off with my thumb. Clyde sat proudly in the photo surrounded by his two wives and five children. "These must be your oldest kids?"

Clyde had been on his way to the shop area to get busy, but he clomped over and stood next to me. I was well aware that he towered above me and had to have a hundred pounds, probably more on me. "That's them, all right."

"Nice photo." I put it back on the shelf and then scrounged around but couldn't find my usual Baby Ruth or Mars Bar. Instead, I grabbed a KitKat and slapped down the dollar. Based on what he'd said at the pump, the ages of his children, what I knew about Lynlee from the report folder, I pointed at the oldest girl in that same photo and said, "She looks kind of familiar. Who's this?"

"Who's who?" he asked. I pointed again. For a moment, his face flushed and he appeared unable to answer. Then he stammered, "Oh, why, that's Elizabeth, my oldest."

"Your oldest. The one who is twenty-two now?"

Clyde picked up my dollar and put it into the register. I noticed that he didn't ring it up. Since I'm a police chief, not an internal revenue agent, I didn't really care, but I kept my eyes on him.

The interesting thing? He didn't answer my question. "Well, gotta get to work on that car. The guy's expecting it later today. Like I said: always good to see you, Chief."

"Same to you," I said, as I turned to leave. "See you when the tank nears empty."

Clyde sniggered a bit and waved me off, and I walked outside crunching my candy bar. As soon as I climbed into the Suburban, I put in a call to Stef. As I drove off, the gas station disappeared in the rearview mirror.

"Yeah, Chief," Stef said. "What have you got for me?"

"Clyde Benson tells me that his older kids, which should include Lynlee, went to the public school in town. But you said that you checked those records?"

"I called and asked them to look Danny and Lynlee up. The secretary said she did and didn't find anything on the computer."

"Okay, well, Danny they might not have. What I'm hearing is that Clyde Benson told folks that Lynlee took Danny and ran away when he was still young. I'm thinking not long after she filed that report."

"But Lynlee was just a kid, too," Stef said.

"Yeah, she was. And something's not right here. Clyde has family photos in the station. Based on the ages of the kids, I'm pretty sure I pointed at a photo of Lynlee and he claimed it was a different daughter."

"So you confronted him?"

"No. I wasn't there to do that. Not yet. I dropped in on him to worm some information out of him. Based on what he told me, I want you to go to the school and ask to see the physical records for that time period. Look up Lynlee. If you find anything, make copies and bring it back to the station. I'm heading to the morgue for a consult with Doc. I'll check in with you when I'm done."

"Got it. But, Chief?"

"Yes, Stef. What?"

"When we arrest Clyde, I want to put the cuffs on."

I sucked in a sigh. "Just get those records."

Max was already at the morgue hobnobbing with Doc when I showed up, but Ash Crawford hadn't yet arrived. "Did our ex-marshal get bored and take off to solve another case?" I heard the sarcasm in my voice.

"He'll be here in a few minutes. I told him not to rush," Doc said with a grimace.

"Good for you."

"Clara, quit goading me," Doc warned.

Max stood far enough behind Doc that the old man couldn't see him, and I could tell he was loving that Doc and I were sparring. Just then, a gravelly voice boomed from behind me: "Glad you waited for me. But we can get busy now."

Height-wise with the hat on, Crawford filled up a good bit of the doorway and had a look on his face like he'd caught me at an awkward moment. Too bad for him—I wasn't embarrassed.

Doc shook his head and sighed, while Max jumped in and changed the subject: "Ash is right. Where's the body?"

"This way," Doc said, shooting me a disappointed glance.

Crawford stewed, a frown on his face, as we followed Doc to the far autopsy table, the one near the back windows, frosted to keep anyone from seeing in. He'd cleaned the bones, scraped off the remaining muscle and tissue and sent samples to the state lab's toxicology department for analysis. The bones were then washed in a solution of hot water and detergent and arranged as they were inside the body, the result resembling a skeleton nearly clean and complete enough to hang in a doctor's office. Beside the mother, Doc had laid out the baby's tiny bones.

"On the off-chance that the girl's not from around here, I'm having a test done that can peg environmental influences on the body, to test for elements prevalent in people who live in different parts of the country, the Midwest, the East or West Coasts."

"They can do that?" Crawford asked, sounding impressed.

"Yes, your friend at the lab can do that," Doc said as we spread out around the stainless-steel table. "It'll take a while, though. I hope we have her identified before then."

"What did you find to suggest cause of death?" I asked. "Anything?"

Crawford crouched down and scanned the bones. "Bullet holes? Scrapes from a knife?"

"No sign of damage from a bullet," Doc said. "And no knicks or cuts in the bones that would indicate that a sharp weapon had been used."

"Fractures?" I asked. "Besides the damage to the skull done by the construction crew?"

"No fractures," Doc said. "I don't see any evidence of blunt-force trauma."

"So we don't know any more than when I left here this morning after the CT scan, I guess?" Crawford looked disappointed, maybe more than that. Perhaps a touch angry.

"Actually, we know a lot more," I countered. He grimaced, then shook his head.

"Clara means that we know what didn't happen to her," Max said to the ex-marshal.

"Yes. We know she probably wasn't shot or knifed, or bludgeoned to death," Doc said. "Other forms of homicide leave more subtle clues, I'm afraid. So I think this is one that's going to take some time. We'll have to hope toxicology shows something."

"Or that we get that facial reconstruction back and identify her. That might give us clues on how she died." Turning to our interloper, I asked, "When can we expect that the reconstruction will be done?"

"Not exactly sure when, but later today," Crawford answered.

I was surprised, and I had to fight the urge to compliment him. A same-day turnaround on a facial reconstruction sounded nearly impossible. Clearly, as much as I hated to admit it, Crawford did have valuable connections.

"Right now they're inputting the images from the CT scan into the computer," he explained. "Once that's done, the program will calculate skin depth and draw the face."

Doc took off his glasses and grinned so wide his ears notched up half an inch. "Technology is incredible. It can do in an hour what it takes a human days or more to accomplish." Then he turned and looked directly at me. "And we should be glad we have it, or a case like this might never be solved."

"I'll get a rush on that tox screen, too," Crawford said. Doc nodded, and the retired marshal took his leave.

After Crawford left, I walked Max to the morgue door, and he leaned close and whispered, "I'm expecting a phone call from you tonight. One missed night, okay to skip our call, but not two. Okay?"

I considered how we had two lives: our work and our personal relationship. So far, we'd been able to keep those separate, but Max ran his hand down my arm before he walked out the door. I turned and saw Doc watching, a keen interest in his expression.

"So, you and Max Anderson, huh?" He seemed to ponder that for a moment. "I thought earlier that I was picking up on chemistry between the two of you."

"We're just really good friends."

Doc scrunched his nose. "Didn't look that way."

Eager to change the subject, I asked, "Any more information about my mother?"

Doc released an "Oh!"

"There is, I guess."

"Yes, I meant to tell you. The neurologist and I had a phone consult while I waited for you to arrive. He suspects your mother has done this to herself."

I thought of Mother and what Sariah and Naomi had said, how she'd been troubled by the family finances. "Stress?"

"No. Not that. At least, not exactly, although that may have been one factor." Doc shook his head. "I know that your mother is an herbalist, that she makes and sells potions, poultices, and the like to folks throughout the area. I've heard stories that she's quite good at it."

I envisioned my mother's kitchen: buckets filled with herbs suspended in various solutions that she funneled into small bottles with eyedroppers. Handwritten labels for her sleep potion; headache relief; indigestion; toothache; hair growth; skin disorders. From the ceiling she hung herbs and flowers to dry, and she bought cheesecloth by the bolt to wrap her poultices. "Yes, she is, Doc. Mother treats nearly every illness with some kind of a mixture of herbs and flowers, weeds she pulls out of the ground in the woods. Why is this important?"

"Does she treat herself?"

I thought back to my childhood, working in the kitchen with Mother, how she bent over the stove breathing in herbs to treat her coughs, the time she cut herself while chopping carrots and had me tie a poultice on her wound. "Yes, she does."

"The neurologist thought so."

"Explain what you're getting at," I prodded, losing patience. "Did Mother poison herself?"

"No, no, nothing like that. Well, maybe in a sense. He thinks she overmedicated herself. His theory is that your mother has been ingesting some form of willow. That arch in her back suggests that she's suffering with arthritis throughout her body. A condition like hers can be very painful, so it's not surprising that she tried to find something to relieve it."

"Willow?" I remembered going out to the forest with Mother, afternoons spent in the rich air, surrounded by green, breathing in the fresh breeze as we scrounged on the ground and pulled up herbs, the times mother stopped at a white willow tree along the river and scraped the bark. "As in willow bark tea?"

"Yes, that would have done it."

"Done what?"

"Well, the Ancient Egyptians first used willow bark to treat aches and pains, headaches, backaches and such," Doc explained. "The bark has salicin in it, a type of painkiller that predates aspirin. Salicin is the basis for salicylic acid, which reacts in a similar way to aspirin in the body."

"So this salicin got into Mother's brain and caused the stroke?"

"Not exactly. The neurologist is speculating that your mother took heavy doses to treat her back pain. Like aspirin, salicin also acts as a blood thinner. He's determined that your mother suffered a hemorrhagic stroke. We believe she probably has a tumor in her brain, and that since her blood is dangerously thin, it caused a bleed."

I took in a deep breath. I thought about Mother, so dead set against Gentile doctors, mainstream medicine. She'd always been smug, bragging that she knew more than any doctor who'd gone through medical school. As a child, I had helped her concoct her potions and listened to her murmur about the wisdom of the ages. "These recipes came down from my great-grandmother," she'd cooed. "They are the backbone of our knowledge on medicine."

"Doc, Mother always talked about how her herbs were nature's gift. How they were so much healthier than prescription medicines."

"Many people think that because something is natural it can't hurt them," he replied. "That isn't always true."

"So what's next?"

"The neurologist is running a scan this afternoon to take a better look at that tumor. We need to find out if it's cancer."

Alarmed, I repeated, "Cancer?"

Doc's voice grew cautioning: "Let's not get ahead of ourselves, Clara. Maybe it's not that at all."

I had to get back to work, but I took the elevator upstairs and stood beside Mother's hospital bed. In the hallway outside the open door, nurses buzzed past rushing to the rooms of other patients. The oxygen still flowed; the machines still beeped. When I took her hand, Mother stirred but didn't wake. I didn't know if I wanted her to or not. I hoped that if she did, she'd be happy to see me, but I doubted she'd react that way. More likely? She'd send me packing.

Doc had said the swelling had begun to subside and that they would awaken Mother the next day, by weaning her off the medicines. Before that happened, I wanted this time alone with her. How sad that this was the only way we could be together, with her unable to open her eyes and see me, talk to me, hear me. I traced her profile with my right hand, while I did the same with my left on my own face. Even through touch, we were a match, so very much alike, and yet worlds apart.

CHAPTER FIFTEEN

A man with an overflowing cart pulled up to the checkout at the Pine City Walmart. The cashier in lane eleven, Edie McPherson, had worked at the store next to the highway for twenty-four years. She'd started as a bagger, worked in electronics for ten years, then moved to the cash registers after she had a run-in with the manager. The guy blamed her when someone stole a digital tape recorder. He thought Edie should have been watching the racks at the same time she was busy helping customers. It had happened on Black Friday, when the store was packed. The whole thing struck her as ludicrous.

Mostly, Edie liked to work at the registers because she could talk to folks as they went through her line. That and she took an interest in what they were buying. Sometimes the items matched the person, other times not so much. What she noticed about the man unloading on the belt was that most of what he'd bought looked like baby supplies, for a newborn.

"Your wife having a baby?" she asked, as she scanned a six-pack of onesies and flopped them into one of the plastic bags on the carousel. "These are super cute. My kids wore onesies all the time. They really come in handy."

"Yeah." The man looked at his watch and frowned at her.

No reason for that, Edie thought, but she wanted him to be happy. The customer was always right, after all. "I'm one of the fastest cashiers in the store. I'll get you out of here quick, no worries."

"Thanks. That would help." The guy shot her a grin, but what he said next didn't sound particularly friendly. "That and less conversation."

Edie molded her lips into a straight line, trying not to frown, and kept silent. That only lasted long enough to scan a shaker of baby powder and a pump bottle of lotion. "I guess you don't know what it is, huh?"

The guy gave her a strange look.

"The baby," Edie clarified. "All the onesies you're buying are yellow, white or green. No pink or blue. Usually when folks know the sex, they buy the really cute pink ones with flowers for the girls and the blue giraffes and trucks for the boys."

The guy didn't appear amused. "No. I don't know. As long as it's healthy, like they say, it doesn't matter."

"That's the important thing. Absolutely."

Edie kept working, scanning the newborn-size disposable diapers, a pacifier. Next came a case of infant formula and plastic bottles.

"Not nursing, I guess," she said. The man shot her an impatient glance. "Not saying your wife needs to, just that most moms do."

The guy grunted but didn't answer.

As the cart emptied, the items at its base came into view. Instead of more baby supplies, the man had jugs of lye drain cleaner along with a case of large black plastic bags, bleach and jumbo-size rolls of paper towels.

Something about it struck Edie as funny. An aficionado of true crime television shows, she laughed and said, "Looks like you've got everything you'd need to get rid of a body except the handsaw."

The guy blinked hard. He gaped at her as if she'd said something wrong. To clear up any misunderstanding, she explained: "On the shows I watch, you'd be pegged right away for a killer. The lye to dissolve the body and the bags to put the bones in to cart them away. Bleach and paper towels to clean up. But the bad guys usually cut the corpse up first, so you'd need a saw."

The man continued to stare at her, his face devoid of expression. His teeth clenched, he ordered, "Just finish this up."

The way he said it sent a shiver through Edie as she hit the total on the machine. It was her biggest sale of the day. "That'll be three-hundred-seventy-six dollars and fifty-seven cents."

Usually, especially for an order that expensive, folks paid with credit cards, but this guy pulled out his wallet and handed her four hundred-dollar bills. While she counted out his change, he loaded the bulging bags into the cart.

Trying not to let her eyes meet his, Edie did her best to smile and said, "Thank you, come again." He didn't respond.

As soon as he turned to leave, Edie nervously began to scan the items from the next cart, but as he shuffled off, she glanced over to watch the man make his way to the doors.

CHAPTER SIXTEEN

Leaving the hospital, I considered what to do while we waited for the facial reconstruction to come in. It could be hours. We'd be lucky to get preliminary results on the lab work the next day. And the DNA? Days, maybe a full week.

Cases like this, ones where a crime took place months or years earlier, weren't usually sprints but marathons. While we waited on more evidence, Max was back at his office working on another case. No telling where Ash Crawford went when he left the morgue. I could have put the case away for the day, but I kept seeing the woman's body before Doc cleaned the bones, the mummified tissue stretched across her swollen abdomen and the baby's skull visible. Something wrong had happened. People didn't bury pregnant women who died of natural causes in unmarked graves.

Thanks to Doc's autopsy, I did have more information—approximate age and height, a guess on when she died. So, I decided to head back to the station and scout around NCIC again on my computer. Not long after, I was at my desk doing just that, scrolling through the FBI's database. I'd expanded the geographical area to include Nevada, New Mexico, Arizona and other neighboring states. The results were depressing: forty missing teenage girls in the past two years. Then I considered what Doc had said, that our Jane Doe may have been in the ground up to five years. When I went back that far, I had sixty-two.

I narrowed down the height parameters to between five feet and five feet four, giving Doc's assessment a wider range, just in case he was off a bit. Nothing, of course, was rock certain. I read the case files, abandoned those that didn't fit, and kept honing down the prospects.

I ended up with four girls who looked to be possible matches. I ran off their photos and the brief summaries of their cases.

An hour or so later, I took my search further by logging on to NAMUS, another government database of missing persons. I scouted around for a while, used different parameters to change things up, and gradually, it happened.

I found two more who could have been our girl.

I kept expanding the timeline, working ahead, looking for other girls who might have been in the same condition, and found another.

By the time I finished, I'd printed off seven profiles—the most likely candidates. All were in the right age range, had brown hair and, based on the dead woman's prairie dress, they'd disappeared from or near towns populated by fundamentalist Mormon polygamous sects. I felt uneasy looking at their photos, wondering if they'd left voluntarily, where they were and what might have happened to them.

Once I finished with the official websites, I took one more step. Sometimes cases don't get reported as they should, so I started a general Google search of missing girls in the Utah area. Nothing showed up that I didn't already have until I happened upon a search result entitled 'MISSING EDEN YOUNG.' I clicked on it, and landed on a photo of a girl, one who had enough similarities to make it possible that she matched our bones. The problem: the information on the site, an amateurish offering begun by an aunt, was scarce. There was no date for Eden's disappearance, no description of where she'd last been seen, or any information on how she'd vanished. Nothing. It seemed odd that her parents weren't the ones looking, and that no one had filed an official report to show up on NCIC or NAMUS. Also interesting, the girl had disappeared from a ranch in Max's jurisdiction, Smith County.

After I printed off a copy of that final photo and what little information there was on the website, I sorted all the potential matches into a binder. None of the profiles mentioned anything about a pregnancy. Just to be certain, I expanded the search again and added two more girls to my binder, ones who'd been missing for longer periods of time. Finally, I clicked onto the file on Christina Bradshaw. Nothing Doc had said had ruled her out, so she belonged in the mix. I ran off more blow-ups of the photos of all eleven girls and carried them into the conference room, where I had a large magnetic whiteboard. Starting on the top left, I arranged the photos by order of disappearance and ended on the lower right-hand corner with the most recent. I didn't have a date for Eden Young's disappearance, so I decided to place her last.

While I stood back and looked at all the photos, a terrible thought percolated in the back of my mind: what if the girl found on the mountain wasn't an isolated case? What if two or more of these missing girl cases were related? The crime scene team had scoured that part of the mountainside and hadn't found any other graves, but that didn't mean there weren't more somewhere. And I wondered if, even now, other girls could be in danger.

Staring at the photos, I felt ill.

Yet while it seemed possible, I had no clues suggesting a link. And with nothing to work with, there was nothing more I could do. Not yet. Not until we had something to go on. Our best bet was the sketch the lab was making, based on the dead girl's skull. Until I had that, I had to put the case away.

As I straightened up and tried to shake off the feeling, Stef stuck her head in my door. Her usual cornrows were gone, and she had her hair pulled back with a headband into an afro. I liked it.

"Chief, have you got a minute?"

"Sure, did you go by the school?" Stef nodded, and I asked, "Did you find anything on Lynlee Benson?"

Out of a blue folder, Stef pulled a small pile of papers. The first sheet was a blow-up of Lynlee's school photo the last year she attended the local school, sixteen years ago. Behind it was a report with attendance records. I checked the dates. "So now we have a timeline. Now we know for sure when she disappeared. How close is this to the day she talked to the police about Danny's beating?"

Stef pulled out the report from the Tombs. "Lynlee's last day of school was two weeks to the day after she filed that report."

I thought about the power fathers had over their families in closed communities like ours, and, also, how few options the abused had. Alber didn't have a social worker or therapist for a victim to ask for help. Until Hannah opened the shelter, we didn't have anywhere for an abused woman or child to run.

"Did you read her school record through?"

"Yes, Chief. I didn't find anything surprising. Run-of-the-mill stuff. Lynlee had good grades, no behavioral problems, nothing to suggest she'd run away."

I considered my stop at the body shop. I didn't know a lot about Clyde, but he didn't strike me as a touchy-feely, forgiving kind of guy. I could easily see him losing his temper with a daughter who reported him to the police. And I thought about the Alber cops and how for decades they ignored domestic violence and child abuse cases. "I bet the reporting officer or the chief at the time told Clyde about Lynlee's allegations, and it didn't go well for her and Danny. That's why two weeks later, they disappeared."

"I'm thinking the same thing," Stef said.

I thought again about my talk with Clyde that morning, how he'd never mentioned Lynlee and Danny. It was as if they'd simply never existed. We had to find out what had happened to them. The next step seemed obvious: we needed to question the parents.

The plan came together quickly. I instructed Stef to drive out to the Bensons' house to talk to Clyde's wives. "Ask about Lynlee and Danny. Collect whatever information you can. Bring xeroxes of the kids' photos with you and Lynlee's school paperwork, so if they play dumb and try to tell you the kids didn't exist, you can call them on it."

"Sure," Stef said. "What if Clyde shows up? It could get ugly fast."

"He won't. I'll take Conroy with me to the garage, and we'll make sure that he's not an issue. We'll ask Clyde the same questions, try to pin him down."

Stef glanced at her phone, checking the office schedule. "Conroy won't start for another couple of hours. Not until three. He's got an evening shift today because he worked last night, remember?"

"It'll take a while for you to find the Benson house. He moved years back, and I'm not sure where. Run it down through the tax rolls," I explained. "Once you get there, stand down until I let you know we have Clyde contained. Then make your move."

"You've got it, Chief." Stef started toward the door.

"Oh, and tell Kellie to ask Conroy to come in early and check in with me as soon as he arrives," I called out after her. "Actually, ask her to give him a call and see if he can come in ASAP."

Stef gave me a thumbs up and was gone.

I checked my email on the off-chance that the facial reconstruction had arrived. It hadn't. So while I waited for Conroy, I built a timeline on Lynlee and Danny Benson, going through the girl's school records. I was pleased when Conroy rushed in only half an hour after Stef walked out the door. His hair was wet, like he'd just gotten out of the shower, and he looked excited. I didn't know if it was about logging in some overtime or helping me. My young officer had a good attitude; he seemed to enjoy each new case that came his way. "What's up?" he asked.

I grabbed the folder with copies of Danny's and Lynlee's photos inside and my old brown leather bag off the coatrack. "I'll tell you on the way."

This time, Clyde was hard at work on the Chevy when we drove up. He stood under the lift with a wrench in his hand trying to tighten something on the undercarriage. He didn't appear pleased to see me. "You can't need more gas," he called out. "I filled that Suburban of yours to the brim. Unless you've been driving the whole time. Is that what cops do for entertainment?"

His eyes narrowed on me when I said, "No gas this time, Clyde."

Conroy stood directly behind me. On the way, he had told me that Clyde was related to him through one of his six mothers, although they weren't close and hadn't spent any time together except at big family gatherings. Conroy didn't remember Danny or Lynlee, doubted that he'd ever met them, but he'd heard rumors through the family that Clyde had a mean streak.

"Howdy, Clyde," Conroy said with a grin. That appeared to put the older man at ease at least a bit, and he grabbed that oil-stained rag out of his coverall pocket and wiped off the wrench as he meandered toward us.

"Hey, Bill. What can I do for the two of you?"

We had decided during the drive that Conroy would initiate the conversation, try to set it up as nonconfrontationally as possible, keep the threat level low. I wanted Clyde to talk, not tell me to hightail it off his property.

"The chief here has a few questions," Conroy said, that grin growing ever wider. "Just trying to pin something down that came up at the station."

Clyde's hazel eyes darkened, and he came down hard on that wad of chew. "What would that be?"

"Just a little family history," I said. "Hoping you can clear something up for me."

"If it don't take too long, Chief." Clyde sucked in a deep breath and motioned back at the car on the lift. "Like I told you earlier, I got the owner waiting to pick up that old Chevy."

"Sure," I said. "Shouldn't take long at all."

I came to a stop a few feet from Clyde, close enough that I could smell onions on his breath, maybe from a late-lunch burger. I noticed that he was sweating on what was a temperate spring day. It'd be a couple more months before summer set in and brought any real heat. I looked at his coveralls and didn't see any sweat stains. Maybe the perspiration had begun collecting on his brow when he saw me for the second time in one day.

"You know when I was here before and I asked about your family, Clyde?"

He had his eyes full on me. Parted his lips and sneered slightly. "I do."

"Well, after I left, I thought about which kids of yours I remembered, and a daughter came to mind, one who should have been older than Elizabeth."

"Yeah, say so?"

"The chief here was telling me that she remembers a daughter of yours named Lynlee," Conroy said, that grin that showed off his grill still on his face. The kid was good at this, acting as if everything was nonthreatening, but under that coat of sweat Clyde paled.

"Lynlee? Now why would you be asking about her?"

"You know, I just thought it was odd that you didn't mention her." I kept my voice even, made sure there wasn't anything accusing in my tone.

A long pause, and I assumed Clyde was considering his response. "Well, she run off a long time ago. I don't talk about her no more. Never mention her name, because she done what you did, Chief."

I thought about how he looked so calm, but the sweat kept building a sheen on his forehead. "She did, did she?"

"Yeah, Lynlee disgraced her family when she defied me and took off." At that Clyde kept his eyes on me while he spit what was left of that slimy wad of tobacco into one of his greasy hands and threw it into a trash barrel between the pumps. As he wiped his hands on the rag, he said, "You know how Elijah's People feel about apostates. You know what the prophet teaches."

"I do," I said, thinking about how he must be enjoying this, for the first time telling me what he truly thought of me. "That was Lynlee in that photo earlier, the girl I pointed at, right?"

He didn't look certain about answering but then nodded. "That was her, but like I said, she's gone. Disappeared a couple of years after that photo was taken. I haven't talked about her since."

"Danny, either?" I asked.

Clyde's round cheeks rose and squinted his eyes, wrinkles forming webs around them. The chew gone, he folded in his lower lip and bit down on it, all the while watching me. "Now why would you be asking about Danny?"

"We heard in town that they disappeared about the same time," I said.

For a moment, no one spoke. In the distance, I heard a bird let loose a long, sharp caw, maybe calling its mate, and the susurrus of nascent leaves from a stand of scrawny canyon maples. The air smelled of dust and motor oil, and that noxious onion. Clyde kept half that lower lip sucked in as he sized me up, I figured wondering what, if anything, I knew.

"Clyde, we'd like you to do us a favor," Conroy said, that gentlemanly smile of his pasted across his face. "The chief here ran a check for records on Lynlee and came up with some old paperwork. We're hoping you'll come downtown and look at it with us, go over this report that's in our files and explain it to us."

"A report?"

"Old paperwork on a report Lynlee filed," I said. "We'd like to show you."

"About Danny and Lynlee?"

I wouldn't have described Clyde's demeanor as panicked—more concerned. Then I fed him the line that almost always works with sociopaths. It fits into their overwhelming world view: that they can talk their way out of pretty much anything. "We figure if you look at the report, you'll be able to tell us what all this is about and talk us through it, clear it up."

Clyde slumped and dropped his right shoulder. I didn't know if we had him. I started to think maybe not. But then: "Sure, I'll follow you there. Just give me a minute to lock the place up."

Conroy escorted Clyde Benson into interview room number one, while I flicked the switch on the video equipment. I wasn't sure where this was going, but I wanted to make sure we had a record of everything that was said. Early on, when I was a rookie cop in Dallas, I'd thought I was interviewing a guy about a dog found gutted on a neighbor's porch. While grisly and disappointing, cruelty to animals wasn't a major crime, and I didn't turn on my tape recorder. I learned a lesson when halfway through the interview the guy confessed to conspiring to kill the dog's owner as well. My chief at the time had read me the riot act.

"So, Clyde, I'm recording this to make sure I don't misremember anything. That okay with you?" I asked when I walked in the room. Clyde nodded and I took a seat across from him, Conroy between us at the end of the table. When I'd walked in, Conroy had been talking family with our suspect, trying to put him at ease, but Clyde appeared on edge. His right knee bounced with nervous energy.

"Okay, so I want to explain statutes of limitations to you first." I then launched into a brief synopsis of the law, and I explained that the statute on physical child abuse was only four years. "Clyde, this report I'm about to show you is sixteen years old."

Clyde gave me a curious glance. He looked as nervous as a raccoon trapped in a tree with a bear climbing up the trunk. "So you can't prosecute, no matter what I say?"

"Charges for *physical* child abuse, like I said, can only be filed within four years of the offense," I repeated. "Got that?"

"Yeah." He slumped back into the chair, hauled one knee up, held it in his hands while he took a few slow, even breaths. Just what I wanted to see; he was calming down.

"Okay then." On the table between us, I laid out the photo of Danny with the black eye and a copy of the never-pursued police report. "What happened here, Clyde? Lynlee told the officers you beat the kid up. That true?"

Since I'd laid the groundwork, explained that we couldn't prosecute him for the kid's black eye, it didn't take long. "I got carried away," he said, a sheepish nod. "You know how it is. Sometimes kids get on your nerves."

"Okay," I said. "That's good. Thanks for being honest."

"So, we done now?"

"You know, what we're curious about, the reason we brought you in here…"

"Yeah, I was wondering about that," he said, suddenly miffed at the thought that we'd torn him away from the body shop to ask questions. "Why'd you take me away from my work for something like this that happened all those years ago?"

"We want to know where Lynlee and Danny are. We need to find them. Just to talk to them, to be sure we've got the whole story here."

Clyde scrunched his shoulders up to his ears. "Hell if I know."

Conroy and I worked him, asking from every direction, taking every tack that occurred to us, trying to get information on the whereabouts of two of his children. The guy was a rock. He never budged off his story that the two of them had left together, even when I pointed out that Lynlee, the older of the two, was only twelve at the time.

"Someone must have helped them," he insisted. "You find out who and you'll find them, I bet. I've got no doubt they're somewhere living in sin in the Gentile world, turning their backs on their faith. I got no use for them, two apostates who've disgraced the family and our prophet, so I've never gone looking."

It became clear that we were making no progress, and before long we gave up. Conroy drove Clyde back to his body shop, and I waited to hear from Stef. When she called in, she gave me the blow-by-blow. The younger wife hadn't been in the family at the time, and she had little to offer. But Clyde's first wife laid out an account that matched what their husband had said: that Lynlee took off with Danny and neither one had been heard from since. Like Clyde, she speculated that the kids had help, but she couldn't, or didn't, say from whom.

"So, nothing. No other information?"

"Sorry, Chief. I guess we've hit a dead end."

I considered trying to get a search warrant for the Bensons' farm, but then wrote that off. We didn't have any probable cause. The judge would never agree. "There must be something we can—"

Another call beeped in. It was Doc, and my thoughts immediately jumped back to the girl on the mountain. Did we have a sketch of her face? I felt a surge of nervous adrenaline anticipating that we might finally have something concrete to follow up on. "Stef. I've got another call. I have to go."

"What do you want me to do?" she asked.

"Keep working the Benson case. We need to find those kids, figure out what happened to them. I don't like that they just disappeared. It's possible Clyde did something to them. I'll check in with you later."

CHAPTER SEVENTEEN

By the time I clicked over, Doc had hung up. Before I could call him back, my phone dinged. On my laptop, I opened an email from Doc's address. Under a heading that read "Smith County Medical Examiner," I saw a thumbnail of a black and white sketch. Excited at the prospect of seeing our girl's face, I clicked on the sketch and blew it up. A cute thing, she had big round eyes and a button nose. I printed off half a dozen copies.

In the conference room, I held the emailed sketch next to the first photo on the whiteboard, the girl who'd been missing the longest. The eyes looked fairly similar but the nose and the chin were completely off. I removed the magnets and took down that photo, leaving ten. The second girl had a wider mouth and rounder cheeks. The third had a pointed chin, one of those that juts forward. In the sketch the girl's chin appeared more rounded.

I kept going.

Others looked promising, with enough similarities to leave them on the board. The girl with the closest resemblance was Carrie Sue Carter. She'd disappeared two years earlier, and her family lived on a farm just over the county line. I also kept the photo of Eden Young. Not an exact match, but a maybe. The final girl I compared the drawing to was Christina Bradshaw. I held her photo up and examined their facial structures. I felt an overwhelming disappointment when I noticed subtle differences, yet they did look a bit similar. Although doubtful, I didn't want to let go of that particular possibility. I couldn't bear to put Christina in the pile with the discards, so I left her in the display with the could-bes.

When I finished, I had only Carrie Sue Carter, Eden Young, and Christina Bradshaw's photos hanging on the whiteboard.

"Anyone look familiar?" Max asked, when I got him on the phone.

"I've got a line-up of three missing girls who could match. One is Christina. I'll email all of them to you. Anything on your end?"

"No, I've been working a robbery case all afternoon waiting on the sketch to arrive. I just got a confession out of the guy and he's on his way to the jail. I haven't had time to work the bone case. Besides, knowing you, Clara, I felt certain you'd run with it, so there was no need for me to duplicate your work."

Maybe I should have been insulted that Max found me that predictable, but then, it was hard to argue since I'd done exactly as he'd expected.

"Now that we have it, my office will email the sketch to the press along with a media advisory," he said. "It'll be in the hands of reporters throughout the state and the region within the hour. On TV this evening, I'm sure."

I felt my hopes rising, the sense that we were moving forward, that I finally had in my hands what I needed to piece the clues together and uncover the answers. All across Utah folks would turn on their televisions and see the sketch. It had to help. "We've got a real shot at this. Someone's probably going to recognize her, Max. Don't you think?"

"Hope so, but you know how these things are. Sometimes that doesn't happen," he cautioned. I knew that, of course. This was far from my first missing person case. But I had to believe we had a good shot. Max paused for just a second, then asked, "How do you want to handle the leads you've dug up?"

"I'll email one of the girl's photos to you: Carrie Sue Carter. How about you run out to her family's place? It's a half hour or so from your office. Talk to her parents. Meanwhile, since Christina Bradshaw is one of the maybes, I'll drive to her sister's place."

"You think it's Christina?"

"I don't know, but she does look a little like the sketch."

"What about the third one? Do you want me to take it?" he asked.

"Let's do that one together. It's a girl named Eden Young. I found her on a website asking for information on her disappearance." I went over what I'd been able to make out about the case from the website, mentioning that Eden's disappearance hadn't been reported to NCIC, and that basic information like the date of her disappearance was missing. "The Young family lives in Smith County, your jurisdiction."

"I don't remember seeing any reports on that case," Max said. "I would remember, I think. Who did you say runs the website?"

"Her aunt."

The phone was quiet, and I assumed Max was thinking that through. "And there's no date. That is odd. Any mention of a pregnancy?"

"No. Nothing. It could be a waste of time, but there's just not enough information to know."

"Do you want me to pick you up?" Max asked.

Instead I suggested that we meet at his office when we finished our separate interviews. I felt anxious, wondering if we were chasing red herrings or truly making progress. My mind kept churning over the fear that the dead girl might not be an isolated case. Before we hung up, I had to ask: "Max, I'm wondering: The thing is, it didn't take me long to find these three missing girls, and I have a file of others I dug up this afternoon from other parts of the state. I know kids disappear, some run away, bad things happen to others, but…"

I hesitated, and he asked, "You're worried that this isn't an isolated case? That there could be more girls like the one we found buried?"

"Max, it's just that…" I gulped hard. I felt sick even saying it. "Yes. I am."

CHAPTER EIGHTEEN

On the drive to the Carter house, Max mulled over what Clara had said, her fears that the murder of the girl found on the mountainside might be part of a series. Although they didn't have any evidence pointing in that direction, he understood her concerns. Eight months earlier the disappearance of one girl had led them on a trail that revealed the brutal killings of others. So it wasn't surprising that Clara's instincts would dissect the current situation and lead her in that direction.

Max thought back to the terrible scenes, the desecrated bodies. *God, I hope not. Please, not again.*

The miles clicked past and he saw the Carter place up ahead, a sprawling one-story house surrounded by acres of farmland. The first thing he noticed was that the fields hadn't been plowed to get ready for spring planting, as they should have been. The house, too, looked worn-out and ill-kept, its white paint faded and peeling off the wood siding. As he got out of his squad car, he took a better look at the fields. The shape they were in, he suspected it had been a couple of years since they'd last been planted, probably as long as Carrie Sue had been missing.

He knocked on the door, and a woman in her forties, faded brown hair and sad hazel eyes, answered. When she took in Max's uniform and glanced at his badge, she looked frightened. "Can... can I help you, officer?"

"I'm Chief Deputy Max Anderson from Smith County. I'd like to talk to you and your husband about your daughter, Carrie Sue."

"Oh, Lord!" the woman cried out. She turned back to the house, "Father, sisters, come. Come quick! It's about Carrie Sue!"

Max found himself being almost pulled into the house, surrounded by two more women, a man in his fifties with salt-and-pepper hair, and a swarm of teenagers and younger children.

"I'm Joshua Carter, Carrie Sue's father," the man said. "Have you found her?"

A murmur went through the room, the children gasping, and one of the women sprang into action, rounding the young ones up, worried about what might be said, not wanting them to hear. "Everybody outside, now. Outside!"

The teenagers protested, but the three sister-wives stretched their arms around them and pushed them all toward the back door. As they rushed out, one girl sobbed and covered her face with her hands. "Carrie Sue's dead, isn't she, Mother?" she whispered.

The woman the girl addressed bent close and hugged her, gave her a kiss. "Go outside, dear. We'll call you when we know."

When Max turned back to the man, he noticed that Joshua Carter's hands were trembling ever so slightly and his eyes had become moist. Max took a hard gulp. These were tough calls, families suffering. He cleared his throat, not wanting to tell them about the discovery of a girl's body.

"Mr. Carter, ladies, I'm here because of the listing for your daughter on NCIC. It's my understanding that Carrie Sue disappeared about two years ago. Can you tell me what happened?"

"She ran away," one of the women shouted. "Just left, and disappeared."

"We think she left on her own, but we're not sure," said another of the women. "Carrie Sue went to school that morning, and everything seemed fine. But she never came home."

"The local police investigated and said she was seen walking off into the woods behind the school. She must have run," the first woman said again. "What else could have happened? But we don't know why."

The man turned to them and shook his head to quiet them. His voice gravel, he asked, "Why are you here? Did you find her?"

"I don't know." Max cleared his throat again as he looked around at the women, who were all bunched together. With each passing second, Joshua Carter appeared increasingly distraught.

"If it's bad news, you need to tell us," the man said, a crack of emotion in his voice. "We've been on pins and needles in this house for two years, dreading bad news. Don't keep us waiting."

Max nodded. "I don't know if we've found her. I have some questions. Can you tell me, was there any reason to believe Carrie Sue might have been pregnant?"

At that, they all hushed and looked from one to the other. "Pregnant?" one of the women questioned. "Why pregnant?"

"Just tell me," Max insisted. "Could she have been pregnant?"

The father released a deep sigh. "If she was, we didn't know about it. But if she did run away, that might explain it. We'd been upset with her. She was sneaking out with a boy from a nearby town. They were sweet on each other."

"But you didn't know if—" Max started.

"No, she didn't tell us that," the man said.

"If she was, she must have been scared," one woman said, her eyes wild with worry. She turned to her sister-wives. "Didn't she know that we would have taken care of her?"

"Wouldn't she know that we'd still love her?" the woman who'd answered the door whispered. "Is that why she left?"

"No, no, I'm not saying that," Max interrupted, trying to refocus them. "Let's sit down."

At that, they insisted he take the leather recliner in the corner, and they sat across from him on a gray plaid couch. Max fingered the file he'd carried in as he spoke. He told them why he was there, what had been found: a pregnant teenage girl's buried body. As he spoke, the women moved closer to their husband, one put her arm around his shoulders, and he held the hands of the other two.

When he asked, the man's voice barely reached a whisper. "Can we see the sketch, please?"

Max pursed his lips and opened the file, handed it across to the father. "Do you think this looks like it could be your daughter?"

All of them barely breathed as they stared at the sketch. The man turned it one way then another, showed it to one of the women, then the other. Each time, their faces seemed to drain of more color. One of the women shook her head. "That's not her. Can't be. Carrie Sue's eyes are brighter."

"It's in black and white, sister," one of the other women said, pointing at the sketch. "The chin and the nose look like hers, don't you think, husband?"

The man nodded.

They talked among themselves, and Max didn't rush them. One of the wives walked over to a small table against a wall. Max hadn't noticed it until then, but there were candles, small angel statues, and a photo of Carrie Sue in the center. It was a memorial to their lost daughter. The woman picked up the photo—the same one that had been on the NCIC website, Carrie's last one before she vanished. She handed it lovingly to her husband, who held it side by side with the sketch. They all grew quiet as they compared the two. Time passed without comment, until Max finally asked, "What do you think? Could it be her?"

The man looked at his wives, who barely reacted, except for one who gave a soft shrug. All had eyes overflowing with tears as they whispered among themselves. Turning back to Max, Joshua Carter said, "We don't know. It looks a little like our girl, but we can't tell."

Max did his best not to appear disappointed. The women and their husband had tried hard, he knew, had done all they could. Identifying someone from a sketch was difficult. There were too many variables. The computer had drawn the face with hair pulled back. Carrie Sue wore bangs. The eyes had no color. The mouth was a straight line giving no expression.

"Maybe if she was smiling, we could tell," one of the women said. "Carrie Sue was the happiest girl. She was always smiling."

Before he left, Max took out a collection kit he'd brought and had the man run the swab inside his mouth to collect a DNA sample. Not long after, Max drove off the property in his squad car. He'd made no progress with the visit. He hadn't known if it was Carrie Sue when he arrived; he still didn't know. Joshua Carter and his wives had wept openly as Max had walked away to the car. To lose a child? What did that do to a family? To a father? To a mother? That made Max consider his own tragedy. It had been more than three years since his wife, Miriam, had died, since he nearly lost Brooke in the car accident. He'd fought so hard to reclaim their lives. Without Brooke, would he have been able to continue living?

Driving toward the office, he thought of Clara. He hoped she was having better luck with Christina Bradshaw's family, getting a clear answer. Clara on his mind, Max reflected on how she'd changed his life. Now that they were together, he and Brooke were no longer like that unplowed field, left abandoned.

CHAPTER NINETEEN

I found Jessica exactly the way I'd first seen her, working on the ranch. The place brought back bad memories. I'd been there the previous August when my sister was missing and all I could think of was that I had to find her.

Last time, Jessica had been cutting grass on a small tractor. This time, she was aerating a plot of land on the side of the house to ready it to plant summer squash. She'd seen me drive up but didn't walk over to greet me, and I understood why. Seeing me frightened her: After all, I may have been bringing very bad news, that her sister was dead. Under those circumstances, it wasn't unusual for families to experience a confusion of emotions, including panic. I waved at her and smiled, and she stood and knocked some of the dirt off the skirt of her careworn prairie dress.

As I plodded closer, she called out: "Is it Christina?"

I took a long breath and smelled the mossy soil she'd turned up in the garden. In the spring, our mountain valley enjoys frequent rains, and the wet earth looked rich, the dark brown of used coffee grounds. Although I didn't want to make her wait, I didn't speak until I stood beside her. "I'm not sure."

Christina threw her head back, not in relief but I assumed in overwhelming exasperation. A missing loved one does that to families, preys on their minds, keeps them on edge, as if they're always waiting for bad news. "What do you mean, you don't know? Haven't you gotten the face yet?"

"I have it with me, but you're a better judge than I am. I didn't know your sister." I didn't want to influence her opinion, so I didn't tell her mine: that it seemed like a long shot. I said only, "If you walk over to the Suburban with me, you can take a look."

"Okay."

We trudged toward my SUV as solemnly as mourners who truly didn't want to arrive at the grave. Once we got there, I grabbed the folder out of the front passenger seat. I took out the computer-generated sketch. I left the photo of Christina in the folder because I wanted Jessica to assess the face strictly from memory. At first, her face gave no clue to her thoughts. She picked the drawing up, held it in her hands, examined it. She ran a finger down the outline, stopped at the lips and traced them, considered. I didn't rush her.

As long as it took, I waited. Then, Jessica let her hand holding the drawing fall to her side. She slumped against the SUV's bumper. I thought for a moment that she might collapse on the ground.

"No," she said. "I-I don't think so."

"Are you sure?" I asked.

Her hands were coated in dirt from digging, but Jessica didn't seem to notice. She left behind a trace of mud on her face when she wiped away a thin trail of tears. "Yes. I think so. As much as I can be. It's been a while, but I don't remember Christina looking like this."

"Would looking at a photo of your sister help?"

She gulped hard, then nodded. Out of the folder, I pulled the copy of the photo I'd printed of Christina and handed it to Jessica. Again, silence, then Jessica shook her head. "It's not her."

I couldn't hide my disappointment. Jessica handed me back the copy of the sketch. She still held her sister's photo in her hand. "May I keep this?"

"Sure," I said. "Absolutely."

The tears kept coming, and although I had to meet Max, I couldn't bring myself to push Jessica away. A deep sadness washed over me when she whispered, "Is it wrong of me to wish it had been her? I mean, if it was her, she'd be dead. Since it wasn't, there's at least some chance that Christina is still alive, right?"

I hated to answer. I couldn't imagine an outcome that would bring her sister back to her alive. Yet, on the surface, that all made sense. Still, my response didn't go in that direction. I couldn't bear to offer false hope. "It's not wrong of you. It's a perfectly normal reaction. You and your whole family need answers. It's natural to want to know."

I felt the weight of Jessica's disappointment like a physical presence pressing down on my shoulders. Cases where families endured year after year without learning the fates of their loved ones were the most difficult. Not knowing was simply heartbreaking. I felt relieved for the distraction when my phone rang just as I was driving off.

"I'm finished at the Carter place," Max said. "They don't know if it's Carrie Sue. Said maybe, but none of them were sure. You?"

Listening to the sadness in Max's voice, my heart felt heavy. Then I thought: perhaps I should have been grateful for Jessica's decisiveness. At least I had one clear answer: "It's not Christina. Jessica is sure of it."

"Shoot," Max murmured. "Damn sad that we had to put the family through all that, thinking maybe we'd found Christina, and then it turns out not to be her. The Carters went through hell while I was there, and it might all be for nothing. Life's far from fair at times."

"Yes. True." I sighed, thinking of Max, and how when no one else did, he understood. "I'll be at your office in fifteen. Let's go see our final girl's parents."

CHAPTER TWENTY

By the time I arrived, Max was waiting on the steps outside the courthouse, rather than in the sheriff's office at the back of the building. The lot was close to empty, the business day ended. He looked as glum as I felt. I had a second folder on the backseat, this one with the computer drawing and a photo of fifteen-year-old Eden Young. "Did you check a map while you were waiting so we know where we're going?" I asked.

"Yup. Have I ever disappointed you?"

"Well," I said, giving him a noncommittal glance. "Maybe once or twice."

Max chuckled as we pulled out of the lot, and I grinned over at him. The mood in the car lifted. Even at gruesome crime scenes, you'll hear cops quip and tell stupid jokes. It's a necessary distraction. A coping mechanism. If we didn't shake off the sadness, working on a case like this one could consume us.

Max glanced down at the navigation program on his phone. "Take the highway east, about twenty minutes."

I looked at my dashboard clock. Behind the mountains, the sun was low in the sky. "Is Brooke staying with Alice tonight?"

"Yes, thank goodness. I don't know what I'd do without her."

I thought about Brooke and felt guilty for taking her dad away from her for the evening. "Max, maybe I should take you back to the office. You can go get Brooke and have dinner together. She'll miss seeing you. I don't know that I need you to—"

"I'm coming." Max gave me a stern look, one that said this wasn't optional. "I want to find out whose bones Doc has at the morgue just like you do. Plus, I'm sure I don't have to remind you, but I will, that Eden's disappearance and the bones on the mountainside are both Smith County Sheriff's cases, neither one in Alber PD's jurisdiction."

"Of course," I said. Partly, I knew, Max was just enjoying giving me a hard time, but he was right. I was only involved because he'd called me in.

"Now that we've got that settled, you'll turn left after the bridge over Screaming Hollow Creek, in about six miles."

As we drove, he filled me in on more of what had transpired at the Carter place. "They seem like a good family. Devastated by their daughter's disappearance."

"I wish we had answers for them. You got a DNA sample from the dad?"

"It's on its way to the lab in the morning."

In the approaching twilight, I saw the farmhouse ahead, a quaint-looking place. When we drove up the husband and his two wives were sitting in old metal rockers on the porch, probably enjoying an evening talk. A pack of children ran around in a side yard, and behind the house the fields looked ready for spring planting.

Eden's father, Sam Young, walked toward the Suburban before either one of us climbed out, and his two wives followed a few steps behind. He had a stern look on his face, and I wondered what he was thinking to see a police car in his driveway, Max and I walking toward him in our uniforms. I considered how Jessica had both hoped and feared that the bones were Christina's. What had Eden's disappearance done to her family?

"Mr. Young. Ladies. We won't take a lot of your time," I said as I approached them. "We're here to ask you some questions about your daughter, Eden."

"Eden? Why are you here about her?" If his daughter were missing, Sam Young's irritated expression seemed odd, as if he saw us as a nuisance. The women watched us, appearing wary. We weren't wanted here. They didn't trust us. I thought not for the first time about the frustrations of investigating cases in polygamous towns, where folks so often refused to cooperate with law enforcement. I wondered if men like Sam Young realized that isolating their families as they did made them more vulnerable to those who would harm them.

"We're here because we found a missing person page started by your sister, Mr. Young, claiming that Eden has disappeared," I said, keeping my voice even, fighting not to show my irritation. "We need to know what you can tell us about your daughter, and if she's truly vanished."

"Eden ran away," the man said, biting off each word and rather defiantly folding his arms across his chest. The two women stood behind him, the younger one clutching the older one, whose face had contorted in what appeared to be an effort to keep silent. I assumed that she had to be Eden's mother. "My hare-brained sister put up that page, that's true, but not with our consent. Eden took off after she and I had an argument. She's gone."

"What was the argument about?" I asked.

"None of your business," he said.

This wasn't going well. I stepped back a bit and gave Max a nod. Sometimes men took things better coming from other men. It was simply a reality of our patriarchal culture, and since Max was with me, there wasn't any reason not to let him take the lead.

Understanding what I wanted, Max backed things up a bit and formally introduced both of us. "Chief Jefferies here is the police chief in Alber, and I'm Chief Deputy Max Anderson from the county sheriff's office. We have a case we're working. A body found on the mountainside."

At that, the older of the two women brought her hand up to her throat and let out a gasp. Her husband's head swiveled toward her, and I saw a warning there to stay silent. In response, she gulped and turned her head toward her sister-wife, who wrapped her arms around her.

The tension palpable, Max paused and took a deep breath. Meanwhile, Sam Young scowled at both of us.

"Mr. Young, when did Eden disappear? If not an exact date, give us an approximate timeline." Max stared at the man, a cold, hard glare.

Both the women did as ordered and remained silent, as their husband slowly shook his head and muttered, "No. It is no business of—"

"Missing teenagers are our business, Mr. Young," Max insisted. His anger was growing, just like mine. All we needed were simple answers to simple questions. Why wouldn't the man cooperate? "We're investigating a case and we need to know. Tell us."

"You have no right to come onto my land and make any demands of me," the man said. "This is my family." His face was growing flush, a red stain spreading from beneath his white shirt collar. He pointed toward the driveway, the road. "Now leave."

"Mr. Young, answer our questions," Max demanded.

I'd had enough. "Why not help us? If it isn't Eden, we'll be on our way. Why not tell Chief Deputy Anderson—"

"Because this is family business," Sam Young bellowed. "Because it has nothing to do with the two of you. No one called you. We have no need for the police."

Fighting to maintain at least an appearance of calm, I attempted to swallow my building anger. I'd heard variations of this my entire life. The wall of secrecy was rising, and I knew only too well the result—he intended to stonewall us.

I was about to lay into him when the older of the women, the one I'd pegged as Eden's mother, cautiously shuffled toward her husband and put her hand on his shoulder. He turned to her, and she whispered in his ear. Again, he shook his head and I heard him whisper, "No."

If she couldn't convince him, I wondered what I could say that might make a difference. Rather than argue, I decided to simply forge ahead. I had the folder with me, and I took out the sketch and held it up. "This is the girl whose remains we found. Does it look like your daughter?"

The older woman clutched her chest. She let loose a long sigh, and I wondered what that meant. Was it relief I saw on her face, or fear? I couldn't tell. Meanwhile, their husband's mouth formed a straight line. I had no sense of what he might be thinking. I'd failed. I'd hoped someone would give a sign, shout something out or react in a way I could interpret. That hadn't happened. I'd played my best card and gotten nothing in return. Through a clenched jaw, Sam Young ordered the younger wife, "Take her back to the house."

My ploy hadn't worked. We'd learned nothing. I'd come up empty, so Max switched to another tack. His voice became pleading. "No. Please. Don't do that. We need to talk to your wives. Mr. Young, help us. Tell us about Eden."

The women hesitated, looked at us, then back at their husband. He said nothing more, just watched them through stern eyes. Seeing no reprieve, they turned and began to shuffle off.

We were losing them. I took over, talking loudly so the women could hear: "As Chief Deputy Anderson said, we're not asking a lot here. We just need to fill in the blanks in Eden's missing person report." He stared at me, and I could see that I wasn't getting anywhere. It was time to lay it all out. "Was Eden pregnant at the time she disappeared?"

I'd hoped to force a reaction from them, and I succeeded. An agonized cry escaped the lips of the older woman. She turned back, but her sister-wife pulled her forward. In contrast, their husband became even more stoic, and his face twisted into a dismissive frown so all-encompassing that I could feel the hatred. "Leave. Leave now."

"But Mr. Young," Max again pleaded, "why not answer our questions? Why not help us?"

The sun had taken its last dip behind the mountains, sending a halo of gold shimmering over the peaks. A beautiful spring evening, but on the Young ranch, none of us were watching it set.

Even in the diminishing light, I could see Sam Young's rage. He addressed the women, who'd paused perhaps a dozen feet away, and repeated his order: "Go to the house!" This time, perhaps, they understood that they had no more leeway. They shrugged off. Once they were a distance away, their husband returned his attention to us, seething. "How dare you come here and say such things about our daughter? You've upset her mothers, and me. To cast such aspersions on Eden reflects on our entire family."

Watching him, I understood: he didn't want any attention given to Eden's disappearance. As I thought it through, Max again took over, his eyes slits, staring the man down and asking: "You haven't answered the chief's question. Again, Mr. Young, was Eden pregnant at the time that she disappeared?"

He glared at us, hatred in his eyes. "No. Our daughter is a good girl. She listens and obeys."

"But you said that she ran away. Are you sure she—" I began, but he cut me off.

"You question me yet again? Here on my own property, where I am in charge? You cast slanders upon our family? Cause my wives to weep?"

Max looked at me, and we both knew that this was a waste of time. "We didn't mean to upset anyone We're here to get information. The police chief and I are worried that if Eden is missing, she may be in danger. Can you at least tell us when she left? Just that one piece of information."

I thought that might cause Sam Young to reconsider, to become more cooperative. My hopes were dashed when he again shot an accusation at us. "You have insulted us by suggesting our girl would do anything like that, get pregnant when she wasn't sealed by the prophet and married in the eyes of the Lord. Eden is a runaway, and that is all."

At that, he surveyed us as if we were long and bitter enemies. Without uttering another word, he marched toward his house, an incensed father defending the honor of a daughter.

The inside of the Suburban was deathly quiet on the drive back toward Pine City. The skies over the mountains had turned a navy blue. Max asked, "So what do we think about Eden Young?"

"Her mother? Such a strong reaction, but I don't know." I paused for a moment, considered. "All I'm sure of is that Sam Young is hiding something. There must be some reason he won't answer a single question."

"I agree," Max said. "And you're right, the way the women reacted, gave me the impression—"

I finished Max's point: "That they thought it might be Eden."

We drove on, and I hoped again that the case would fall into place when we identified the bones. "When do you think DNA will come in? We can track down that aunt, the one who put up the website, and get a sample of hers to see if those are Eden's bones."

"Ash asked them to move it up the chain, so—"

It had been a long day, and I didn't react well to the mention of the ex-marshal's name. "Ash Crawford again."

This time, Max didn't respond. He knew that I was wound up, upset. I kept thinking about Carrie Sue Carter and Eden Young. I wondered if both were somewhere alone and in trouble, needing help. I thought of the teenager's bones, the baby's remains laid out on the stainless-steel autopsy table at the morgue, and my heart sank in my chest. But there was nothing I could do for them until we had some kind of a lead. Night had come, and I had nothing to work with.

Max must have read my thoughts. "Clara, you can't fight every battle alone. You have to be willing to let others help."

"I know, Max. But what if…" I ended there, unsure what to say, not wanting to repeat the same concerns about Crawford I'd already voiced. I felt lost and tired. I wondered what Eden's mother had said to her husband after we drove away, if he'd let her say anything or ordered her to be silent. I had no doubt that Sam Young ran that house with an iron hand.

Ahead lay the cutoff to the river road. Max put his hand on mine. Still upset, frustrated, I didn't want to go back to my empty room at the shelter. Maybe Max sensed that, because he whispered, "Clara, Brooke is with Alice. It's been a tough couple of days for both of us. Tomorrow will come soon enough, and maybe it will bring an identification from someone who saw the sketch on television or in the newspaper. Something will turn up. Some evidence. Some lead. But maybe, tonight, we can just be together? Why don't you pull off here?"

The sky dark above us, gauzy streaks of white clouds overhead, scattered stars, we walked the path to the river. Max carried an old blanket out of the back of the SUV, and he had one arm around my waist. I had my stash out of the trunk, emergency vittles I kept in case I was ever stuck somewhere, energy bars and bottled water. It wasn't much of a dinner, but we had so little time truly alone together.

The river was a special place for us. As teenagers we'd shared our first kiss on its banks. Max spread the blanket out on the damp ground. The current ran fast, powered by the runoff from the snow melting on top of the mountains. The air smelled rich with oxygen, and I caught the sweet scent of wildflowers blooming along the shoreline. Spring. The world reawakening.

We munched on my meager offerings, while we gazed up at the stars in silence. Before long, Max laid down and I cuddled against him. Worried I might miss something, I sat up and unclipped my phone from my belt and made sure the signal was strong. It was. I checked for emails, texts, missed phone calls. No one appeared to be looking for me. I thought of Mother at the hospital. I considered that she was alone there. I felt the guilt of a daughter who should be at her side. Yet I knew she wouldn't want me there.

"Come back here," Max said.

The expression on his face tore into my heart. I felt it in every nerve. It made my skin tingle with desire at the same time my mind again warned me that I shouldn't open myself up to a man, to the hurt that can follow. Yet this was Max, a man I trusted, someone I desired as much as he desired me. Despite all my fears, I laid down next to him, tucked my body beside his and gazed up at the heavens.

"Max, you remember yesterday, that route we took to the ski lift?"

He was busy, undoing his equipment belt. The buckle opened and he pulled it off, put his holster off to the side next to my own. He reached out for me, put his hand on my waist. I felt the heat of his lips against my neck, while he removed the two pins that held the bun at the nape of my neck. My dark hair fell from its nest, and he ran his fingers through it. Hungry.

"Sure, I remember," he said, his voice hoarse with desire. "Why?"

I took a ragged breath, thinking this wasn't the time. Yet I wanted him to know. I needed him to understand. "It took us past the Second Coming Ranch."

Max pulled away. From high above us, the moonlight filtered through the trees and illuminated his profile. "Oh."

I paused, thought about what I wanted to say. "I saw him, driving onto the ranch with his oldest son."

I couldn't see Max's eyes but I felt them, questioning. "Did you let them know it was you? Did you talk to them?"

"No, I just kept driving. I-I thought about pulling into the driveway behind them, but just for a moment. Maybe to confront them about all they'd done, all I'd suffered on that ranch. But I drove on."

"Do you think they knew it was you?"

"They must have recognized me. I mean, I was in the SUV with the seal on the side. He must know that I'm back, that I'm the police chief. Nothing that happened in Alber ever escaped his notice."

Max appeared unsure what to do, because he pulled his legs up and sat crossways on the blanket. He gazed at the stars, silent, then turned toward me. He said nothing for what seemed like a thousand heartbeats. Then he whispered, "Clara, I'm sorry."

"I know you are, but you shouldn't be. You have nothing to regret. You're not him."

With that, Max again moved toward me. He wrapped me in his arms and held me, and I leaned into him so close that not even the memory of the man who'd once been my husband could wedge between us. I put my hands around Max's neck and pulled him to me, brought my lips to his. Moments passed, and the warmth of his kiss wiped the knot in my stomach away, if not forever, for as long as we lay under the stars together. My hands trembling, I began unbuttoning his uniform shirt, and he whispered, "Clara, you're upset. I understand if you're tired and being with me tonight isn't…"

All I could think of to say, the one thing that explained it all, was to repeat, "You're not him."

CHAPTER TWENTY-ONE

A mild delirium had taken over. Violet felt warm and wondered if she might be running a fever. The contractions came and went, no set pattern, and she wondered why it was taking so long. Shouldn't the baby have come by now? Was something wrong?

Her nose itched, and she tried to scratch it, but couldn't move her hands from where they were tied to the railings. She couldn't bend to bring her face to her hand, not with her feet anchored the way they were to the bed. Instead, she turned and brushed her face against the coarse pillowcase.

All afternoon, Disney movies played on the television in the corner, and *Frozen* had blared off and on for so long that she'd memorized all the words to 'Let It Go.' The song came on again, and she opened one eye wide enough to see the screen. Elsa was throwing snow and building her ice castle, celebrating freedom, making Violet feel even more boxed in, confined.

As Elsa sang, Violet thought back to another afternoon, the final time she'd snuck up the stairwell to talk to her friend. At the top, she'd again hidden behind the door. Nurse Gantt and the man from the bus station had stood in the hallway, talking.

"How much longer do you think?" she'd heard him say.

"Not long. A few days. Do you have everything in place?" Nurse Gantt asked.

"Yup," he'd replied. "We have six couples who want the baby. All desperate for it. They've agreed to an auction. The baby will go to the highest bidder, as always."

Nurse Gantt lowered her voice, serious. "Do they know that it's incest? Are they aware that it might make it more likely that the child would have some form of… inherited defects?"

Incest? With that one word, Violet realized that Nurse Gantt had to be talking about Samantha and her baby.

"No reason to tell them that. All we're agreeing to deliver is a healthy baby."

"What if the infant has some sort of deformity? Something visible?" Nurse Gantt asked.

Violet's skin turned cold when she heard the man reply. "Then, we'll do what we've done in the past. After all, our clients want perfect babies."

As she listened, bile worked its way up to Violet's throat, churned inside of her. She considered retreating downstairs, but then she heard the man turn the conversation to her: "How long before that other girl, the one with the violet eyes, is ready?"

"A month. A little more," Nurse Gantt said.

Violet's hands shook. She wanted to flee, to get away. But as she eased the door shut, the hinges rubbed and released a high-pitched, bird-like screech.

In the hallway, Nurse Gantt and the man stared in her direction.

Violet ran down the stairs. On the second floor, she threw the door open. Down the corridor, Lori stood, her eyes big, watching from behind the medicine cart. Violet slammed the door to her room shut behind her.

Footsteps grew closer. Then Violet heard Nurse Gantt in the hallway: "Did any of the girls come running out of the staircase door?"

An agonizing pause, then Lori's soft voice: "No. Was someone on the staircase?"

"Whoever it was must be on the first floor," the man said. At that, the girl heard more footsteps, this time fading away toward the staircase.

All went quiet. Violet's hands still shaky, she walked to the window and looked out, wishing she were somewhere, anywhere else. She thought back to what the man had said, that if Samantha's baby wasn't perfect, none of the people would want it. She wondered what happened to the imperfect babies.

At that moment, the door to her room had eased open. Lori had walked in. The aide closed the door behind her, and then she'd turned to Violet and smiled.

CHAPTER TWENTY-TWO

We woke at daybreak to the sound of the river and the calls of the birds greeting the morning sun. I opened my eyes and looked into Max's. I wondered how long he'd been awake, watching me sleep. He leaned in to kiss me. When our lips parted, he whispered, "I would like to start every morning like this."

I couldn't answer. To do so would have made a commitment I wasn't ready for. Instead, I kissed him back.

At some point during the night, Max had raided the Suburban to retrieve another blanket and the parka I keep there. He had us well covered, but my nose and cheeks felt ice-cube cold. The spring night must have gotten down to the fifties, maybe cooler. My uniform was wrinkled and damp from the morning dew.

Max explained that he'd called Alice and had Brooke spend the night with her, as I drove us to his office and dropped him in the courthouse parking lot. Before he reported for work, he had to run home, shower and dress. It was early, going on seven, but I worried that he'd be seen and questions would be asked. "Will the sheriff be looking for you?"

"Nothing to fear. I'll handle it." Before he closed the door, he peeked back in. "Even if he is, I don't care. I wouldn't have missed it."

The door slammed, and I watched him lope off to his car.

I should have gone to the shelter to change, but instead I headed to the hospital to see Mother. I felt guilty that I hadn't stopped in the evening before, but I found her sleeping peacefully in her bed in the ICU. I held her hand, thought about all she'd gone through and the uncertainty that lay ahead. What if when she awoke, she couldn't walk or speak? What if her hands, her right one still in a ball, didn't work well enough to cook dinner, button a child's shirt, or drive the family van to the store for the grocery shopping? What if she could no longer concoct her potions to sell? Who would support the family?

The agony of not knowing hung heavy on me, as I considered all that could wait ahead. Yet I had no ability to cure her.

From the ICU, I took the elevator to the first floor, then made tracks to the back of the building. Doc Wiley stood just inside the morgue doors with Ash Crawford towering beside him. "Well, there she is. Speak of the devil," Crawford bellowed.

"Doc—"

"Clara, we were just talking about you. Marshal Crawford is waiting for an update on the case. What have you and Max found out?"

I noticed something in Doc's hands, a small bag with instructions written on the front, the form to submit a sample to the lab. I tried to read it, but only saw "ASH CRAWFORD" written in the section for the patient's name. Before I could see what test was being run, Doc turned the form away from me.

"Getting some free medical advice, Ash?" I asked.

Crawford shot me a not unfriendly glance, but one that I didn't interpret as any sign of great affection. "I've hired Doc as my personal physician. But it's not really any of your business."

I wondered why he'd go to the county medical examiner for any kind of a test. Doc was an internist, but he conducted those examinations in his medical office, not within the confines of the morgue. At any rate, I moved on. Ignoring Crawford, I told Doc, "I came to talk about my mother. Alone?"

The ex-US marshal shot Doc a glance, then shrugged. "I'll wait here."

Doc motioned for me to follow him, and Crawford called out as we left him standing at the door, "Chief Jefferies, I do want an update on the case when you're finished."

I didn't answer.

I followed Doc past the stainless-steel mortuary cabinets, the refrigerators where bodies were kept, and the autopsy tables. The bones found on the mountainside—the teenager and her unborn child—were still perfectly arranged on the table closest to the window.

In Doc's office, he opened a desk drawer and put the bag holding Crawford's test sample, whatever it was, inside, I assumed to hide it from my inquiring eyes.

Once he had it safely stowed, Doc turned to me. "Did you see your mother this morning?"

"Yes, she seems unchanged."

"She is. But as I explained, we'll be waking her soon." Doc then went into detail describing how she would be weaned off the medications. Meanwhile, her scan results had come back. Mother did have a tumor, a small one, in her brain, and that was the site of the bleeding. "We're sure it's benign, and we think it's very slow-growing. So rather than risk any surgery at this time, we'll watch it."

"That's good, right?"

"Very good," he said. "If she's lucky, nothing will need to be done. If the tumor does expand, we'll assess options."

"Okay, good. Then she'll be back to normal soon?" The look on Doc's face, the wariness I saw, frightened me. "What's wrong?"

Doc cleared his throat. "Let's sit down."

I did as instructed. Doc plopped down onto the chair across from me and leaned toward me. "Clara, Ardeth may have a lot of challenges ahead. We don't know what type of rehabilitation she'll need, but there's been some damage. This could be a long and expensive road."

I took a deep breath, saddened and worried. "I've promised Sariah and Naomi that I will help pay for Mother's care. I have some money put away. And I've been told that my brother Aaron has agreed to help as well. We'll make sure she gets everything she needs."

At that, Doc sat back in the chair. "That's good."

Something else worried me. "What's the likelihood that she'll have more strokes?"

Doc's shoulders rose a bit, and he winced, as if unsure. "Without the willow bark tea, she should be all right. But she shouldn't experience a lot of stress. It's not good for her to get overly upset."

Doc's warning about my mother followed me as I left the morgue. The door slammed behind me, and I spotted Ash Crawford waiting in the hospital corridor. He must have been able to see that I was upset. "If this is a bad time…" he started.

"I don't know that there'll be a good time," I snapped, my voice harsher than I'd intended.

I remembered Doc's lecture, that it was to our benefit to have Crawford on our side. I thought about the dead girl and her baby. We'd gotten no closer to identifying them. Again, I wondered if other girls could be in peril while we made no headway on the case. Despite my concerns about his motives, I had to agree that the downside of letting Crawford help didn't seem significant compared to what we had to gain from him. That we'd gotten the sketch in such short order confirmed that he had the influence he claimed. Yet, as early as it was, I was having a tough day, and I didn't have a lot of patience. He followed as I rushed toward the exit. My voice fraying at the edges, I said, "Let's just get it all out in the open. What do you want to know?"

The retired marshal frowned. "Chief Jefferies, stop walking."

At that, Crawford planted his feet. Off to the side, the blue-haired lady who runs the information desk sipped her morning coffee. Outside, the sun had risen high enough to send shafts of light through the hospital's front doors and form spotlights on the tile floor. I came to a halt a few feet ahead of him, turned and looked back. "Okay. I've stopped."

"Good," he said. "I don't want a lot, just a rundown on where the case stands. If I know where it's leading, I'll have a better idea of how my friends at the state lab can help you."

I hesitated. My doubts still nagged at me, but in that moment, I couldn't think of a valid reason to keep fighting Crawford. "Let's go out to my SUV, and I'll show you where we are."

At the Suburban, I grabbed the paperwork. I flipped through the binder and pulled out the photos of the girls on my list, all three that I initially thought might match our teenage girl from the mountain. Crawford rifled through, looking at the images, the names of the girls written in the margins. When he finished, I gave him a verbal rundown, explaining that Jessica had ruled her sister out while Carrie Sue Carter's parents thought the sketch bore at least some resemblance to their daughter.

"You agree with the sister, that it's not Christina Bradshaw?"

"I do. I don't think there are enough similarities. But we have Christina's DNA, so we'll know for sure when the report comes in."

"I've got the lab pushing the DNA. We should have it soon. A day, maybe two," Crawford said. "Who is this girl in the last photo? Tell me about Eden Young."

I went over the details, described the encounter with the parents, how one of the women—presumably Eden's mother—reacted so strongly. How Sam Young shouted at us and told us that we'd violated his family's honor by suggesting that his daughter would become pregnant out of wedlock.

"That seems odd," he said. "Don't you think?"

"Well, yes, but not entirely." I went through the drill with him, explained how unlike the rest of the world the polygamous towns were, and that parents didn't always react the ways that they did in the outside world. "When the dad said we insulted the family by suggesting his daughter could be pregnant, he was referring to the dictates of the sect, how they view girls who don't maintain their chastity until marriage, those who lose their virginity, as spoiled."

"Spoiled?"

"Fallen. They're labeled as fallen girls, unsuitable for marriage."

"Of all the hogwash," he said, visibly angry. "To deny a daughter over gossip? Foolish!"

I agreed but said nothing.

"You seem to know a lot about this culture." Crawford gave me a curious look.

I considered how to respond, then settled on telling the truth: "I grew up in Alber, in a polygamous family. I have three mothers. But I left the faith years ago."

"Ah," he said, knowingly, as if that explained something. I wasn't sure what. "So Eden Young is another possible match? You haven't ruled her out?"

"Yes, she and Carrie Sue are the question marks." I then explained how iffy it all was, that Eden's father had not only refused to closely consider the sketch but wouldn't give us basic information, including when she'd disappeared. When Crawford asked who reported the girl missing, I brought him up to date on the website and Eden's aunt.

Crawford chewed on the inside of his cheek, appearing to assess it all. "Since one of these two girls may be our victim, I'd like to review their case folders. I may pick up on something that could help. Maybe come up with a way to further assist you. If it gets to the point that you start searching for any of these girls, that's my specialty. I have a lot of experience in tracking fugitives that could work for missing persons."

I sucked in a deep breath and thought about the deputy US marshal Max had called. He'd said that Crawford had become interested in the important cases, ones like this where folks paid the ultimate price: their lives. Maybe we could work together. "Only if you promise that you'll share any ideas with me, and that you won't investigate on your own."

Crawford chuckled, raised his right hand as if taking a pledge and said, "I promise."

I glanced at my watch; it was going on eight. I needed to get to the office. "I was up all night, out working on another case. I have to change clothes," I said, explaining away my disheveled appearance. "I'll meet you at the Alber police station in an hour to go over the girls' case files. Just so you know, there's not much in them, but you can see what we have."

He nodded, and I took off. Halfway out the door, he shouted after me.

I pivoted back toward him. "Yes?"

"Thank you."

From the way he looked at me, I had no reason to doubt his sincerity.

CHAPTER TWENTY-THREE

As I drove to the shelter, I wondered what Crawford had thought when he saw my wrinkled clothes. Doc seemed pretty sure he'd noticed something between Max and me. That brought to mind the notes in my desk drawer that condemned me for not following the faith and demanded that I quit my job and leave Alber. I considered my mother in her hospital bed, my family barely letting me in. If the town and my family knew about Max and me, what would they think? What would they do? But I wasn't giving the relationship up. I couldn't do that. My work and Max were the only parts of my life that truly made sense.

A call came in on my cell. "Yes, Stef, what's up?"

"Chief, I'm not getting anywhere on this search for Lynlee and Danny Benson. I've exhausted all the ideas I've been able to come up with."

I questioned her, went down a list of possibilities, and confirmed that she'd tried all the obvious tactics. "Let me think about it," I said. "I'll be at the station soon. We can talk then."

I parked in front of the shelter, jogged past a clutch of prairie-dress-clad women watching a group of preschool children playing on the sidewalk. "Well, I'll be…" one of them murmured, her air accusing, as if she suspected I'd been up to no good.

"Guess she didn't make it home last night," someone said with a chuckle.

"Not the first time," another said. "I hear she has a tattoo."

"She'd be the type," the first woman contended.

I kept running. If I stopped and acted concerned, they'd interpret it as proof of a guilty conscience.

Once inside, I bolted up the stairs to my room, peeled off my dirty uniform and got in the shower. Soaped up, I thought of the disapproving looks of the women I'd encountered. Apparently, word of my tat had spread quickly. I wasn't surprised that those who judged me added it to my list of indiscretions. Of course, they had mistakenly judged it as more evidence of my rebellion. They'd never understand that my eagle had always reminded me of Alber, of my roots, of home. As I rinsed off, I recalled that day in the tattoo parlor. Ten years ago, the artist had handed me the stencil and told me to put it where I wanted the tattoo. I hadn't really thought it through, but I looked down at my arm and remembered the X-ray Doc had shown me of the jagged fracture. "Put it there," I said, as I placed the stencil over where the break had been.

Maybe I thought tattooing over it would make the memory fade. In hindsight, I understood that while my broken arm had healed, despite the camouflage I still bore the scars of my painful past.

I dressed and threw the dirty uniform into a laundry bag and left it outside the door. I'd made an arrangement to pay one of the women who lived in the shelter to wash and press my clothes. Running down the stairs while buckling my holster, I saw Hannah carrying a load of towels. "Clara, how's your mother?"

I waited until we were close enough to talk without others hearing. "She's stable. They're bringing her out of the coma today."

"Oh, you should be there. You should see her when she opens her eyes."

"No." Hannah looked confused, perhaps because I bit the word off with such intensity, but I didn't explain. I couldn't talk about it. Not yet. I was still thinking through what Doc had said, that stress could cause another stroke. Mindful of our troubled relationship, what if my being in her room sent Mother's blood pressure soaring? "I have work to do. I'll talk to Sariah later and find out how Mother is."

"Oh, okay, well, you know what's best," Hannah mumbled.

At that, I thought about Lynlee and Danny, and what Clyde had insisted about his children: that he believed someone had helped them flee. Hannah Jessop, this dear woman looking at me with such concern, was the one who'd aided me nearly eleven years ago. At my lowest point, I feared that if I didn't escape, some night I'd disappear and my body would never be found. My husband had threatened that so often, boasted about how powerful he was as the brother of the prophet and that no one would question if I had simply vanished.

"Hannah, back a while, say sixteen years ago, was anyone in Alber helping children escape abusive parents?"

Her eyes flashed with surprise, and I saw something there, a glimmer. She took me by the arm and walked me into the parlor, to the farthest corner where no one could hear us. "Why do you ask?"

"Clyde Benson says someone must have helped Lynlee and Danny when they fled. They were too young to have left on their own."

Hannah hesitated. "Clara, there are things I can't tell even you."

I wasn't sure how to interpret that. Hannah and I were close, and I couldn't imagine anything about herself she couldn't tell me. Then I realized that this involved another person, someone who might not want to be exposed.

"Hannah, I need to find out where the Benson kids are. I need to know if their father is telling the truth or if it's all a lie and he's done something to them. You need to tell me what you know."

Hannah appeared to consider that. She'd been so willing to help during my months back in Alber that I almost didn't believe what I was hearing when she said, "No. I can't. But I will make inquiries with certain people. Does that work?"

If I'd been honest, I would have said no. I wanted that information, not just for this case but if something like it popped up in the future. I more than wanted it; I needed it. "Hannah, tell me the name. Is this someone you're close to?"

Hannah surprised me again, this time by physically pulling back, putting distance between us, and looking at me as if I were pushing too hard. It seemed evident that this was something very delicate, a deep secret. "I can't answer that. I can't tell you anything. These are things that no one talks about. And they involve confidences I can't divulge. But I can try to find Lynlee and Danny Benson for you."

At a dead end, I didn't really have any other options. I didn't try to hide my disappointment when I said, "Okay. Let's do it."

Ash Crawford had his long legs crossed as he slouched in a waiting room chair when I arrived at the station. Kellie handed me a pile of message slips as I walked past her. She had on a skimpy royal-blue T-shirt and a pair of body-hugging satiny black jeans along with those same strappy heels. I turned to Ash. "Go ahead to the conference room. It's straight ahead behind the windows. I'll grab the files and meet you there."

He nodded and took off.

"Okay, what's going on with you and Officer Conroy?" I asked Kellie as soon as we were alone.

She blanched. "Nothing, Chief."

"Uh-huh." I thought briefly that I sounded a little like my mother. "Listen, we can't have distractions. If you two date, you can't let it get in the way here at the office. Understand?"

"Well, we're not serious, at least not yet, but..."

"And those jeans and that shirt may be great for a date, but not in the office. Got it?"

Kellie didn't look pleased, but she nodded.

*

In my office, Ash Crawford read through the meager files, then again eyed the photos of Carrie Sue Carter and Eden Young. Carrie Sue's photo was full-face, and he lined it up with the sketch, took a good look and announced: "I can see a slight resemblance, but there are differences, like the lips. I don't know. It could be, but…"

He then turned his attention to Eden Young. In that case, we had a problem: the only photo I had was copied off the website, and it was taken with her head partially turned away from the camera, at an angle, making it difficult to compare with the face-forward image in the sketch.

"It could be Eden, don't you think?" I asked.

"They are a little similar, but…" Deep grooves creased his forehead as he considered, then he said, "I'm going to run out to the truck to get my laptop."

Waiting for Crawford to return, I flipped through the message slips Kellie had handed me. Only one caught my eye. A few minutes before I'd walked in the door, Doc had called about toxicology. The results were in. I considered whether or not to call him and let Crawford listen in. Despite giving him some access to the case, my instincts said not to. I decided to wait and call Doc later.

Moments passed and Crawford shuffled back into the room. He turned his computer on and pulled up a scan of the skull from the CT. Then he went to the website, copied the photo of Eden—the same one I'd just shown him—and enlarged it. "Let's see if she could be our girl."

On the screen he opened a facial recognition program, one I'd read about but had never used, mainly because we didn't have money in the Alber PD budget to pay for what the town council would label a luxury. It was another reminder that Crawford had resources Max and I lacked. The ex-marshal uploaded both images into the program and put them on a split screen. He then rotated the skull, lining it up so that the angle was approximately the same as the photo. He hit a command, and the program superimposed the face over the skull. The program locked in various anchor points: the arc of the nose, the top of the forehead, the cheekbone and the chin. The result was a ghostlike image of a translucent face with the hard-white lines of the skull beneath it.

To my eyes, it looked as if they were fairly similar. "What do you think?"

"Well, give me a minute." Unhappy with the resolution, I gathered, he adjusted the image slightly. When he finished, Ash leaned back in the chair and stared at the screen. Then he grimaced and shook his head. "It could be her, but there are some differences. It's hard, even with the computer, to get them exact."

Ash logged off the program and handed me the files. "So we're at a dead end. What are we going to do about it?"

I'd been thinking about that since the evening before, when we'd been run off by Sam Young. "I'm going to talk to the aunt. She's the one who filed the report. Get her to take a look at the sketch and find out what else she knows about Eden's disappearance."

"Good idea." Crawford cocked his head to the side and smiled at me. "But you must have other cases to look into. I could track her down for you. We could move on this faster if I were more involved."

I felt taken aback by the suggestion. I'd opened up a bit, let him see the files because he had resources I didn't. But it had to end there. While I appreciated his eagerness to help, what he suggested crossed a line. "Not gonna happen. You're not law enforcement. You retired. You can consult, but nothing more. No interviewing witnesses."

Crawford's eyes turned dead cold. Furious, he grabbed his cowboy hat off the conference room table, picked up his laptop and shoved it under his arm. "You're a hard woman, Chief."

I gave him a stern look, considered how to respond and landed on, "And you're no longer a cop. Get used to it."

*

I had every intention of doing what I'd told Ash. But first, I put in a call to Hannah. I wanted to get Stef back working on the Benson case, and I needed a break in it to know what to tell her to do. "Any luck on Lynlee and Danny?"

"You're a pushy one," Hannah said, with a short laugh. "Actually, I was just about to call you. I have made inquiries, and I should have an answer for you today. Not sure when."

"Thanks," I said. "I owe you one."

"Actually, a few," Hannah said, and, of course, she was right. The most important thing: my freedom. Without her, I never would have had the courage to leave Alber all those years ago. But for the past eight months she'd also been a valuable source of information. "Not that I'm keeping track."

I chuckled. "Okay, absolutely. So, what can I do for you?"

"Make time for lunch today," she said. "I'm beginning to worry that you'll keep shrinking until you disappear."

I had been losing weight, not by design, and I felt touched that she noticed and worried. "Will do."

"Talk to you later."

As soon as I hung up, I called Doc. Before I inquired about the lab results, I asked, "How's my mother?"

"Ardeth is starting to come around. We're monitoring her condition."

"No indication yet of how much damage the stroke caused?"

"Not yet. I'll update you when I know more. Okay?"

"Sure," I said. "So, what's the tox report say about our girl?"

"Well, it's somewhat inconclusive. There's just too much deterioration. The body was buried too long for most of the tests to come back with any real insight. But they found no traces of poisons, no arsenic, lead or other heavy metals. Those were ruled out."

"That's it?" It was disappointing news. Without some idea of cause of death, we had little to go on.

"Well, we did find one thing that's pretty unusual, but maybe not entirely based on the girl's condition."

"Her pregnancy?"

"Yes, that's what I'm referring to."

"What did they find?"

"This isn't definite, Clara. The lab is doing more tests to verify. A tech found faint remnants of oxytocin, the hormone that brings on labor. But what's really odd is that it's a synthetic oxytocin."

"Synthetic oxytocin. Why would they find that?"

"It appears that our girl was injected with Pitocin, the drug that's administered to induce contractions, most likely not long before she died. And for there still to be any in the tissue, someone gave her a mammoth dose."

"Huh," I said, as I thought this through. "What happens when there's an overdose of Pitocin?"

"It can cause fetal distress, a drop in the heart rate, and infant death."

"And for the mother?"

"Improperly administered, Pitocin can overstimulate the uterus and cause it to rupture," he explained. "Untreated, that can also lead to death. The thing is: there's no way this high a dosage could have been given by accident. It's carefully administered through an IV."

"So such a high amount of the hormone would cause the death of both the mother and her child?"

"Absolutely."

I'd known from the moment I saw the girl's shallow grave, the bones of her unborn child, that this case was suspect. Neither Max or I believed that it would turn out that they'd died of natural causes. The next thing Doc said confirmed our suspicions: "Clara, these are murders."

CHAPTER TWENTY-FOUR

Not understanding how long she'd been asleep, Violet woke to the baby shifting inside her womb. She'd begun thinking of him as a boy and given him a name. "Josh," she whispered. "Hey little guy. Hang in there. Hang on!"

Her eyes opened, and she found no one in the room with her. The television had gone silent, the most recent movie not even a memory. The scant sleep she'd managed had come between intense contractions that left her feeling bruised and battered. She ran her hands over her sore, bulging abdomen and her eyes filled with unspent tears.

"If only I could change it all. Start over. Then I would…"

Footsteps on the stairs, and the wood creaked. Her pulse skyrocketed as she prayed, "Please, don't let it be him."

As she waited with dread to see who would walk through the door, the girl thought back to the terrible weeks after Samantha vanished, the room she'd been in on the third floor empty. When the girl had asked for her friend, Nurse Gantt had snickered and said, "She's gone."

"Where?"

"You don't need to worry about that," the head nurse insisted as she handed Violet a juice box along with a small white paper cup with vitamins inside.

But Violet had worried. She'd thought of little else besides what the man and Nurse Gantt would do to her baby. She hadn't forgotten how they'd talked of auctioning off the infants and getting rid of those who weren't perfectly formed or healthy enough to be sold. When she'd pondered what to do, Violet didn't believe Nurse Gantt would simply let her walk out the door. So she'd fantasized about ways to escape, but she'd never landed on any ideas that seemed even remotely possible.

With Samantha gone, the aide, Lori, had become Violet's only friend. The girl often thought back to the day she'd run down the staircase, and Lori had covered for her. Lori seemed to instinctively understand the girl's turmoil. One afternoon in the living room, she'd leaned close to Violet and whispered: "If you want to keep your baby, I know a way."

"You do?"

"If you stay here, you won't have any choice but to give the baby away," Lori had warned. "But, if you want me to, I can help you."

The girl's chest had swelled with gratitude; she'd beamed at Lori, believing she'd found a savior.

But that day when Lori had offered to help lay in the past.

Tied to the bed, Violet trembled, as the heavy footsteps on the stairs grew closer.

CHAPTER TWENTY-FIVE

"Hannah Jessop on line one, Chief," Kellie announced over the intercom.

Seated behind my desk, I hit a button and answered: "I'll take it. Thanks."

"Well, she'll talk to you," Hannah said. "I didn't think she would. I figured I'd have to act as the intermediary. But she said it's okay. She's trusting you because we're friends."

Pleased, I asked, "Does this person have a name?"

Hannah chuckled. "Dolores. She's the woman who ran kind of an underground railroad out of Alber."

As much as I knew about my hometown, I felt surprised. I'd read about the underground railroads, a secret network of volunteers and safe houses who helped runaways escape the horrors of slavery in the early to mid-1800s. It was more evidence of how repressive our culture had been under the prophet's rule that someone had felt it necessary to run a similar operation in Alber to aid those who fled violence. "There was an underground railroad in Alber? When was this?"

"It went on for thirty years," Hannah explained. "I would have thought you would have heard something about it as police chief."

"Not a word."

At that, Hannah laid out the basics: Hiding her activities even from her own husband and family, Dolores orchestrated escapes for abused women and children. She made the plans, set them in motion, and delivered her charges to folks who transported them to safe houses in Salt Lake City, where men and women, most of them mainstream Mormons, aided them in building new lives.

"Rather like you did for me," I pointed out.

"I learned from Dolores. She was something of a mentor."

I'd never considered that someone had shown Hannah the ropes. "Does Dolores remember Lynlee and Danny Benson?"

"She does. She wants to talk to you before she decides if she'll help you, though."

Eager to get the information I needed, I asked when the woman would reach out to me.

Hannah sighed. I had the feeling she'd grown weary of my insistence. "Dolores has your phone number. It will come through as an unidentified number, so pick up. She'll call when she's ready."

The search for the Benson kids progressing, I called Stef to tell her I was working an angle and I hoped that I'd get back with her soon. After I hung up, I thought over what Doc had told me. Someone had administered a massive overdose of a drug to the girl and her baby found on the mountainside. We had a murder on our hands, and I needed to find out who was responsible.

Max picked up on the first ring. "Chief Jefferies. Glad to hear from you." In a lower voice he whispered, "I'm still thinking about last night."

I was glad he wasn't in the room with me to see me blush. "Max, I'm calling about work: the pregnant girl on the mountainside."

"That's a coincidence, or maybe not so much. I guess Doc called you, too. I just hung up with him. Pitocin, huh? What do you make of it?"

We knocked it around, repeating many of the things Doc had said, that the girl and her baby had been given an overdose that ended both their lives. Max agreed that gave us an angle to work. "I've been thinking about who could have done this, and, of course, the first possibility that came to mind is a doctor. The thing is, we don't have a lot of them in the area. Only a handful. And I can't see any of them burying a patient. If they lost a mom during childbirth, even from a medical mistake…"

"The family would have been told their daughter died, and the girl would have gotten a proper burial," I said, finishing his sentence. "Yes, I think you're right. I can't imagine it's one of the docs either. Especially based on the amount of the drug Doc said the girl was given. But how did someone else get it? A drug like that must be regulated."

"Well, that's kind of interesting," he said. "When I hung up with Doc, I scouted around on the internet. Guess what?"

"Pitocin is on Amazon, next-day delivery?"

Max chuckled. "Not exactly. Supposedly you can't buy it in the US without a prescription, but there are international importers that'll ship it into the country. They only require that customers check a box agreeing that they won't administer it to human beings."

"So what are they buying it for?"

"Not a clue. But I'm writing subpoenas for the websites. The catch is that it may be hard to get cooperation. Since they're not US companies, they aren't required to comply. But I'll have the paperwork on Judge Crockett's desk within the hour. We'll ask for information on anyone in Utah who's purchased Pitocin in the past five years. That covers Doc's estimate on how long the body was buried: at least one, no more than five years."

I thought about Max, his instincts, how well we meshed. "Is there a way to speed this up? What can we do?"

"Not really, except that I'll keep bugging them. Unfortunately, Ash's influence doesn't extend outside of Utah, so he can't help us. Our only hope is that the drug companies cooperate."

I thought again about Ash Crawford and his resources. I felt a sense of envy and, for the first time, perhaps gratitude. Certain that we had a killer to find, with little in the way of concrete evidence, we needed all the help we could get.

The ex-US marshal's name having come up, I filled Max in on my encounter with Crawford, explaining that he'd agreed that Carrie Sue Carter looked enough like the sketch to be a potential match. Then I described how he used his laptop to compare Eden Young's photo to the CT scan. Although it didn't give a clear answer, Ash hadn't eliminated her either. That led to what I'd planned for the afternoon. "While you work on the subpoenas, I'll head out to Eden's aunt's place, find out what she knows about her niece's disappearance. I'll bring the sketch to show her. And I'll get that DNA sample we talked about."

"Great. With the parents not cooperating, this may be our only option," Max said. Then he asked, "What about tonight?"

"Tonight? Do we have plans?"

"No, but I'd like to make some. Assuming we're not chasing leads, how about dinner at the house with Brooke? She was pretty disappointed about pizza night."

I thought about Brooke. I wondered what I was doing, and if she could end up being hurt if Max and I didn't work out. We'd been careful to keep it light, but if I showed up too much, wouldn't she guess? And then I thought about my mother. "Not tonight. I need to talk to Doc, to find out about Mother's condition."

That was something Max had no argument to counter.

Remembering my promise to Hannah, I stopped at Danny's Diner on Main Street and ran inside to grab lunch. A few minutes later, I emerged with a turkey and swiss sandwich and a water. Hannah was right. I wasn't paying enough attention to my health. Like Mother, I had a bad habit of letting stress get to me.

As I followed the navigation program on my phone, I munched on the sandwich. The aunt's name was Miranda Young Johns. The

Johns were a fairly well-to-do family by Alber standards. They
weren't as prosperous as the Johanssons, who owned the bison farm
where there'd been the mass killings the previous fall, but they were
comfortable. The drive wasn't a long one. I'd assumed the address
would take me to the main house on their farm, but I passed it
and kept driving until my phone announced: "You have arrived."

Off the road sat a neatly kept trailer. I parked on a gravel
driveway and clambered out of the SUV.

The place was in fairly good shape, as trailers in Alber go.
Most of the ones in town, including the one my family lived in,
were careworn. A single-wide, this one had bright white sides and
black shutters. I scrambled up the stairs hoping to find Miranda
Johns home.

The sun was high in the sky, and it beat down on the back
of my neck. The smell of overturned earth surrounded me, and
plow lines in a corn field behind the trailer stretched out from the
road toward the horizon. The grass around the trailer—most of it
cut weeds—was just beginning to green. Standing on the stoop,
I banged on the metal door, which rattled and sent off a tinny
sound that reverberated around me.

"Mrs. Johns, it's Chief Clara Jefferies from the Alber Police
Department. I just have a few questions for you."

No answer.

I knocked again. "Mrs. Johns. I'm Chief Jefferies. I'd like to talk
to you about your niece Eden and the website you made about
her disappearance."

Again, no answer.

I heard sounds inside, shuffling like someone was walking to
the door. "Is anyone home? Please open up."

At that, someone with a faint, high voice said, "My mom says
I can't open the door. Not for anyone. So go away."

She sounded like a young girl, and I answered, "That's good
that you're listening to your mom. I bet she'd be proud of you."

"Yeah, she says never open it. Not for anyone."

"Okay. I understand. Where is your mother? Will she be home soon?"

The child hesitated. "Momma drove off after the man showed her a picture. She got real mad, told me to stay here, and she got in her truck and left. The man followed her. If you're police, will you make sure he doesn't hurt my mom?"

"What man?"

"A tall man. Do you know him?"

I wished she'd open the door so we could talk face to face, but she was doing the right thing. I didn't want to imply otherwise. "I might. What does he look like?"

"He's super tall, like a tree. And he had on a big hat. And he showed Mom the picture, and she got upset. Madder than she used to get at my dad before she threw plates at him and we left him."

I knew, but I asked to be sure. "What kind of hat did the man have on?"

From behind the door a pause, then, "Like the ones in the cowboy shows on television."

Ash Crawford had beat me to the trailer, ignoring his promise to stay out of it. I'd trusted him enough to let him see the file, and he'd gone around me. He'd have hell to pay for this, I told myself as I bid the kid goodbye and headed toward my SUV. As I climbed inside, my phone rang.

"Chief?" Kellie asked. "We've got a situation."

"What kind?"

"It's at the Young ranch, where you were yesterday. One of the wives called nine-one-one to report it, said her husband is outside shouting at some people. She says there's a guy there who claims that he's a US marshal. Her husband's sister is there, too, and everyone's upset. The husband has a rifle."

"Hell," I muttered.

"Chief Deputy Anderson is on his way. He'll meet you there."

I thought about the kid in the trailer who didn't sound anywhere near old enough to be left alone. "Kellie, send Stef out to watch over this kid until her mother gets home." I rattled off the address. "Stef doesn't have to go in, just sit outside in her car. Tell her to let the kid know she's out there, so she doesn't get scared."

"Sure thing, Chief," Kellie said. "I'll tell her ASAP."

"Damn, when I get a hold of Crawford…"

"Did you say something, Chief?"

"No. Just tell Max I'm on my way."

CHAPTER TWENTY-SIX

I had a longer drive, so by the time I pulled up, Max was already there. Two pickups, Crawford's and one I didn't recognize, were parked in the driveway with Max's squad beside them. Sam Young had handed his rifle over to Max, who had it pointed at the ground, but a woman standing beside Crawford was shouting with every ounce of oxygen in her lungs at Young.

"I told you that Eden was in trouble," the woman I assumed must have been his sister, Miranda, screamed. "And they come here with a sketch that could be her, and you tell them to go away. Don't you care about your own daughter?"

"Miranda, just leave us the hell alone," Young shouted back. "It's no one's business but mine and my family's what happened to Eden. Not yours, for sure. Mother always said you were a gossip and a busybody!"

I took a position next to Max to try to figure out how to help, as I shot Crawford a contemptuous glance to let him know that he had a lot to answer for.

"Mr. Young, we really need to talk to you about Eden. If something has happened to her—" Max didn't get to finish the thought because Miranda walked up to her brother and punched him in the chest, harder than I thought such a tiny woman, little more than five feet and maybe a 110 pounds, could muster. I remembered what her young daughter had said, that Miranda had left her husband after throwing plates at him. This woman had a hell of a temper, and I thought I kind of liked her. That to the side, I needed her to shut up. We weren't getting anywhere with all the yelling.

"Mrs. Johns, please, be still!" I shouted.

"Who the heck are you and why should I—" she started.

I grabbed the cuffs off my belt and held them up. "I'm the one who is going to take you in and book you if you don't shut up and stand down so we can get to the bottom of this."

At that, Miranda huffed, scrunched her mouth shut, and stepped back. "Do what you want with him. Mother always said that Sam didn't have a lick of sense in his head. I'm surprised they let him stay in Alber. They forced out a lot of good boys and kept him for some reason I've never been able to understand."

The tension crackled as I turned to Crawford. "Wait for us in your truck." He didn't immediately move, but eyed me, noticeably unhappy. I wasn't buying it. He had no room to complain. "Now!"

While the former marshal shuffled off, Max and I separated the sister and brother. He took Miranda over to her truck, stood off to the side and talked to her, which left me with a very angry Sam Young.

Rubbing his chest, he demanded, "You going to take her in and book her for assault? She hit me. You all saw it."

"I could. I could also take you in and charge you with lying to a cop and impeding an investigation."

"I don't have to tell you anything." A flush covered his face and his cheeks rose in indignation. "And I'm not telling you anything. Not a chance."

"You will, or I'll tell you what I'm going to do." I still had those handcuffs in my hand, and I again held them up. "I'm going to take you in to the station and book you on everything I can think of, keep you there until you open up and talk."

"I don't have to talk to you. The prophet says that when there's an apostate—"

I tried to calm down, to slow my breathing. I'd been trained not to overreact, but this guy pushed all my buttons. I'd had it, and I wasn't backing down. "The prophet is in prison, rotting away, without any way to help you. He's not in charge of the police anymore. I am. And you better tell me what you know, or this isn't going to end well for you."

Young sucked on his cheek, gave me a withering stare and shook his head. "When women forget who they are, their place in the world—"

I hadn't been this angry in a long time. "I know who I am. I'm the one wearing the badge. And I know what I can do to you if you don't cooperate." In truth, refusing to answer a cop's questions wasn't a crime, but I was banking on the fact that he didn't know that.

Time passed, his eyes boring into mine, and I could feel the hate. I didn't wait for permission. I started pushing for answers. "Mr. Young, does that sketch look like your daughter Eden?"

He reared up and stared down at me. "That couldn't be my daughter. Eden wouldn't be pregnant. To insinuate that insults the entire family, that a daughter of mine would…"

I couldn't tell if he'd stopped talking because he was unsure what to say, or that his anger, so visible on his face, choked off the words. Not to be quieted, I pushed again. "Does that sketch look like your daughter?"

Nothing. No answer. But then he looked back at the house, where his two wives were on the front porch. One, the older of the two women, was sobbing, her hands across her eyes and her chest heaving. At that, something changed, and he turned toward me. While it wasn't a welcoming glance, he no longer sized me up as if the devil stood before me.

"I… the truth is, I don't know," he stammered. "It does look a little like her, but I'm not sure."

"Do your wives believe it's Eden?"

This time, he shrugged. "None of us are sure. It kind of looks like her, but not really."

"Call them down here. I want to talk to them."

He waved his hand and the younger wife wrapped an arm around the sobbing woman and escorted her toward us. As she did, I glanced over at Max. He had one of the DNA kits I'd brought with me in his hand. He held it up to me, all the while talking to Miranda Johns, I guessed about her missing niece. I plodded over, grabbed the kit from Max, then returned to my station. Soon I had Sam Young leaning against an oak tree alongside both of his wives. They were arguing, taking swipes at one another, disagreeing about if the sketch looked like their daughter.

"Since none of you are sure, we can determine if it is Eden with a DNA test." I turned to the older woman. "Mrs. Young, you're her mother?" She nodded and I opened up the kit and handed her the swab, explaining how to run it along the inside of her cheek. Still crying, she did and handed it back to me. I put it in the storage tube and closed it up in the bag, wrote the woman's name on it and the date. Then I asked them to tell me about the day Eden vanished. It turned out that she'd disappeared four months earlier. As soon as they gave me a timeline, I knew Eden wasn't the girl we'd found on the mountainside. I'd eventually tell them that, but not until I had every bit of information I wanted. They had a missing daughter, and I wanted to understand what had happened.

"What was the argument about the day Eden left? The one that started all this?"

Sam again shot his wives the kind of arrogant glance that ordered silence; he still wasn't completely cooperating. But Eden's mom had apparently had enough. She turned from him and said, "My husband found out that she was seeing a boy, sneaking off with him. Sam was furious. He told her she had disgraced the family. He took her with him to town, grocery shopping, so they could talk, and when he returned home, he was alone."

"What happened?" I asked him.

"Eden took off," he said. "Slunk away like the guilty child she was. We argued on the way there, and I had her sit in the car while I shopped. When I walked back out, she wasn't there."

"Do you have any idea where she would go?" Max asked.

"No," Eden's mother said. "I wanted Sam to drive around and look for her, but he refused."

"It wasn't to be tolerated," her husband seethed. "The boy she was seeing is a bad seed, not one who will be allowed to remain. Not one the prophet will assign wives to under the law of placement. Eden spending time with such a boy out of wedlock? It would have caused a scandal. Our family would have been ostracized by the entire community."

Once the questioning stopped, I explained that, based on the timeline, the girl on the mountainside couldn't be their daughter. Eden's father showed no emotion, but her mother threw her arms around my neck and hugged me. I asked them to go to the sheriff's department and file an official report on Eden's disappearance. The women looked hopefully at their husband, but he made no commitment, saying only, "I'll pray on it."

At that, the family turned and left. As angry as Sam and Miranda had been with each other, she went with them. Max and I watched until they disappeared inside the house.

"What did you find out from Sam's sister?" I asked him.

"Miranda's madder than a wet hen at her brother. When he told her Eden had run away, he refused to take any action, and she put up that website without his blessing. He didn't want anyone to know."

That made sense, given how sensitive Sam Young was to gossip about the family. I then explained the situation to Max, that Eden hadn't been missing long enough to be our victim. He thought about that. "But she was seeing a boy. What if she were pregnant?

Her parents might not even know. My wife didn't show for a long time with Brooke. Sometimes, especially with a first pregnancy, women hide it well. In a long prairie dress? Couldn't she have been pretty far along?"

I shook my head. "Even if she was, there wasn't time for her body to decay like the bones we found."

Max instantly recognized the problem. "Of course."

"I keep thinking, Max, like I said before…" I paused, and he gave me a worried look. "What if whoever did this is preying on other young girls? What if Eden, Carrie Sue, others are at risk? Girls whose photos I have in that file at the office, off the NCIC website. Maybe some of these cases are related."

Max's brow furrowed. "I, well, Clara, it could be… but, there's no evidence. We have no reports, no other bodies. As far as we know both Carrie Sue and Eden are runaways, like their parents said."

I couldn't argue with that, but I still asked, "But what if I'm right?"

Worry pinched his eyes together and bent the corners of his mouth down. "Clara, all we can do is work the case, follow the leads, find out who's behind this. If there are more, that's the way we'll stop whoever is responsible."

"But if they're out there…" I let the sentence dwindle away, and Max's frown deepened. I'd brought up a possibility that neither one of us truly wanted to believe, but also one that I couldn't shake.

"What do we do about him?" Max asked, motioning toward Crawford. He had his cowboy hat back on, and he was leaning against his pickup, arms folded, staring at us as if we embodied every problem he had in the world.

"We put the fear of God in him," I said. With that, I turned and walked toward Crawford, Max following beside me. As soon as I got close enough, I shouted, "What the hell were you thinking?"

"That I could—"

"We had a deal! You were to stand down," I said. "Tell the chief deputy here how you agreed not to interfere, after I was kind and let you look at the files. Go ahead. Tell him!"

"Chief Jefferies, I was simply attempting to assist local law enforcement—"

"Damn it, Crawford, you aren't law enforcement." Max's face flushed angry, and he looked spitting mad. "We're not under any obligation to work with you. To include you in anything. Get that through your damn head."

"Why, I—"

"This is over," I said. "Done. You're out."

"That's not…" Crawford looked like he'd swallowed a rotten egg and it was about to come back up. "I can be of service in the case, and I—"

"Why the hell are you here?" I demanded. "What is it about you and this case? Tell us the truth."

Crawford glared at me and turned away. He stalked toward his pickup's door, but I didn't stop shouting at him. "You better keep out of this, Crawford. Any more interference, and I'll charge you with impersonating law enforcement. You told those people you were a cop. Let me remind you. You aren't. Not anymore."

At that, Crawford took a deep breath, and I figured he was trying hard to hold his anger. He said nothing, just scrambled into his pickup, and a moment later he had taken off down the road.

Max and I said goodbye and headed out ourselves. He still had the subpoenas for the companies selling Pitocin to check on, and I had plans of my own. My distrust of Ash Crawford renewed, I'd decided to do what I should have done early on. I was going to do all I could to check up on the man, find out who he was and try to figure out why he was so invested in our case.

But the phone rang. An unidentified number. I almost didn't pick up. Then I remembered that I'd been expecting the phone call.

"Chief Clara Jefferies?" The woman sounded aged, her voice wavering.

"Yes, who's this?"

"My name is Dolores. I believe we have a mutual friend, Hannah Jessop."

"Yes, we do. I'm glad you called. When can you see me?"

CHAPTER TWENTY-SEVEN

"Would you like a cup of tea?"

The dining room had a long oak table covered by a white lace cloth. In the center was a crystal punch bowl that looked like one Mother had when I was a girl. I momentarily wondered where it was, where all the beautiful things my family had owned before my father's death were. Sold, I assumed, to support the family. Thinking of father's passing, I regretted yet again that I would never be able to confront him. I'd grown up idolizing him, but he'd turned his back on me to follow his prophet's orders. It felt like unfinished business, and it weighed on me, as did my shattered relationships with the rest of my family. I'd called Sariah on my way to the meeting to find out about my mother. All Sariah had heard was that Mother was showing signs of waking soon.

I considered visiting later that afternoon, but then recalled Doc's warning that Mother shouldn't be upset. It was better if I stayed away.

Dolores lived in one of the big mansions in town, a rambling structure that faced the main street with a large bay window. The furnishings were as old or older than she was, I guessed. Around the yard there were small cottages where her sister-wives lived. In our brief conversation before we turned our attention to why I was there, she explained that she'd been the first of eight wives married to one of the church elders, a former stake president who ruled over all of Alber's wards. He'd died nearly a decade ago and left her in control of the family funds. As such, she had a great deal of power over the family.

She poured our tea into the thinnest of bone china cups. She added three sugar cubes to hers, took a sip and appeared pleased. A tiny woman, frail-looking, she had to be in her eighties. Her features fine, her eyes clouded over but still remarkably blue, her pale skin had the look of parchment stained by age.

"So tell me about Lynlee and Danny Benson," I asked. "You helped them leave?"

Despite so many living in the house, all eight wives and a handful of their children, most adults, we were alone. I suspected Dolores had sent the others off when she knew I would be visiting. As she'd instructed, I'd parked my car three blocks away, then approached through an alley to get to the house. I couldn't guarantee no one had seen me, but I'd done my best not to arouse gossip.

"That episode with Lynlee and Danny was a long time ago. Fifteen years or more," she said. "What I need to know is why you're asking, before I decide if I'll help you."

I explained the situation, that I'd found the old report in the Tombs.

Dolores shook her head, her mouth twisted in disgust. "I'd heard they had secret files at the police department. I believed it, but hearing that it's true, and that they buried child abuse, I imagine domestic violence, sexual assaults?"

"Yes," I verified. "All those crimes and more. Most of them I can't pursue, because the statutes of limitations have lapsed. My hands are tied."

"Such a disgrace. And this from men who claimed to represent the Almighty." I nodded in agreement, and she inquired, "But you can go ahead with Danny's?"

"Perhaps. I need to talk to him, to determine if the elements of the case are right."

"All these years later?" she asked, sounding surprised.

"Based on some questions I'd like to ask Danny, there is that possibility. But I need to talk to him in person to find out what he wants to do and whether or not the case qualifies."

That didn't appear to sit well with Dolores. She sat back, said nothing, and tapped the table with the long unpainted nails of her bony fingers. She seemed in deep thought.

"Would you be able to reach Danny for me?"

She didn't answer, just kept quiet, and I fell silent, too. Then, she peered over a pair of wire-rimmed glasses at me and said, "I'm not sure this is something I should do."

"Well, I think he should be the one to decide if he wants to talk to me. I know it's been a long time, but he may want to proceed, if that's a possibility."

"Hmm." Again, silence. I didn't try to rush her, and before long she said, "I'll think about this. I'll pray on it. And I'll let you know."

"But Dolores, consider the circumstances here. Clyde may be abusing other children. If Danny wants to, and we can go forward with this, it could be a way to stop Clyde. You have an obligation to help, don't you think?"

While she'd been welcoming, hospitable, at that her mood soured. "You're asking me to upend the boy's life. To remind him of the horror of living in that house with that man, everything that happened to him. I won't be rushed. Before I agree to do that, I am going to give it serious thought."

"You'll let me know?"

"I'll sleep on it. If I think it's best to call Danny, I will. And I'll let you know if I have and what he's decided."

As she walked me to the door, she looked up at me. I towered over her by more than a foot. "We were worried about you, you know."

"What do you mean?"

"All those years ago when Hannah told me about you, explained what was happening… especially with who you were married to, a man with that kind of power... we thought something very bad could happen to you."

"You knew?"

"The church had total control over Alber back then, but a small group of us monitored such things. We knew who the men to watch were. The ones who had a reputation for such things. When someone appeared to be in trouble, we reached out to them, as Hannah did to you."

I remembered that day after I left Doc's office. I had my long sleeves on my prairie dress pulled down, covering the splint and bandage. I'd walked out, and Hannah had appeared. It was as if she just happened to be there, that fate had crossed our paths. I'd never suspected anything more.

"It wasn't happenstance that Hannah was outside the doctor's office door that day?"

Dolores said nothing more, but she wrapped her arms around me. She felt reed-thin, but I sensed there was a strength there, a determination.

"Thank you," I whispered.

On the drive back to the station, I passed the house I'd grown up in. An eighteen-wheeler was parked out front and boxes were piled up on the front porch. It appeared the homeowners were moving out. I gathered that they hadn't waited to sell the place. The sign remained in the front yard and it didn't have a "SOLD" placard on the top. I slowed down in the SUV, then I pulled over and parked. I sat there for a little while, staring at the house. I thought of the Christmas tree Mother decorated every year, the stockings she hung like washing on a line from a string she pulled across the archway into the dining room. Father in the backyard pointing up at Samuel's Peak and the humps that formed the camel, telling us about the three wise men. Easter egg hunts. I'd been so angry for so long, and I'd thought little about my childhood before my life had been turned upside down. I pictured Mother in the hospital bed and I wondered if Sariah or Naomi, my brother Aaron or any of my many siblings would be there when she opened her eyes.

The day had evaporated, and when I walked into the police station the evening shift was starting to come in. Conroy was again seated across from Kellie in the reception area. The usual drill; as I walked in the door, Kellie handed me a few message slips. I flipped through them, found nothing except a note from Doc asking me to call.

When I reached him, Doc sounded tired. "I wanted to give you a heads-up about your mother." His voice flat, I knew the news wouldn't be good.

"What is it, Doc?"

"Clara, Ardeth is going to need care. She… how best to put this…"

I didn't rush him. He was struggling. Seconds passed, and I said, "Doc, just tell me."

I heard a long, sad sigh. "The stroke has weakened her right side."

"How weak?"

"She should be able to care for herself, Clara, but she'll need help. She'll be able to walk, but at least in the beginning she'll need a wheelchair, in a little while a walker. Perhaps for the rest of her life she'll walk with a limp, but if she's lucky maybe eventually with a cane."

"And her hands?"

"The right hand is paralyzed."

I took in a deep breath, struggling to remain calm. "Anything else?"

"So far," Doc said, his voice rough with emotion, "it appears that Ardeth is incapable of speech."

*

After I hung up, I sat at my desk for a long time. Occasionally, I heard someone walk past my door, but no one knocked, my phone didn't ring, the office had fallen quiet, as if the powers that be understood that at that moment, I couldn't take any more bad news. I thought of Mother's pride, her stern bearing before these past years when time weighed so heavy on her. This would be a bitter pill. I considered my family's home, the dilapidated double-wide in the trailer park that rimmed the mountains. Only recently had water been connected to the kitchen. They still used the old outhouse in the backyard. Mother would have difficulties living there, especially with so many people in such a small place.

I wondered again if I'd had anything to do with the stress that led to her stroke, if any of the guilt was mine for running away, then returning and not leaving as she'd asked me to.

Father would have known what to do, I realized. We had issues, my father and I. He'd raised me to believe I was exceptional and that I would always be cared for and loved, and then he turned me over at the prophet's direction to a man who didn't deserve me. A man who would never love or cherish me. A man who would always see me as a possession, who'd blame me for his own shortcomings.

Still, Father loved Mother. He loved all three of my mothers. And he would have cared for them. He loved his children, too, although sometimes I wondered if maybe not enough. But he was dead, gone, and we were alone.

I picked up the phone and called the sawmill. "Aaron Jefferies, please."

"Who's calling?" a woman asked.

"His sister Clara."

Silence. Then the woman said, "I'll ask if he'll take the call."

My brother and I had only briefly spoken since my return, and it hadn't been particularly friendly. I considered that he might simply hang up, but I waited, then waited longer, and finally I heard his voice. "You've heard about Mother?"

"Yes," I said. "That's why I've called."

Our conversation was short; we didn't bring up the past, only talked of the future and what our mother would need. Aaron and I agreed we'd pay the hospital bill and for her rehabilitation. I had some money not because I'd been frugal, but because I had no life outside of work, nowhere to spend what I made. "Clara, I know the family hasn't welcomed you back with open arms." Aaron sounded, if not repentant, as if he thought he should explain. "I'm sorry, with you being an apostate, it's just…"

"Difficult," I said, and he didn't contradict me.

Outside, the sun was going down. After I hung up, I brought up files on the computer and made notes on the two cases I was working. We were waiting on DNA on the bones found on the mountainside. Max had the subpoenas out to the internet companies that sold Pitocin. I noted on the second file that I expected to hear from a source in the morning about whether or not she'd help me reach out to Lynlee and Danny Benson.

The evening stretched ahead. I wanted to call Max, to make arrangements to meet, maybe at the river where we could again sleep under the stars. I thought about waking up this past morning and the first thing I saw being him, watching me. I'd put my hand up and traced the curve of his smile, and he'd kissed me long and hard. I wanted to curl against him, feel his warmth, and have him hold me while I told him of the sad turn my mother's life had taken and all my family had lost.

I gathered my bag and packed up my laptop. Kellie had gone for the evening, and Gladys manned the dispatch desk. "I'm off. Be back in the morning."

She was on a call and waved at me, and I was gone.

I drove through the darkness. Instead of pulling into the lot at the shelter, I continued on until I saw the house again, the one where I'd grown up. The moving van was still out front, the lights were on inside and it glowed. For more than an hour, I sat in the Suburban and watched the movers, children running in and out and their parents calling to them to stay out of the way.

Finally, the truck pulled away, and I started the engine and drove back to the shelter. In my room, I lay on my bed. I picked up my phone, intending to call Max, but instead I texted him.

Mother will need rehab. Not good news. I'm going to bed early so not calling.

He texted back:

I can meet you. I'll call Alice to watch Brooke. You shouldn't be alone.

It was a kind offer, a desired one. But I wouldn't take Max away from Brooke for another night. He was hers more than he was mine. She needed him as much as I did.

Thanks but not necessary. We'll talk in the morning. Good night.

After I sent off that last text, I hung up my uniform and pulled a big T-shirt over my head. I lay back down thinking I wouldn't be able to sleep. But I soon drifted off.

In my dreams, I floated over my body in the bed. As I hovered, Mother appeared at my bedside. My eyes closed, I looked as unreachable as she had in the hospital. As I had with her, she sat with me and held my hand. I felt at peace. Calm. I knew what I had to do.

Over and over Mother whispered: "Clara, you are my daughter, and I do love you."

The night passed and morning approached. In the moments before my eyes opened, I stood outside a house I didn't recognize, where a woman I didn't know pummeled a faded rug that hung across a clothesline with an old black metal rug beater. Over and over she pulled it back and swung. Each time, clouds of dust rose around her. The air filled, until it appeared that she stood in a foggy haze. When she finished, she turned as if to walk toward the house, but instead she confronted me. Her eyes held mine.

"Stop them," she pleaded. "You have to find the girls, before it's too late."

CHAPTER TWENTY-EIGHT

I woke up thinking of Carrie Sue Carter, Eden Young, and the other missing girls whose photos I'd copied off the internet. I hit the office early, before six, and turned on my computer. The dream had left me with a disquieted feeling. Anxiety. I skipped breakfast, and my whole body felt unsettled. I was missing something. What?

Before seven, I was on the phone with Doc, who had no news about the DNA. When I complained that Ash Crawford had promised to speed up results, Doc told me to calm down. "Crawford has done what he can. DNA takes time. And these types of cases, found remains, are marathons not sprints. You know that, Clara. You need to bide your time. We'll have it soon."

It was all true, but, for some reason, I couldn't just wait. I pulled out the folders on Carrie Sue and Eden. I went over my notes and Max's, hoping to find another avenue to investigate. Nothing popped up. Instead, I returned to what I'd set aside when I'd gotten the bad news about mother the evening before: finding out everything I could about Ash Crawford to try to figure out what was behind his obsession with our case.

First thing: I looked Crawford up on NCIC. Cop addresses aren't always available, but I found an old one in Salt Lake, then a recent move to a ranch north of Alber, in the shadow of the mountains. I wrote the latest address down, looked it up on Google Earth and snipped a photo of an old farmhouse surrounded by fields bordered by a split rail fence. I saved it to my phone and copied it to the case files on the computer.

Then I began an internet search. Pages of articles popped up, starting with the most recent. The first was an announcement of his retirement. It had a link to a letter issued by the US Marshal Service's Washington DC-area headquarters, thanking him for his many years of service. In articles announcing his departure, his colleagues and others in law enforcement throughout the US praised Crawford. They called him dedicated, determined and fair. All were good traits when it came to law enforcement. Two years earlier, he'd investigated the disappearance of a convicted killer who'd escaped from a prison in northern Utah. The guy had been on the lam for a couple of decades. He'd disappeared into the background, lived as a model citizen and hadn't raised an eyebrow in years. But Ash Crawford tracked him down, found him living in a Provo suburb with a new wife. They had children and grandchildren, and the neighbors thought he was "just the nicest guy."

Some of the articles mentioned Crawford in the headlines, but in others his name was buried deep in the texts. I clicked from one screen to the next. I kept looking for something, anything that would explain the man I'd met, the one who wouldn't take no for an answer when it came to intruding on our case.

In an old article, I found a photo of Ash with his wife at an award ceremony where he was recognized for aiding the FBI in tracking a ring of sex-trafficking suspects. Her name was Justine, and she was as petite as he was tall.

With that bit of information, I began searching for information on Justine Crawford. It turned out there were only a couple of dozen women in the US with that name. I looked at the photo again. I'd found Ash's age at one point: sixty-four. In the photo, Justine looked a bit younger, so I narrowed the list down to only those who were fifty-five to sixty-five, and I kept searching. I scrolled and read. As hard as I tried, it seemed that Ash Crawford's personal life was unknowable. Nothing appeared that gave justification for his interest in the bones.

I couldn't explain how I finally landed on it. I had nearly given up, decided there simply wasn't anything to be found, when I made one last attempt by scrolling back and starting over. This time I typed in "Ash Crawford" and "buried bones." The reason I hadn't noticed the article earlier was that it wasn't in a Utah newspaper, but one out of a small town in Nevada.

The headline read: PREGNANT WOMAN'S BONES FOUND IN SHALLOW GRAVE.

The body of the article described a familiar circumstance, the decomposed body of a young woman—a pregnant teenager— found in a rocky grave in a field outside of the city. The body, like the one we'd found, had nothing with it that helped identify the girl. A reconstruction depicted a face that looked a little bit like the sketch of the teenager we'd found: long brown hair, slightly built, about five feet two.

"What is this?" I mumbled. "So strange."

Crawford's name first appeared low in the article, a mention that he had volunteered to consult on the case. "US Marshal Ash Crawford will work with local law enforcement to help identify the girl and determine the cause of her death," the piece concluded.

I searched for more on the story. Two months after the grave was discovered, the girl had been IDed. Photos of the sketch ran beside a photo of a young girl from a nearby city. Her mother was quoted as saying that her sixteen-year-old had gotten pregnant and ran away from home. "We don't know where she was during the time she was missing or what happened to her," the girl's father had said. "We'd appreciate any information anyone might have that could lead to answers on what happened to our daughter."

I found a mention of a detective who'd worked the case, and I looked up the phone number for the agency. When I introduced myself, I explained that I was calling about Ash Crawford.

"What's he doing now?" the detective asked.

"We have a case here in Smith County, Utah, sounds a lot like yours. A pregnant teenage girl found buried."

"Let me guess: Crawford is all over it."

When I confirmed that was why I was reaching out to him, the detective launched into a litany of complaints about how Crawford had moved in and taken over the case, barricading out local law enforcement and pushing the boundaries until the case imploded. "Looking back, we would have had a better shot at solving the case without him. But when a US marshal offers to help? You take him up on it. He had resources we didn't have. But in the end, he kept getting in the way."

"I don't understand," I said. "We talked to someone at the US marshal's office and they described Crawford as a great investigator."

"So I've heard," the guy said. "Wasn't our experience."

We compared the two cases and I soon realized that they weren't as similar as I'd thought. The girl in Nevada had only been a couple of months pregnant, and the autopsy had found evidence of a gunshot wound. "Somebody put a bullet right through that girl's head," the detective said. When it came to suspects, the primary one was the girl's boyfriend, the biological father. "We felt good about charging him, that we had circumstantial evidence, but the kid has an alibi."

"One that stood up?" I asked.

"As far as we can tell he wasn't even in the state around the time she went missing. He was taking classes a thousand miles away. We're still hoping to solve the case, but we haven't gotten there yet."

"No other suspects?"

"Only Ash Crawford."

Despite my dealings with the retired marshal, that took me by surprise. "Crawford was a suspect? Based on what?"

"Based on the fact that he seemed inordinately interested in the case, and that he kept getting in the way while we tried to solve it."

"But a suspect?"

"Chief, think about it. Haven't you ever had a case where the bad guy tried to get involved in the investigation?"

It didn't take me long to realize he had a point. "Sure, I have. Actually a couple, when I worked in Dallas, including an arsonist who doubled as a volunteer fireman. He showed up to help put out the fires he set."

The guy laughed. "So how would this be any different?"

The Nevada cop's words echoed in my mind after I hung up the phone: *inordinately interested in the case… How would this be any different?*

I called Max. "You busy?"

"Just jumping through hoops. I'm trying to get some company in Denmark to work with me on this Pitocin angle. I've been on and off the phone with them. That said, things are pretty normal around here. As you'd expect, Sheriff Holmes is on the warpath about the international phone charges."

"Figures." Still, I didn't blame the sheriff. I knew how hard it was to balance a rural agency's budget. "Listen, if you've got the time, I'd like to tell you what I've found out about Ash Crawford."

Once I'd laid it all out, Max was quiet, as if thinking it through. "So, they think the girl's boyfriend murdered her, but if he didn't, they honestly think Ash may be involved?"

Max sounded dubious, and I understood why. But in a twisted way, it made sense.

"They didn't have anything concrete, just suspicions based on the way Crawford wouldn't let go of the case. The detective said Crawford got in the way of the investigation, things like what happened with us yesterday at Sam Young's place, when Ash got Miranda all riled up and we ended up having to put out a fire to get everyone to talk."

"Huh, that's odd."

"Sure is."

CHAPTER TWENTY-NINE

The heavy footsteps stopped at the door. Violet kept her eyes shut and waited, pretended to be sleeping. Whoever it was, the man or one of the sister-wives, turned and left.

Relieved, Violet tried to still her pounding heart. But then she felt it coming, another contraction. She grabbed the railings and held tight. Violet had begged for something to ease the pain, but they'd given her nothing. If only they'd untie her, at least until the baby came. What she ached to do was roll on her side and cradle her abdomen.

As the iron hands of the contraction encircled her body and tightened, she tried not to scream. But the intensity built, and it became her only release. "Oh, please, no!" A shiver ran through her followed by another wave of jaw-clenching pain. Her shrill cries ricocheted off the walls. Once it passed, she waited, terrified, but the man didn't saunter back into the room, or the women. She was alone.

Once the contractions temporarily released their hold on her body, Violet thought of her mother, of home, of the bed she shared with two of her sisters, shelves that held dolls in bright dresses.

"Home," she whispered. "If I could only go home."

That's where I should have gone, she thought. *When I fled, I should have run to my family.* Instead her mind filled with memories of the night she left the unwed mother's home with Lori.

*

"We're still doing this? Tonight?" In her blue scrubs, her blond hair piled on top of her head, Lori had peered into Violet's room. The aide had a bright smile on her face and looked excited at the prospect of what waited ahead.

"I'm ready," Violet had whispered, an impish grin on her face. "Are you?"

Lori nodded. "Remember the plan."

Nurse Gantt had ordered Violet onto bed rest the day before. For the final few weeks of her pregnancy, she wasn't to budge off the mattress except to use the bathroom. It had all seemed peculiar to the teenager, who felt healthy and strong. Her baby bump had grown to the size of a watermelon, which made moving around awkward, but she hadn't had any indications of any problems.

"I'll wait in the car for you. Right after lights out, I'll leave the door to the staircase unlocked. Okay?"

"Okay." Every morning and night when Violet said her prayers, she thanked God for Lori. She was the only one willing to help Violet and baby Josh. If Lori hadn't offered, what would have happened to them?

The afternoon dragged. With no television in her room, Violet combed through old magazines. The only one she had any interest in had an article on homeschooling. Violet wondered if she should do that with Josh, but even if Lori found Violet and Josh a family to live with—which she'd promised to do—Violet would need a job.

As the hours passed, her nerves pricked with expectation. After bed check, she dressed in a white maternity top and jeans with the stretchy panel in front, then hid in bed, the blanket up to her chin, until lights out. The house finally darkened, and she eased from bed.

Violet cracked the door open. The overhead light had dimmed, and she saw no one. Her heart pounding, she slipped into the hallway. Carrying her shoes, in her stocking feet, she tried the door. Unlocked.

No lights on in the staircase, Violet carefully analyzed each step by touch, lining up her heel to the riser. Her feet slippery in the socks, she clutched the bannister. At the second-floor landing, Violet heard voices.

"Shouldn't you be gone by now?" Nurse Gantt called out.

"I'm leaving," Lori replied. "I was just downstairs talking to one of the girls. I walked her up here to make sure she went to bed."

"You spend too much time with them," Miss Gantt criticized. "You shouldn't get close to them. If you get too close, you lose sight of what we're doing."

Violet couldn't hear Lori's answer. She wished she could have told Nurse Gantt the truth: that Lori was the only one who'd made the facility feel even a little bit like a real home.

"I'm on my way out," Lori shouted. "See you tomorrow."

At that, Violet again began picking her way down the stairs. She arrived on the first-floor landing and slowly opened the door. A moment's pause, and she slipped through. A brisk clip through the living room and kitchen, then to the back door. She was nearly out of the house when she heard shoes shuffling in the hallway.

"Yes, the girl with the violet eyes is nearly ready. If she doesn't go into labor on her own, we'll hook her up and get her going in two weeks, three at the most. The baby will be a little early, but it should be fine. Have you scheduled the auction?"

Quiet. Violet had assumed that Nurse Gantt was listening to the man on the other end of the phone. "Glad that's taken care of." A pause, and then she said, "No. I'm not anticipating any problems. These prairie-dress girls have been taught to obey."

The man must have said something.

"Samantha, yes, I know, she was a disappointment, but Violet is more compliant. I'm not worried. You'll see."

Through the window, Violet saw Lori flick her car lights on and off, the signal to hurry. Thinking about what Nurse Gantt had said, Violet eased open the back door. The hinges squeaked.

She hesitated, fearful Nurse Gantt would round the corner. Only silence.

Outside in the cool evening air, Violet rushed to the car.

"We're off," Lori whispered, with a playful cackle.

Unaware of the danger that lay ahead, Violet watched over her shoulder as the home disappeared behind her, grateful that the yard lights hadn't turned on and that Nurse Gantt hadn't run out screaming at them to stop.

CHAPTER THIRTY

How could Ash be behind all this? Max wondered.

He felt as if he was walking a tightrope. From the moment Clara met Ash Crawford, she'd been suspicious of him, and Max had tried to smooth the tension between them. Max understood why Clara worried: the guy was acting strange. But a suspect? That, well, that was over the top. Ash Crawford, Max decided, was no more a killer preying on young pregnant girls than Max was a circus acrobat. *Heck, I can barely balance my checkbook, much less twirl plates while walking on stilts.*

Behind his desk, Max swiveled his chair to look out the window at the parking lot, the field behind the courthouse. In the distance, he saw the mountains. Sometimes they pulled at him, and he had to fight the urge to chuck it all, grab his rod, bait box and waders, spend the day in the river fishing for trout. Let his mind clear of all the pain and suffering he saw on the job. Weed through the remnants of his life and pull out the bad stuff.

Max figured he had a lot to deal with, more than most folks, he judged. Forced out of his family by his father, the death of his wife haunting him, a daughter in a wheelchair to raise, so much to worry about.

Clara had helped with that. Being with her, those hours together, they were better for him than anything else he'd experienced since Miriam's death. For so long, nothing had been normal. Nothing with the exception of Brooke had mattered to him. But his time with his daughter—as priceless as it was—carried with it a shadow of remorse for not driving the night of the accident. Sometimes he pictured Miriam as she was that evening when she slid into the driver's seat, eyes bright, smiling over at him. He'd loved her. He truly had.

So much regret.

The only one who'd been able to pull him out of the cycle of guilt was Clara.

He thought of the prior weekend at the cabin, then coming home to the bones on the mountainside. Maybe that was the way a cop's life went: a mixture of the best and the worst. Maybe he'd always known it would be like that. He saw such sadness in his work, witnessed evil that the average person wouldn't be able to tolerate. It wore on him, he knew.

Max thought about how long Ash Crawford had been a cop. Probably three, maybe even four decades. All Ash must have seen during those years, experienced. Sometimes that changed a person. Had it changed Ash? Was Clara right? Maybe, but... Max couldn't get there. He couldn't deny that Clara had a good sense about people. He'd teased her that she had womanly intuition. But this time, this time she had to be wrong.

Max didn't care what the Nevada cop said: not Ash Crawford.

That decided, Max swung his chair back around to his desk, picked up the subpoena for the internet drug company he'd been working on when Clara called. That was how they were going to find out what happened to the teenager and her baby: narrow down the list and come up with the name of the person who bought Pitocin, the one who'd injected that poor kid and killed her and the baby. And he was going to get it done.

CHAPTER THIRTY-ONE

I knew from the hesitancy of his voice that Max didn't believe what the Nevada cop had said about Ash Crawford. One thing Max and I did agree on: that he was going to keep working the drug trail, searching for the buyer of the Pitocin. Meanwhile, I continued to surf the internet, trying to find out more about our mysterious ex-marshal. Crawford had acted oddly enough that no matter what Max thought, I was forging ahead. Besides, I was stymied on the investigation into the bones until the DNA report came in. One search engine to another, pages of news articles, but not much turned up about Crawford or his wife, Justine. I was considering what to do next when Dolores called.

"He'll talk to you," she said.

"Danny Benson will talk to me?"

"That's right. I gave him your phone number, and he'll call this morning. He's living in St. George, so you'll have to see him there."

"Lynlee?"

"She's agreed, too."

The drive to St. George took a couple of hours, even though the address was on the closer, northern end of the city, and my navigation system guided me to a small white clapboard house. I clomped up the stairs and rang the bell, and a pretty woman with a swath of pale freckles across her nose answered. She stuck out her hand. "I'm Lynlee, Chief Jefferies. Nice to meet you."

The kitchen was cozy, roosters decorating everything from towels and tiles to napkin holders and a breadbox. Lynlee poured me a cup of coffee. "We need to talk first. Then, if this all sounds okay, I'll call Danny and he'll join us."

I agreed, and answered questions. I explained that I'd found the report she'd filled out, praising her for protecting her brother at such a young age. "It seems like you're still watching over him."

"I am. Danny's had, well, a rough time. Dad was brutal with him. It's left him, both of us, with a lot of bad memories."

"How is his life?"

"Danny's okay. We were taken care of for a long time by a family here in St. George, and we took their last names. Without them and Dolores, who saved us, I don't know what we would have done. I'm married and have a little girl. Danny still lives with our adoptive family."

At that, Lynlee asked for an account of everything I knew and what I wanted to talk to Danny about. I was as thorough as I could be, but I left out one thing: that the only way charging her father would be a possibility was if he had sexually abused a child. Danny was so young when they fled, not even in kindergarten, bringing up that hitch had to be done carefully. I still had the district attorney's cautions to consider: that I could unwittingly plant a false memory.

"So it's up to Danny if he wants to press charges against our father?"

"Yes. But the case also has to fit certain parameters to be eligible after so many years. If it qualifies and he wants to proceed, I'll take it to the DA, and we'll see if he'll take the charges."

Lynlee sighed. "I've been wondering about the other children."

"Other children?"

"My brothers and sisters, half-brothers and half-sisters. My father always had to have someone to pick on. Before Danny, Dad abused another of my brothers. So I worry that when Danny and I left, Dad found a new target."

"I understand. I've been worrying about the same thing, that your father hasn't stopped abusing his children. That there are other victims. It's one of the reasons I pushed to go ahead even though so many years have passed." I felt relieved, grateful that she understood the seriousness of the case. "It makes it more important that we stop him, doesn't it? Some child could be suffering right now."

Lynlee paused, as if thinking that through. "I agree, but this has to be up to Danny. If there's one thing the therapists taught both of us, it's that we need to take control of our lives. Not let others decide for us."

"Good advice."

Not long after, it appeared that Lynlee must have reached out to Danny with a text, because he shuffled in the door. At twenty, I could see the little boy in the photo, the cute kid with shaggy hair. As a young man, Danny seemed a bit timid, and I wondered if that was because of who I was and why I'd come, or if those early years had imprinted on his personality and he'd never been able to shake them.

We gathered around the kitchen table, a bowl of artificial peonies in the center. "Danny, your sister and Dolores explained why I'm here and what I want to talk to you about?"

He nodded. "I'm not sure how I feel about this."

I hesitated, trying to decide how to proceed. I didn't want to do any further damage to the kid, and as much as I could, I wanted to be honest. "There are statutes of limitations on crimes, and I'm not sure if we can pursue anything against your father. It depends on what happened all those years ago. But if the case qualifies, you can still decide not to go ahead. It will be up to you."

"Thanks," he said. "That helps."

"Tell me what you remember about your father."

For the next hour, Danny struggled through an account of horrific abuse. Clyde hadn't just hit him that day he blackened his eye, but pushed him, shoved him, smacked him across the face and clutched him by the collar and squeezed. "One day, I don't remember doing anything wrong, but then I never did understand what I'd done. Dad, well, he grabbed me by the hair and he pulled me across the room. For years after we fled, I had a circle of hair missing from the top of my head. I'd yelled and screamed and cried and begged him to stop, but he wouldn't let go."

I envisioned how Danny must have suffered, considered what that must have been like for a little kid.

When Danny finished his account, I asked, "Was the abuse purely physical, hitting and such, the types of assaults you've described?"

At that, Danny shot Lynlee an uneasy glance. Something seemed odd about it, as if he were asking her permission. She shook her head so slightly that I almost missed it.

When he didn't answer, I asked again: "Do you remember any other types of abuse?"

Danny again stared at Lynlee, whose frown deepened. Time passed, until he eventually asked: "Isn't that enough?"

"Of course." I considered the way he kept looking at his sister. Was he asking for her permission to tell more? "Danny, what your father did to you is horrible. You shouldn't ever have had to endure all you went through."

Danny appeared to consider that. "Is there enough to make it possible to charge Dad? If I want to?"

I sat back in the high-backed wooden chair wondering if this were a Pandora's Box I shouldn't have opened. Despite all the horror of what he'd told me, none of it extended the statute of limitations. The offense had to be sexual. "I don't know that it is enough, Danny. I'm sorry. What you endured is horrific, but the statute requires more than physical abuse."

"Oh, I see." He leaned forward in his chair and planted his forearms on his thighs, clasped his hands and stared down at the floor.

"Why did you bother us then?" Lynlee asked. I glanced over and saw her anger, and I understood. Maybe this had all been a mistake. "Did my father have to kill Danny? Is that the only thing that would have made it serious enough?"

"No, no, of course that's not it. It's just that. Sometimes when there's one type of abuse, there are others. I thought perhaps…" I struggled with how to go forward. "I'm just looking for the truth, so we can figure out what the options are."

"That's what I remember he did to me, just what I've told you," Danny said, his eyes locked on his sister. She avoided looking at him and seemed agitated. I felt guilty that I'd barged into their lives and convinced them to resurrect such a painful past. Yet I had the feeling that there was more, something else at play here. Something involving not Danny, but his sister.

"Lynlee, why did you leave home?" I asked.

At that, she gave Danny a stern glance I interpreted as an order to stay silent. Looking directly at me, she insisted, "I left with my brother. To protect him."

Danny craned his neck to the side and narrowed his eyes at her. He appeared upset, but he said nothing. They were communicating without words, the silent conversation of a sister and brother who'd been through hell together and were so close they read each other's thoughts.

"No other reason?" I asked.

At that, I turned back to Danny just in time to catch him mouthing: *Tell her.*

That answered my question. At that moment, I knew what was unspoken and who it happened to.

"Tell me what, Lynlee?" I asked. Neither one spoke, and I waited. The pressure built in the silence until it formed a presence in the room, a ghostlike apparition that hovered over all of us. Foreseeing no way around it, I asked, "Lynlee, did your father do something to you?"

At that, Lynlee bolted out of the chair. "I appreciate your driving all the way here to see us, but you need to leave. My husband and our child will be home soon."

I remained seated. I felt certain I wasn't misinterpreting. Everything from Danny's body language to the pleading look in his eyes telegraphed the message. But I couldn't feed it to her. I needed her to say it: "Lynlee, won't you tell me what your father did to you?"

Her hand to her forehead, Lynlee appeared ready to run, to flee from the room and the house, and leave us there.

Danny stood and approached his sister, wrapped his arms around her. I heard him whisper, "Why should we let him get away with what he did to us? Why is it our burden to carry? Remember what the counselors told us: take control."

Pushing him away, Lynlee would have none of it. "Please, leave," she ordered. "Now."

Watching them, I saw something in their faces, a shared sadness that touched my heart. I felt an overwhelming regret. It appeared that all I'd accomplished was to dig up very bad memories, to no one's benefit.

As much as I wanted to argue with Lynlee, to convince her to open up about all she'd suffered, I did as she asked. But on my way out the door I handed each of them my card with my private phone number. "Whatever you decide, whatever you choose, is the right thing. I'm not questioning that. Just make sure it's your decision, and that you're not letting your father control your lives any longer. If you do want to pursue this, there's not a lot of time. The clock is ticking."

Lynlee appeared puzzled. "What do you mean?"

This time, I focused only on her. "If I'm not mistaken, you'll be twenty-eight in a few months? Once you are, you're ten years past adulthood, and the door closes. Even if you want to, we won't be able to pursue charges."

CHAPTER THIRTY-TWO

By the time I reached Alber, it was mid-afternoon. I felt at loose ends, and I didn't know where to turn. I needed to bring something to a conclusion. I needed closure, if not on Clyde Benson, then I needed to track down whoever killed our pregnant mom and her baby. Instead of turning onto Main Street and heading back to the station, I drove through Alber and headed toward the mountains. I wondered if Jerry Cummings had his crew back out working on the ski lift, if they'd finished the pier that was going to be erected over where the grave had been found.

I kept my eyes straight ahead as I passed the Second Coming Ranch, thinking about Lynlee and Danny, and the therapist who'd advised them to take control of their lives. I reminded myself that no one controlled me any longer, either. As I passed, I saw that tractor in the distance, the one bringing feed to the livestock. I didn't let myself wonder this time if my husband—the man who was once my husband—was driving. It didn't matter, I told myself. He didn't count.

Yet the ranch pulled at me, needled at me. Deep down where I hold the truths that govern my life, I knew that at some point I had to confront what happened there, not slip silently past but stand tall and take it all on.

Once I turned off onto the access road, I slowed down. I saw the ski runs on the mountainside. The closer I drove, the more I wondered why I was there. What did I hope to find? Except that sometimes, when things don't gel, the best thing an investigator can do to move a case forward is to revisit where it began. The dark shape of the ski resort lay ahead, and I saw workers' cars in the lot. As I had three days earlier, I drove around the building to the back and parked closer to the construction site. I recognized Jerry Cummings' lean outline as soon as I got out of the Suburban. He was off to the side, watching his men work and talking to a tall guy with silver hair. A cowboy hat. Ash Crawford.

Neither man saw me at first, which surprised me. I would have thought they'd heard me drive up. But when I clambered out of the SUV, I realized they had a machine compacting the soil, pounding the dirt over and over, to ready it for pouring the foundation for the pier. I considered how they'd have to do this a dozen times to erect the piers to build the ski lift. Building blocks, like the ones we needed to keep adding to our case if it was going to take shape.

"What are you doing here?" I shouted as I approached Cummings and Crawford.

"Watching to make sure the men do it right," Cummings said. "I work here."

"Not you. Him," I said, gesturing toward Crawford. He held an unfolded map in his hands, as if he'd been showing Cummings something on it. "What's *he* doing here?"

Crawford sucked in his lips and pulled them to the side. "I'm talking to Mr. Cummings and looking around. Is there a law against that?"

"This is a crime scene," I said.

"Not any longer," Crawford pointed out. "Your CSI guys released it. Yellow tape's gone. The crew's back at work. I have as much right as anyone to be here. Mr. Cummings doesn't mind, do you Jerry?"

A short shake of the head and the foreman said, "Not a bit."

"So what's your gripe?" Crawford asked.

No need to hold back any punches. "I heard about what you pulled in Nevada. I hear you're not welcome back."

At that, Ash glowered at me as if I'd just called him the vilest of names. "Lots of incompetent cops in the world. Some folks don't know how to investigate a case. Whether they realized it or not, they needed help."

"That's not what the Nevada detective said. And that's not the case here. Max and I have got this. You need to pack up and go home. Enjoy your retirement. Go fishing. Spend some time with the wife. Maybe I ought to stop in and talk to her, ask her why you're hovering over our case?"

"My wife? Hell, you…" Taken aback, he'd started to speak but abruptly stopped, swallowing whatever he'd planned to say. A moment passed before he shook his head then growled, "You have no right to tell me what I can or can't do. And you stay the hell away from my wife. She's got nothing to do with this."

Visibly angry, Crawford stalked off. As he pulled out on the driveway, he gunned the engine. He left in a cloud of dust, gravel dinging his truck's undercarriage.

On the drive into town, I called Max and asked him to meet me at the police station. Thinking it through, I'd decided that by waiting on the DNA, we were letting the forensics run the case. After seeing Crawford with his map, I realized Max and I had to hurry. We needed to take control, before Crawford interfered even more with our case and doomed it to failure, the way he'd done in Nevada.

"So Cummings says Crawford was out there just looking at the spot where the body was found, watching the men ready it for the pier. He had a map with him—he'd circled all the ranches, farms and homes in the area," I explained when Max arrived.

"Sounds like he hasn't stopped investigating this on his own." Max appeared disappointed in the turn of events, but not as angry as I felt about Crawford's interference.

"Max, we can't have Ash Crawford taking over the investigation."

"Clara, I know, but—"

"What do you think he plans to do? Why did he have the map?"

Max scowled at me, the creases across his brow deepening. "Well, it sounds like Ash plans to canvass. I guess he thinks that someone who lives in the area may have seen something that could help solve the case. That's unlikely though, as rural and deserted as that area is. The neighbors out there are miles apart."

"Or he may have decided that the girl may be connected to someone who lives in the area, and folks might be able to ID her," I said. "It's possible, but that's also a long shot, since we don't have any missing person reports in the area except those we're already investigating."

"That's true, too."

"But Max, what Ash is right about is that we've been sitting back waiting for the forensics to bring us answers. With him out there stirring folks up, we can't do that."

Max gave me a weary nod. "I'm afraid you're right."

"We need to question those folks before he has time to mess things up."

In a few minutes, I had aerial photos of the area around the ski lodge on my desk. It was getting late, and we only had a couple of hours of daylight to work with, but I had circles drawn around all the ranches in the area. Everything within a five-mile radius of the burial site.

"Okay, so we've got about a dozen old houses and ranches out there. How about some old-fashioned gumshoeing?"

"Sure, I'll call Alice, ask her to keep Brooke at her house again tonight. Do you want me to drive, or should we take your Suburban?"

"If we're going to get this done before dark, we need to split up. I'll take the ranches on the east side. You take the ones on the southwest."

"I don't know," Max appeared concerned. "Cold-calling like this, you never know what you're walking into. Maybe we should go together?"

I needed some kind of resolution, and I was tired of waiting. "No. Let's get this done." I handed him his list of addresses. He didn't look pleased.

"Listen, I'll take the ones on the east," he said. "You don't have to go to—"

"No," I cut him off. "I chose this side for a reason. I want to do this. I've got to do it."

"You sure? I don't think it's a good idea for you to—"

"It's time," I said.

CHAPTER THIRTY-THREE

The intervals between the contractions grew shorter and the pains lasted longer. "Something's wrong," Violet said to the younger woman the next time she shuffled into the room. "It hurts too much."

The woman seemed odd to Violet; she had since the first day she'd met her, as if everything wasn't right with her. The woman had never talked much, but since they'd tied Violet to the bed, the woman wouldn't even look at her.

"You should let me go," Violet pleaded, her voice weary. "What if I die here?"

Head down, the woman shuffled out of the room without replying.

How long ago had it been? Violet couldn't recall, but she vividly remembered the long drive she'd taken with Lori to the house that night.

Even in the dark, the house had looked ramshackle, with a gray roof stained by mildew and shutters in dire need of painting. At the home, Lori had talked often about her husband and children. She'd mentioned how much fun it was to live in a city. But the house they pulled up to was down lonely country roads and surrounded by nothing but cattle pastures and cornfields.

"Didn't you say you lived in a city?" Violet asked.

"No. I said that I used to live in a city. This is where we live now. But this is better. It's a good place for you to hide," Lori turned and grinned at her. "We'll have to be very careful, Violet. Nurse Gantt will send people to try to find you."

Once inside, Lori said, "We have a place all ready for you. Away from the family, so you can have your privacy."

The house quiet, Violet tried not to make any noise, and Lori led her to a door that opened to the cellar stairs. "Your room is down here."

The basement smelled of decay and with each step the dampness hung heavier on Violet. She followed Lori past shelves holding home-canned vegetables and fruit, to a door at the very back. Lori opened it and flicked on a light. The cement-block walls were painted a pale beige that matched the tile floor. There was a small chest with four drawers and an armoire with a few long dresses hanging in it. In the corner of the cell-like room sat a white wicker bassinet on a stand.

"I think the dresses will fit you, and there are undergarments in the dresser." Lori switched on a dehumidifier that hummed away, then a small electric heater. She opened another door that led to a cubbyhole bathroom with a shower.

"That's a hospital bed." Higher than a regular bed, it had guardrails on the sides. Violet pointed at an IV pole in the corner "Why do you have that in your house?"

"You don't think you're the first girl I've helped, do you? We've delivered other babies."

Violet hadn't been sure how to answer. "You have?"

"Of course. I consider it my calling."

When the sun rose the next morning, the first rays filtered in through the room's only two windows, high rectangles just above ground level. In the daylight, the room looked even more depressing, dusty and forgotten.

After a shower, Violet slipped on a yellow prairie dress that hung loose on her slight shoulders. Hungry for breakfast, she scurried up the steps and grabbed the knob. It wouldn't turn. She tried again. It wouldn't budge. Panic washed through her, anxiety that surged like a flood of adrenaline. "Lori!" she called out, pulling on the handle. No one answered. She pounded and shouted again. Nothing. Inside her womb, Josh kicked hard. "Lori!"

The sound of a lock turning, and the door opened. A man peered at her, a man so big, he filled the doorway. "You must be our new house guest. We were wondering when you'd get up."

Violet walked into the kitchen and found Lori frying bacon and another woman washing dishes. At the home, Violet had always seen Lori in scrubs, and she'd assumed that Lori and her family were Gentiles. But both women wore long prairie dresses, and Violet realized that the other woman, Rachel, had to be Lori's sister-wife.

"Good morning," Lori said. "Take a seat and I'll get your breakfast."

"Why was the door locked?"

"We didn't want you to be disturbed," the man said, as he stared down at her, hard. "You need to stay downstairs in the mornings until the children leave for school. We don't want them to see you. It's safer if you're our little secret."

From that first day, something about the man had given Violet a disquieted feeling. Seated at a table next to the window, she'd looked out at cattle in a pasture. "Where is this place?"

Lori's husband had narrowed his eyes at Violet and said, "It's the end of the earth. No place anyone ever comes."

CHAPTER THIRTY-FOUR

I started with the chicken ranch farthest from Alber, closest to the mountains. An elderly man, Mr. Everett Johnston, and his two wives lived there, folks I'd known as a girl. A double-wide on cement blocks, a deck on the front with some old beige folding chairs, the vinyl seats torn and the legs pocked with rust. The coops sat a short walk from the house, run-down wooden structures that looked fragile enough to be leveled by a stiff breeze. The chickens clucked and walked in circles scratching the dirt in search of feed, surrounded by an eight-foot-high cyclone fence to keep out wolves and a screen mesh cover so the hawks couldn't swoop in and grab them.

Old Mr. Johnston rustled out of the trailer, obviously not happy to see me, since he had a rifle in his hands.

"What're you doing here?" he demanded. "Didn't you see the 'no trespassing' sign?"

I shot him a broad grin, the kind that I reserved for settling down folks who I worry have a fairly loose hold on reality or a jumpy trigger finger. "I just need to ask a couple of questions. Nothing to worry about."

"That's what cops always say, and then, boom!" His hands shook, and I worried more about that rifle pointed in my direction. His face flushed, clearly agitated, he said, "Cops tell you everything's okay, and then they're carting you off in handcuffs."

Maybe Max had been right. I probably should have run background checks on all the folks who lived in these remote ranches before I made the decision to drop in on them unannounced and alone. Mr. Johnston had obviously had some rather unpleasant dealings with police in the past. And with my past, my reputation in town, I wasn't always greeted warmly when I knocked on doors.

"I'm only here to ask you and the wives to look at a sketch of a young woman. I'd like to know if you recognize her."

That seemed to give him pause. "That girl on the TV? The pregnant one? The dead one?"

"Yes, that one." At that, he lowered the rifle but I still didn't feel completely safe. "I'd appreciate it if you'd put the weapon away."

He appeared to think it through, unsure what to do, perhaps. A moment's hesitation and he leaned the rifle across one of the chairs as he shouted, "Wives, come out here and talk to this cop so we can get her on her way." Instantly, two women, one thin and straight as a post, the other so round I doubted she could bend to tie her shoes, tramped out of the trailer and onto the deck. They followed their husband down the wooden steps.

"Who is that girl?" Mr. Johnston shouted, as they approached me. "You think we know her? That's why you're here?"

"We don't know who she is. But her bones were found up where they're building the ski resort, so it's kind of in your neck of the woods."

"The girl on television? The one they showed the drawing of?" the skinny Mrs. Johnston asked. She had one of those faces so heavily wrinkled that it looked like a dried-up apple core. I nodded, and she said, "We've been talking about her all day."

At that, I took a second look at the trailer, this time noticing a satellite dish on the top. Like when I was a kid, most of the folks in Alber still didn't watch regular television, but it appeared that Mr. Johnston had loosened up on following the prophet's edicts to eschew such earthly temptations. Of course, the Johnstons were also breaking rank by talking to me, an apostate. I gathered that

Mr. Johnston had become something of a rebel in his old age. I found that rather surprising, and a touch admirable.

"You don't need to show us that picture. We've been seeing it on the news," Mr. Johnston said. "We don't know her."

"Have you heard anything about any girls disappearing? Any talk at all?"

They looked one to the other and shook their heads nearly in unison. "Nah," the old man declared. "You're wasting your time with us."

I circulated from one lonely ranch to another. Most of the folks didn't have television and hadn't seen the girl's face, and all the others greeted me, if not happily, then without brandishing firearms. Some of those mindful of my status in the faith refused to talk to me directly, but when I held up the sketch they looked it over, then shook their heads. All the visits went quickly. Since I was getting no information, I had no reason to tarry.

"Where are you?" I asked Max. I called him as the sun dropped low in the sky. Another half an hour and it would be dark.

"I'll be at the last house in a few minutes. No luck so far."

"Same here. After the Second Coming Ranch, I'll be done," I said.

Max sighed. "Clara, why are you doing this? You don't have to. I can drive over there and talk to them. There's no reason for you to maybe run into—"

"I do need to." I hadn't had time, with so much going on, to tell Max about the Benson case. So I hadn't confided in him about Lynlee and Danny and how their words had touched me. That they'd worked so hard to gain control of their lives made me realize that I'd let others have too much influence on my own. I'd been thinking about it all day, ever since the drive home from St. George. And I'd come to the conclusion that until I confronted my past, I couldn't truly move on.

Eight months earlier, I'd returned to Alber. I'd faced down the folks in town who shunned me. I'd done what a good cop does and taken on the work. But until I stood up to those who'd tormented me, they had the power to haunt me. I understood Max's concerns, but I didn't really have a choice.

"I wish you wouldn't go to the Second Coming. I'm sure you have your reasons, but—"

"Max, this is my call. I'm doing this because I'm a cop and it's my job. And I need to prove to myself that he doesn't control me any longer."

We were both silent. "If there's a problem, anything goes wrong…" Max said.

"It won't."

My pulse quickened the closer I drove to the Second Coming. I'd worried about how to get through the electronic gate, but it yawned open when I drove up. The sun ever lower in the sky, I considered for a moment that I should have made the ranch my first stop, not my last, but that couldn't be changed. Nothing was to be done. I swung onto the long driveway. Blue cypress, unusual in the mountains, bordered it. The first time I drove onto the property, when I was a seventeen-year-old bride, my husband, who was in his sixties, had patted my hand and bragged about how he'd had the trees shipped from Italy after a trip to Tuscany with four of his wives.

"Someday I'll take you on trips to exotic places. Would you like that?"

"Yes, husband." My voice had sounded weak, even to me.

There would never be such trips, or any evidence of love, just disappointment, heartache and pain.

As I drove past, the horses grazed in the fenced pastures, slender Arabians with long faces and intelligent eyes. They had been my godsend when I lived on the ranch, their stable my refuge. I'd spent hours brushing them down, talking to them softly and telling them my troubles. Once, on a night when a bruise had covered my jaw and my face ached, I'd slept on a bench outside one of the stalls.

I parked near the front steps and peered up at the three-story fortress. The family would be getting ready for dinner, the wives collected in the kitchen in the main house, cooking. A few watching the smaller children as they played in the toy room. How grand the house looked from the outside; how dark and foreboding it had always felt inside.

I'd only made it up to the third step when the door creaked open.

"I knew when I heard you were back that you'd return. And here you are on my very own porch."

Sebastian Barstow's appearance had changed little from the way I remembered him. Sixty-nine when I fled, he had to be closing in on eighty, but he remained a formidable man. His shoulders wide, his hands thick, he stood determinedly erect, as if daring age to bow him. His white hair had thinned, and he combed it straight back. He wore a long-sleeved white shirt tucked into black trousers and a pair of black shoes with rubber soles. I remembered how those shoes of his sounded as he walked down the hallway toward my bedroom.

I'd told myself that seeing him wouldn't affect me, couldn't affect me. Ten years, and I was immune to his influence. He had no power. Yet my heart squeezed into a fist.

I stared at the cane he rested on, a lion's head at the grip. Despite his strength, his money, he wasn't immune to age. It was taking its toll. But then my eyes tracked up to his crumpled face. The decades had faded but not erased the angry glint in his blue eyes, the visible disdain he held for me.

"Sebastian, I'm here on official business. I'm canvassing all the houses in the area." As hard as I fought it, I heard traces of my rising emotions in my voice, and he recognized it as well, his mouth curling up in scorn.

"Is that why you're here? No other reason?"

"No other reason," I said. "I'd like to talk to you, your wives, to have you look at a sketch of a teenage girl who was—"

"Clara Jefferies Barstow, you are one of my wives. Sealed by the prophet," he shouted. "You may have turned your back on Elijah's People, my brother's teachings, but you can't escape them. Remember: I have the ultimate power. It is up to me to decide if you enter the celestial kingdom at the end of your days."

I shot him a cold glance, one I used in interview rooms. He didn't react. Staring up at him, I noticed the faint mark on his cheek, the one left by a cut I gave him the night I threw a hand mirror at him as he had stomped toward me in a rage. After it hit him and drew blood, the mirror had fallen to the floor and shattered, sending shards across the floor. That night, Sebastian had grabbed me by the hair and pulled me to him, and he'd made me kneel on the broken glass. I remembered the sharp pains the glass shards sent up my thighs, the rivers of blood on my legs when I finally stood.

I sucked in a healthy dose of oxygen to calm my nerves. "I'm here for one reason, to show you the photo of a teenage girl whose bones were found near where the ski lift is being built. I'd like you and your wives—"

"Again, Clara. You are my wife. We are married in the eyes of God for eternity." His voice softened, and I remembered this tactic, this other Sebastian, the one that attempted to reason with me, to prove to me that what I knew, saw, felt and suffered, wasn't real. "Come inside and we will talk."

"I am not, and I have never been your legal wife," I said, my voice sandpaper. "You were never my husband."

The man who'd once had the power to do whatever he wanted to me, the man who still tormented my dreams, glowered down at me. He made no move to call the others, or to walk down the steps toward me. I held the sketch up so he could see it. "This is the girl. She's approximately five feet two, brown hair, somewhere in the neighborhood of fifteen years old. Do you know who she is? Have you seen her?"

Instead of examining the drawing, Sebastian focused on me. From behind him, another man emerged, taller, massively built. "Father, is this woman bothering you?"

At the sight of Trench Barstow, my ex-husband's oldest son, my throat squeezed so tight I could barely breathe. Trench had to be in his mid-fifties, and his dark hair had turned a steel gray. The cruelty in that man's eyes hadn't faded.

"Hello, Trench. I was just showing your father this drawing of a teenage girl whose remains were found—"

"You always did bore me," Sebastian sneered, his voice dripping in contempt as he shook his head. "Come inside, Trench. Let this woman be gone."

His face devoid of expression, Trench stared down at me as he held the door open until his aging father disappeared inside the grand house, a building I knew every room in, one where I'd lived for seven years, if what I'd endured could be described as life.

The heavy wooden doors slammed behind them, and I stood statue-like for a moment, the sketch in my hand, considering what to do. I took out a pen and printed on the margin:

PLEASE CALL ALBER PD IF YOU HAVE ANY
INFORMATION ABOUT THIS TEENAGE GIRL.

My knees rubber, I climbed the remaining steps. At the top, I slipped the sketch between the door and the frame, then I inhaled a deep breath, turned and marched away. At the Suburban, I took one last look back toward the house. Trench stood inside at a window, staring out at me.

As calmly and slowly as I could muster, I slid into the driver's seat, turned on the engine, and began down the driveway. I was nearly out when the electronic gates shuddered and began to close. My pulse kicked up as I pressed harder on the gas pedal. I'd barely turned onto the road when the heavy gates slammed shut behind me.

CHAPTER THIRTY-FIVE

Violet kept her eyes closed as someone walked past her bed. She didn't know if it was the man or one of his wives, but she didn't dare open her eyes and risk that it might be him. From the beginning, she'd feared him. Yet he'd done nothing to justify her trepidation, not until the argument. Recalling that evening, she thought again about how that was when she first understood what she'd stumbled into.

By eight most mornings, the children had left for school and Lori and her husband had driven off to work. That meant only Lori's sister-wife, Rachel, remained at home. A placid-looking woman who rarely smiled, she had the body of a man, heavy-boned and thick, strong shoulders. It served her well as she spent much of each day in the fields, tending to the farm.

To hide from the children, Violet ate most of her meals in her cellar room. The first week passed, and Saturday came, and Lori carried a breakfast down to the cellar. "We'll keep the door at the top of the stairs locked over the weekend. We can't have the children see you."

Violet nodded, but she had a disquieted feeling. Little things had continued to bother her, like the day Lori had arrived home from work carrying a small white paper bag. From it, she'd taken pill bottles and vials of a clear liquid she stacked in the cellar room's armoire.

"What's that for?" Violet had asked.

Although she couldn't have explained why, she felt a wave of fear when Lori said, "Medicine, to help you deliver your baby."

"Oh." Violet had said nothing, and later she'd chastised herself for her worries. After all, Lori had done nothing but help her.

Then came the afternoon a car pulled onto the driveway. Lori waved at Violet to hide and then called Rachel over. The two women talked to whoever got out of the car, while Violet watched from the kitchen. She couldn't see the person well enough to tell if it was a man or a woman.

As soon as the car left, Violet walked back outside.

Lori slogged toward her, appearing upset. "We're going to have to be careful."

"Who was that?"

Violet's nerves bristled when Lori said, "Nurse Gantt reported you missing. They're trying to find you."

The rest of that day, Violet felt on edge, but all was calm until late the next evening, when she heard angry voices. She edged quietly up the steps to listen at the door and heard Lori pleading: "The baby isn't ready. If we take it too early, we'll lose it. Why would we—"

"That picture is all over the television," her husband seethed. "We need to get that baby out and get the girl out of the house before it all goes bad."

Josh kicked Violet, and she put her hand over the spot while the voices continued. "That woman who came doesn't know Violet is here. No one knows anything," Lori insisted. "There's no danger."

"That could change. Fast!" Then Lori's husband said something that sent a shiver through Violet: "I don't want to lose the ten grand they're paying for the baby any more than you do, but I'm not going to prison for this. We need that girl out of here."

Lori had lied. She and her husband were selling Violet's baby, just like the home.

Fighting back panic, Violet crawled back downstairs and dressed, then again listened at the door. Once sure everyone had gone to bed, she tried the knob. Locked. She pushed against the door, but it wouldn't give.

Back in the cellar, she searched, hoping to find something, anything she could use to force the door open. She found nothing.

Intent on escaping, she focused on the two windows above the utility sink. To reach them, she stacked the gallon-size jars from the shelves in the sink. One after another, she carried over jars of carrots and peaches, corn and green beans. Finally, she boosted onto the clothes dryer, then stepped onto the highest jars. They swayed, and she grabbed the ledge to regain her balance. She turned the handle and popped the window. Crisp night air rushed in at her.

Breathing in the prospect of freedom, Violet thrust her head through the narrow window, then her shoulders. All went well until her baby bump stopped her. She didn't fit.

All hope lost, Violet crawled back down, tears streaming from her eyes. She returned the jars to the shelves, changed into her nightgown and sobbed herself to sleep.

What felt like minutes later, the sun shone in through the windows and Lori stood at the foot of the bed, glaring at her. "You tried to escape."

"No, I—"

"The jars are on the wrong shelves, the carrots where I keep the beans. And the window over the sink is unlatched."

Violet had never seen Lori so angry. The teenager gulped back strands of sour phlegm caught in her throat. "I didn't—"

Her face a mask of rage, Lori had stalked off. At the base of the stairs, she'd shouted, "Husband, come here, now. We are taking this baby!"

CHAPTER THIRTY-SIX

When Max woke, he reached over and felt the other side of the bed, intending to nudge closer to Clara. He sighed, disappointed, hurt. The sheets were cold. Empty.

She'd arrived unexpectedly the previous night, upset, looking weary and beaten, yet on edge and angry. He'd urged her to talk about what had transpired at the ranch, but she'd refused. "I can't," she'd whispered. "You wouldn't understand."

That had hurt him, and he'd told her so. He reminded her that he had his own painful past, his own unresolved issues with his father. The old man had abandoned Max on a city street on his seventeenth birthday, two hundred dollars in his pocket and no prospect of a place to go or anyone to help him.

"Of course, Max. I'm sorry. If anyone would understand, you would." Then, finally, she'd opened up, whispering about what had happened that evening at the ranch, how the old man had glared at her and claimed her as his wife. Clara had talked, and Max had quietly listened, until she finally confided, "It didn't go as I'd hoped. But I needed to do it."

Max wasn't sure, but he took her in his arms and didn't argue.

An hour after he'd woken up alone in bed, Max was dressed in his uniform and grabbing a hard-boiled egg out of the refrigerator. A note from Clara lay on the table: THANK YOU FOR BEING THERE.

Max took out his wallet, folded the note and slipped it inside.

Maybe Clara didn't realize, he thought, that she never had to thank him. He wanted to be beside her on the tough days as well as the good ones. He thought back to their time at the cabin, how he'd tried to explain, how he wanted her to believe as he did that the world couldn't judge them if they didn't let it. All they needed to do was to live their lives on their own terms. But Clara had pulled away, just as she had that morning. As grateful as she was, she'd left him alone.

If Clara had asked what he thought, Max would have admitted that he worried about her. She'd claimed that yesterday had made her stronger, that seeing her ex-husband, her ex-stepson, had shaken her but set her free. Max didn't see it that way. As far as he could tell, it had only resurrected terrible memories. After they'd fallen asleep, he awoke to her thrashing on the bed. The top sheet balled up in her hands, she'd screamed, "No. Stop. Leave me alone."

CHAPTER THIRTY-SEVEN

I started the day weary after a bad night's sleep. Staring down the old man at the ranch the evening before hadn't proved as liberating as I'd hoped. Standing up to Sebastian, seeing his son Trench, had left me uneasy, jumpy. Being with Max had helped, but not enough to find any real peace. I pulled into the parking lot at the station and met Stef on the walk to the door.

"How's it going, Chief?"

I smiled and said, "Okay here." Looking at her, I thought again of the Benson case, and I wondered if Lynlee had had any second thoughts about pursuing it. Still waiting for the DNA analysis on our Jane Doe and her baby to come in, I had time to kill. I hadn't given up on holding Clyde accountable. "What's on your calendar today?"

"I'm helping Conroy with a safety program at the high school, and then we're setting up a trap on the highway. We're getting complaints that the truckers are speeding again. One woman claimed an eighteen-wheeler stormed past her, going at least a hundred."

"Well, probably not a hundred, but—"

"Yeah, I didn't think so either."

While we talked, the seeds of a plan came to me. I started to pull together an idea, a tactic for pursuing Clyde Benson. I considered changing Stef's plans, having her help me. But mulling it over, I tabled the thought. It was a delicate situation, and having a rookie shadow me could be a distraction. "Stef, I'm going to check back with Lynlee and Danny today, give them one last chance to file charges. If that doesn't work, I'm going to drop in at the Benson farm and talk to Clyde's wives while he's at work, find out what I can from them about the safety of the other kids."

"His other kids?"

"Lynlee mentioned something to me, that her father abused different kids at different times. I'd been worried about that. Some abusers are like that, picking out one child to torment. I may not be able to get justice for what Clyde did to Danny, but I'm sure as hell not going to leave another kid in that house to be used as a punching bag."

"Sounds like a good plan." Then Stef muttered as she held the door for me, "I'd still like to slip cuffs on that POS."

"Wouldn't we both," I agreed.

At my desk, I made two calls: One to Doc to find out the status of the DNA. He offered to check on it and get back with me. The second was to Lynlee. She didn't pick up, and I left a message: "Please call ASAP. I need to talk to you today."

The station was busy, our usual Friday-morning meeting, and my staff, all six of our officers, waited for me in the conference room along with Gladys, who delayed her departure. We went through their questions and comments, talked about two minor robbery cases they were working, and I brought them up to date on the bone case.

When it ended, Max called and asked me to meet him at Danny's Diner for lunch. Before I agreed, I checked my messages. One was from Doc: DNA expected late afternoon.

I skimmed through the rest and found no call from Lynlee.

Max was seated at a window table looking through the menu when I walked in. "I understand the pot roast with dill sauce is quite good."

He peered up at me and chuckled. "A favorite of yours?"

"It's what I ordered for my first dinner here. It's not on the menu, but Danny's wife makes it off and on. Not sure if they'll have it today."

"I may go for a barbecue sandwich," he said. "That *is* on the menu."

"Good choice."

At that, my phone rang: Lynlee, returning the call I'd left hours earlier. "Gotta take this."

For privacy, I stepped out of the diner and onto the sidewalk. Leaning up against the building, after making sure no one was within earshot, I said, "Thanks for calling. I'm checking to see if there's anything I can say to convince you to tell me what happened with your father."

In the silence, I heard her steady breathing, and I felt the tension even though we were many miles apart. I wondered if she'd simply hang up. I wouldn't have blamed her. "I know what you want," she finally said. "But I'm not going to give it to you. It's not that it didn't happen, but I don't want the world to know. My husband and our friends."

"Are you sure?"

"Yes. I've thought long and hard about this. If I tell you and you use it to arrest my father, I'll have to testify in a courtroom and everyone will know what he did to me. I won't do that."

It felt as if a door had slammed shut, and I reminded myself that it wasn't one I had the right to reopen. This wasn't my call. It wasn't my pain. Lynlee, as her therapist had urged, was taking control of her own life. Everyone deserved that, to make their own decisions about what they'd confront and what they'd leave buried. I'd done that just the night before at the ranch.

"Okay. If that's your decision, I respect it."

"I do worry about my brothers and sisters, but I just can't..." she started, but then her voice dropped off.

"Lynlee, it's okay. Remember what I told you?" She didn't respond, so I reminded her. "That no matter what course you chose to take, it would be the right decision."

"Thanks. I appreciate that." I was about to hang up, when she said, "Chief Jefferies, if there's anything you can do to check on my brothers and sisters, make sure they're okay, I would appreciate it. I've lost track, being gone, of how many kids our dad has, but some may still be pretty young. That house? Living there? It was hell."

"I've been thinking about that," I confided. "I'll follow up on it. I don't intend to just drop this. I promise."

She thanked me and the phone went dead.

Walking back through the diner's door, I glanced at my watch. Twelve fifteen. Every time I'd driven by Benson's Body Shop during the past week, I'd watched to see if Clyde left for lunch. Every day, his truck was there. I had hours at my disposal before the DNA report was expected, and I had just made Lynlee a pledge I intended to keep.

"Max, I have to go. A case I need to follow up on," I told him. "Sorry about lunch."

Disappointment rutted his forehead. "You sure it can't wait?"

"I need…" I hesitated, reconsidered, then forged ahead. "I need to do this." Max nodded, and I asked, "Before I take off, anything new on the Pitocin subpoenas?"

"Nothing yet, but I'll check back with the companies after lunch." The diner's owner, Danny Bannion, shuffled to our table with his order pad open and pen poised. Max returned his attention to the menu and said, "Get me a roast beef sandwich to go."

"Anything for you, Chief?" Danny asked.

I considered my promise to Hannah, to be better about working in a meal at least once a day. "Turkey on rye with a water."

"Got it."

*

On the highway, I munched on my sandwich and called Stef to find out where Clyde and his family lived. She gave me an address, but explained that it didn't work in her navigation system, so she described the route and the house, mentioned a few landmarks. "You sure you don't want me to go with you? Since I've met the wives before, I could help."

"No. I'll be fine. You go work with Conroy." As I passed the repair shop, I saw Clyde's truck parked outside of one of the open overhead doors. He wouldn't be closing the shop and heading home for hours, so I didn't have to worry about him interrupting. "I may be a while. I might not make it back to the station today. When I finish at the Benson place, I'm going to drop in on Ash Crawford. I want to push him, see if I can talk to his wife. That guy worries me. There's something wrong there. Ask Kellie to let me know if she hears from Doc. We're still waiting on the DNA on the bones."

"You've got it, Chief."

With Clyde out of the way at the body shop, I followed Stef's directions. The course took me past the turnoff to the mountain, the way that I'd taken the previous evening to do the canvass. I continued on, then turned onto a second road, one I hadn't driven in years. I didn't know any of the folks who lived on this end of town, but I passed a few modest homes as I watched for a driveway with two big oak trees, one on either side, and a green mailbox. The road became increasingly desolate and appeared to dead-end ahead. I worried that I'd missed the Benson farm, when I saw what I was looking for, exactly as Stef had described it. I glanced at my watch. One thirty, a good time to drop in. The children would be at school.

I parked near a two-story house, a modest, careworn place. The west side of the house was buffered from the summer sun by a stand of pines mixed with oaks. I got out of the Suburban, walked up to the back stoop and knocked on a rickety aluminum storm door. No one answered.

I scanned the area. No cars. No trucks. No vehicles. I sighed. Maybe this wasn't such a good idea. Maybe both the wives worked outside the house? Or maybe they were grocery shopping or running errands. I considered leaving and trying another day, but then decided to have a look around.

A shed sat a hundred feet away up a hill, and I trudged over to see if anyone might be inside. The dirt felt slick under my feet, wet from a rain that had come through during the night, and the farm smelled of the barn up on the hill. A dozen head of cattle grazed in a pasture to my left, while off to the right the fields were half plowed for a spring planting.

Once I reached the metal shed, I stuck my head in. "Police. Anyone here?"

Ten by ten, it didn't take me long to determine that no one was inside. I took a visual inventory: heavy chains for the tractor, an extra set of tires, a workbench with shelves covered with jars filled with nails, screws, bolts and the like. Saws. Hammers. And along the far wall, Clyde had lined up three large oil drums.

Well, this doesn't help, I thought, although if asked, I wouldn't have been able to say what I was looking for. I just wanted a feel for the place and the people who lived here. Turning to head back to the Suburban and again considering leaving, I glanced in a corner and noticed six jugs of bleach. That struck me as strange, but then I thought about how folks use bleach for all kinds of tasks. But what sat next to it surprised me even more: jugs of lye drain cleaner.

I turned back and looked at the house. Clyde obviously wasn't using the lye to keep the drains flowing. Why would he need so much for such a modest-size house? Plus, this far out in the country, no town or city around it, the house wasn't on a sewer system. I wondered how much bleach and lye were safe in a septic system. *How odd.*

Backing out of the shed, I saw someone, a woman, on a tractor tilling the field. I waved and shouted: "Mrs. Benson! Chief Jefferies from Alber!"

She kept plowing, and I realized she probably couldn't hear me over the tractor's engine. A moment later, she swung into a U-turn and headed toward me and I waved my arms and shouted, but again, she didn't see me. I noticed a dirt path, one lane wide on the side of the cornfield, and I decided the best option was to drive up to her. Heading back to the Suburban, I thought about the lye again, how peculiar that seemed. I wondered about Clyde, his history of violence. I had no real reason to do it other than a gut instinct, but I decided not to throw away the opportunity to look around more while no one was home to stop me. I glanced back at the field and saw the woman plowing, and I felt sure that I hadn't been seen.

The house was one of those with exposed cement-block cellar walls at the base, the wood siding starting a few feet above the soil line. The first-floor windows hung low enough that I could see inside the house, and it appeared to be a chaotic but normal household. A kitchen and dining area, a living room with a television set. A table off the kitchen was surrounded by chairs. Nothing I saw gave me any reason to be alarmed.

The cellar appeared dark. I hunched down to look through the basement windows. In the shadows, I saw the type of larder homes all over Alber had, filled with glass jars holding home-canned vegetables and fruit. No surprises. I glanced over at the field; the woman on the tractor had disappeared, I assumed at the far end of the cornfield. I decided that I should get in my SUV and drive out to talk to her.

I could have retraced my path to get to the Suburban, but instead circled the house, not for any particular reason. When I arrived at the far side, I noticed lights on in the cellar, two windows glowing softly. I looked back again at the field, still not seeing the woman on the tractor. I hesitated, wondering where she was. I walked toward the windows. Curious. *Why not look?*

I bent down, keeping my knee above the wet, muddy earth, trying not to get my uniform dirty. An old television on a stand stood in a corner of what appeared to be a room, a movie on the screen, some old Disney film I couldn't remember the name of. *Who's down there?*

The rest of the room not visible from that angle, I crouched all the way down. Against the far wall sat an old-fashioned armoire, its doors closed, and next to it a bed. I took in a tattered comforter, then stopped with a jolt when two eyes stared back at me. A woman, or a girl—she looked young—was in the bed, shouting something at me. Her lips moved, her face contorted in pain, or was it fear? I couldn't make out what she was yelling through the glass. Then I noticed that the bed had railings. A hospital bed. Beside it, a clear bag hung from an IV pole with a thin tube running to her arm.

Her arms? My stomach clenched when I realized both of her arms were tied to the railings at the wrists and elbows. I scanned the railings and saw more bindings at her ankles. The girl's belly formed a ball.

Pregnant. The girl was pregnant. I looked at her face, and it looked familiar. Who was she?

I pushed off with my hands to get up, but at that moment, when I was halfway between standing and kneeling, something struck me in the back of the head. Lightning bolts of pain scattered from the point of impact through my skull. My stomach seized, and I thought I would retch on the dirt. I crumpled onto my knees and hands. Then came a second blow and a kaleidoscope of color that vanished when the world went black.

CHAPTER THIRTY-EIGHT

"Chief Deputy Anderson, I'm in St. George," Detective Mullins said. "I've been trying to reach Chief Jefferies for nearly an hour. No one at the station seems to know where she is, but she said she was having lunch with you. Any idea how to get in touch?"

"She got a call and had to leave," Max explained. "She's not answering her radio or her phone?"

"No, but we're still having problems with the radios. There's been a bug in them since last week. We have a repair guy coming out on Monday. And if she's out in the hinterlands, her phone doesn't always pick up. We've had this happen before."

Max looked at his watch. "I saw her around noon. That's not very long ago. Just an hour and a half. She did seem to be in a hurry. We'd talked about lunch, but we ended up both grabbing a sandwich to go."

"Shoot," Mullins said. "It wouldn't matter, but—"

"What do you need? Anything I can help you with?"

"Nah. I don't think so. I'm trying to return stolen property to a robbery victim and he won't take it. Says we broke it. I explained that this is the way we got it when we made the arrest, but he's being an ass. He keeps threatening to sue. Now he's demanding to talk to my boss. Chief Jefferies is good at settling guys like this down. I thought maybe they should talk, so she can get him to back off. But no one can reach her."

Max let loose a brief huff. He reminded himself that Clara was a cop, one who carried a gun she knew how to use. And that in the mountains, a lost signal on a phone was to be expected. Nothing Mullins said was particularly alarming. Still, Max didn't like Clara disappearing. She needed to be better about telling someone where she was heading.

"Have you asked around the station, Mullins? The chief must have given her itinerary to someone there. She wouldn't have not told someone where she was heading."

"I talked to Kellie on dispatch, and the chief told her about lunch with you."

"Call and ask Kellie to put out a call for information to the others. The chief isn't irresponsible. She always makes sure someone knows how to find her."

"That's true. But if you hear from her, you'll ask her to bump me on the radio or put in a call? I'd like to get this guy to ease off, so I can head back to Alber."

"You've got it. And Mullins?"

"Yeah?"

"When you find her, ask her to call me."

"Sure enough."

After he hung up, Max read through the latest subpoena to be returned from the drug companies. He circled an address in an adjacent county, then looked up the number of the sheriff's department there and asked to talk to the lead detective.

"What can I do for you?" the guy asked.

"Have you ever heard of a home for teenage mothers on your turf?"

"No, can't say as I have."

Max thought about that, decided it seemed odd. Why wouldn't the guy know about the place? Usually detectives, cops, they worked with homes for transient youths, the homeless, had their feelers out to them for information and kept an eye on them to keep them safe. But then he'd looked at the map, and this place was way out in the country. On Google Earth, he scanned the area, then blew up the image. It looked like an old three-story Victorian with nothing around it for miles.

Max thought about asking the guy to drive out, do a little investigating, but he didn't know what he was looking for. Not yet. Instead, he thanked the detective and hung up.

When I get in touch with Clara, we can take a drive over there, he thought. *Find out what's going on.*

Max looked at his watch, wondered where Clara was, then picked up another of the subpoenas that had come in and began reading.

CHAPTER THIRTY-NINE

I didn't know where I was, how long I'd been blacked out, and I couldn't understand what had happened to me until I felt a shooting pain radiate from the back of my head. Like electric fingers it spread across my forehead and traveled to my jaw. My neck burned as if it were on fire. Agony shuttered my eyes, but when I opened them a slit, Clyde Benson stood in front of me, his arms crossed and a grin on his face.

"You should have stayed away," he said. "Now look what the hell you've done."

"What did I do? Why are you..." My head tilted to the left, I squinted at him, hoping for an answer. All Clyde did was let loose a belly laugh. My head ached, and I couldn't make sense of any of it. I couldn't remember. I remembered that I'd come to talk to the wives. Why was Clyde home and not at the body shop? What was all this about? I tried to stand up but couldn't. I realized I was tied to a metal chair with a slatted back, my arms behind me, my ankles and waist bound. My stomach lurched. My head hurt so bad that I could feel every pore on my face, every hair on my head. Agony. I remembered seeing something that alarmed me, but I couldn't recall what it was. As if he could read my thoughts and enjoyed my confusion, Clyde let loose another deep, rolling laugh that seemed to vibrate off the cellar walls.

"What's so funny?" the woman behind him said. She had fluffy blond hair and wore blue medical scrubs. Her name tag read "Miss Lori." "What are we going to do with her?"

Clyde shook his head, dismissing her. "Listen, wife, you do as you're told. You get that baby out of that girl in good shape so we get our cash, and I'll take care of the chief here and the girl."

A baby? My gut revolted again, twisted in pain, as I remembered the girl tied to the hospital bed.

Lori walked away in a huff.

"Rachel, come here!" Clyde shouted.

A big-boned woman with the look of a wrestler plodded over. "You sit in that chair and watch her. I've gotta get back to the shop. Got a transmission repair I need to get done. I don't want anyone asking questions about where I've been. I'll hide her vehicle. Before I head home, I'll pick the kids up from school and drop them at their grandparents' house. They can sleep there tonight."

"I'd like 'em home," she said, plopping down onto another metal chair like mine maybe six feet away. "I don't like your mother with the children, she's mean, and she and your dad—"

"No matter what you'd like, we've got too much going on to have those kids at the house. I'll be back after work. Lori should have that baby out by then."

Rachel gave me a strange look, like I'd somehow caused her problems. I tried to smile, but any movement sent shards of pain shooting through my face. My hands tied, I couldn't reach up and check, but I would have been willing to bet that the back of my head had an ostrich-egg-size lump. The rope or whatever he'd used was too tight on my wrists, and my hands throbbed. My fingers felt numb.

Clyde shot me another broad smirk. He looked pleased at the turn of events. He didn't seem at all worried that if he got rid of me the revenue at his station would go down when I didn't swing in for a fill-up and a candy bar. Or, more important, that anyone would come looking for me. "I'll see you later." I tried to remember if I'd told anyone where I was going. I thought I did, but my head ached so, I wasn't sure. Clyde grinned at me, like he was my new best friend. "I'll be thinking this afternoon about all I'm going to do to you. This'll be fun."

I felt my stomach churn again. At that, he was gone.

"Ohhhhhhhhh! It hurts! Make it not hurt," someone groaned. Who was it? I struggled to remember what had happened right before the incredible pain. I remembered a young woman, a girl, pregnant, tied to a hospital bed. She'd looked familiar. But who was she? I'd looked at dozens of photos of teenage girls that week. I gulped hard, fighting back the bile that crawled up my esophagus, sour in my mouth. "Is someone hurt? I saw a girl. Is that her?"

Rachel didn't answer. She had one lazy eye, I realized as she inspected me. Not bad out of focus, but askew to the other. She kept her head twisted to the side as she picked dried grass off of her prairie dress, remains from working in the cornfield, I supposed.

The moaning stopped. I had to get the woman talking, to figure out what was happening. "So, your name is Rachel?" I asked.

My forehead hurt when I opened both eyes, and I had a hard time focusing on her. I looked down. My phone was gone, and my gun. It would have been less painful to put my head back, try to keep calm and not jostle. Every time I moved, my head ached. But once Clyde got home, well, it didn't take a cop to figure out what he had planned for me. It didn't involve either letting me go or letting me live. I thought about the barrels in the shed, each one large enough to hold a body. My insides lurched again as the lye suddenly made sense. Enough of it mixed with water, add a little heat, and a body could be reduced to a dark sludge, the bones made so fragile they could be pounded into powder.

The woman hadn't answered. My pulse hammering inside my chest, I decided to try again. "I've always liked the name Rachel. I had an Aunt Rachel, growing up."

She nodded at that, but said nothing. From the room with the girl, another scream. The other woman, Lori, shouted, "Rachel, come here a minute. I gotta untie the girl's legs and move 'em higher up, bent, so I can get this baby out of her. You need to hold 'em for me."

I thought back to the case I'd been working on, the bones on the hill, the girls whose photos filled my binder. I squeezed my eyes shut to ease the pain, and the girl in the bed's face flashed before me. I knew her.

"What's the girl in that bed's name?" I asked. Rachel didn't answer, so then I shouted as loud as I could, "What would it hurt to tell me who she is? What's her name?"

"Shut the hell up," Lori shouted. "Rachel, get in here. Now!"

It appeared that Rachel blamed me for causing her more trouble; she gave me an irritated glance. She stood and moseyed over, walking as slow as syrup dripping out of a maple tree in winter. *She doesn't want to go in there,* I thought. *She doesn't like this.*

I heard them arguing in the room, working on the girl's ties, I assumed, and I used the time to search around for something, anything I might be able to use to free my hands. Nothing grabbed my attention, but I felt around on the chairback, hoping to find a rough spot. Maybe I could rub the binding across it and fray it off. To my disappointment, the chair was as smooth as one just made, and I had no idea what I was going to do. Hoping to ignore the nagging pain and concentrate on getting free, I tried to think of some way to knock the shelves down on top of Rachel when she walked out of the room, but at the far end, I saw metal braces that anchored them to the wall.

My only hope was to find something sharp.

Shifting in the chair, pushing with my bound feet, advancing a few inches at a time, I worked myself over to the closest shelf. I had on a pair of black ankle boots, leather with a thick sole. My head aching, I brought my feet back, then snapped them forward and kicked one of the jars on the lowest shelf. I'd hoped it would fall toward me, smash on the floor, and I'd be able to pick up a spike of glass. The jar crashed, but in the opposite direction, on the other side of the shelf.

"What the hell's going on out there? Rachel, go check," Lori shouted. "I've gotta take care of this girl."

I heard hurried footsteps. As quick as I could, I hooked my feet around another jar. This time I pulled it toward me. The jar toppled, the glass shattered and sauerkraut flew across the floor. The smell of vinegar clouded around me, glass everywhere. Hoping to grab a piece, I swiveled in the chair and leaned. The chair wobbled, and my heart sank to my stomach. I couldn't reach it. I straightened in the chair just as Rachel rounded the corner.

"You're gonna get me in a mess of trouble," she muttered. "You don't know what they're like. What Lori and Clyde will do to me."

She walked behind me, grabbed the chairback and pulled me toward the wall, away from the broken glass. It didn't matter, I realized. The bindings were too tight, especially the thick rope around my waist that held me to the chair. I couldn't have reached down and scooped up a piece.

Once she had me out of the way, Rachel shook her finger at me. "You're causing trouble! I've gotta get the broom and clean this up, or he'll be mad. And I can't have him mad at me."

Rachel bustled off and I sat there, tied to the chair, thinking about what she'd said, staring at the pieces of glass that I wanted more than anything in the world and couldn't reach. From inside the room, another unholy shriek, a scream so loud and so primitive that it could only be childbirth when all wasn't well.

"Is that girl okay in there?" I shouted. "What's wrong?"

"Just shut the hell up," Lori called back. "I got enough going on without worrying about you."

CHAPTER FORTY

Mullins never did call Max back, but when his phone rang again, it was Stef. "Chief Deputy Anderson, I hate to bother you, but Mullins and I were talking, and…"

The rookie sounded nervous, as if she wasn't sure she should have called him. "It's okay, Stef. Did Mullins find Clara? What do you need?"

"Well, that's the thing: no one's heard from her."

Max looked at his watch and nearly an hour had passed since he'd talked to Mullins.

"You've been calling her?"

"Yes, Mullins first, and I've called, and no answer. It goes right to voicemail."

"Well, she's probably out of range. Have you figured out where she was heading?"

"She told me. First she was stopping over at the Benson house."

"Clyde Benson? The guy who owns the gas station?"

"Yeah." Stef still sounded timid. "The chief wanted to talk to his wives. She's been looking into an old case. Child abuse."

Max asked about where the Bensons lived and then thought about the time that had passed since Clara had left the diner. "Was Clara worried about that stop at all? Any concern there?"

"No. I don't think so. I was there earlier in the week, and they were cooperative."

"Okay, but she hasn't returned yet?"

KATHRYN CASEY

"From the Benson house, she was going out to talk to Marshal Crawford. The chief has seemed kind of agitated about him. She sounded worried about that one."

Max thought that through for a moment. "Out to Crawford's?"

"She said something about getting to the bottom of why he was interested in the bone case. She's been upset about him off and on all week."

"Yeah, well, that's true…" It didn't take long for Max to wonder if Ash and Clara had gotten into an argument out at the ranch. Without him there to calm her down, she might be going after the old guy, and, well, that might not be good. "Do you know where Crawford lives?"

"The chief put the address in the file with the information on the bones."

Max had been working in the same file, one they shared, and he pulled up Clara's reports. Tucked into her latest notes, he found Crawford's address, on a rural postal route. He thought again about the confrontation that could be taking place if Clara lit into Ash Crawford. Nothing good could come of it.

"Listen Stef, I'm sure the chief is fine. But I'll drive past the police station and lead you. We can head out to Crawford's. My guess is that she's finished at the Benson house and is there by now."

CHAPTER FORTY-ONE

Screams echoed through the cellar, eruptions of primal pain. My head ached, magnifying the girl's cries until they pulsed through me. One was so loud, so high, that I thought it might shatter the glass jars on the shelves. Trussed as I was, I couldn't look at my watch, but her contractions seemed to have settled into a rhythm, maybe ten minutes apart. In between, I heard her sobbing, begging the woman named Lori to call for help, to get her a doctor.

"I can handle this. You don't have to worry. Everything is okay." But the woman's voice gave away her doubts.

"What's your name?" I shouted. "What's wrong?"

This time, an answer. "They call me Violet." The girl's voice was breathy and at the same time hoarse. "Help me. Please. The baby, he won't come, and I…"

Violet? I didn't remember any of the girls being named Violet. Maybe this was another girl, one I hadn't even found a report on. But the way she'd said it, that "they" called her that? The raw agony of the girl's next scream tore through me, grabbing the pain that coursed through my brain and twisting it. I felt connected to the girl by some unseen hand. I had to help her. "Lori, untie me, and I'll assist you. Cops go through a birthing class. I've been trained."

"Please, Lori. Please, let her help me," the girl begged.

Lori said nothing, and just then Rachel rounded the corner carrying a black plastic bag, a broom and dustpan. Her hands were shaking, and I noticed her eyelids tremble.

"Rachel, I can help deliver that baby," I pleaded. "I've been trained to—"

"Don't listen to that woman," Lori shouted. "We'll get this baby out soon. You just leave her tied up. Clyde has plans for her."

"Yes, ma'am," Rachel answered.

I thought about the two women, their places in the household. Lori I pegged as somewhere in her fifties. Rachel looked considerably younger, maybe early thirties. She must have been the second wife, and she seemed less switched on; I wondered if she had some kind of intellectual disability. I remembered what she'd said, that Clyde and Lori could be mean, and that she hadn't wanted Clyde to take their children to his parents' house.

"Rachel, we haven't met, but my name is Clara Jefferies."

I tried to sound as friendly as I could with the headache and the tension, but the woman paid no heed. Hunched over, she methodically swept the glass into the dustpan. The sauerkraut smelled ever worse, the rotting cabbage odor wafting through the cellar. Rachel had most of it on the dustpan when she noticed a shard of glass under the bottom shelf. On her knees, just two feet from me, I wondered if I could upend the chair and topple onto her. I debated, missed the opportunity, then judged that it never would have worked with my hands tied. Somehow, I had to get free.

"Have you been married to Clyde long?" I asked. "I'm a customer of his. I buy my gas at his station."

That seemed to interest the woman. She looked up at me. "I go there on Saturdays. I clean and restock."

"Oh, you must be the one who fills the candy dish near the cash register." I did my best to sound light. The girl had been quiet for a while, and I wondered if Lori listened in. Probably not, with the baby to worry about. "I always buy a Baby Ruth or a Mars. When I was there last, I grabbed a KitKat."

Rachel looked at me for a moment, as if unsure how to react, but then she became dead serious. "We're out of a lot of the candy bars. Delivery next week."

"Oh, good. I'll look forward to that," I said, and she nodded. "It's lonely. Can you sit with me? Like Clyde told you to?"

Rachel looked uncertain. "I'm going to throw out the glass and see if Lori needs me first."

"Oh, okay."

Rachel rustled off, and I sat and waited. She seemed to take a long time, and I thought I'd lost her.

Alone, the cellar quiet, I thought back, struggling to pull together the pieces of what had happened. I didn't understand how or why, but somehow my two cases had intersected. A pregnant girl tied to a bed? Clyde Benson had to be involved in the bones on the mountainside, I decided. How could this be purely coincidental? Could he have been the one behind all of it? But what tied him to the girl? What was the link? My head pounding, I struggled to figure it out and couldn't. Then I realized that it didn't matter. There would be time later to work my way through it. At that moment, I had only one objective: to get free and save the girl and her child, or we'd all end up buried in some unmarked grave, bones that might never be found.

From inside the room, Violet's shrieks began again. I could picture her in the bed, the baby not coming out, the pain increasing. The birthing class had relied on video, but I'd seen a few babies born at the Second Coming Ranch during my years there, to my sister-wives. For a long time, I'd wondered why they had babies and our husband wasn't able to with me. He said it was my shortcoming, that I wasn't capable of getting pregnant, but even with the little bit I'd been told, what I'd been able to figure out about how babies were conceived, I knew that it was impossible if the man was unable to—

Screams, back-to-back this time, and Lori shouted: "Just get the hell out of here, Rachel. You're making it worse staring at me like that. Making me nervous. Go watch that woman cop like Clyde told you and leave me alone."

Footsteps again. Rachel's heavy work boots clomped toward me. From the room, another piercing scream.

"Is the girl all right?" I asked Rachel when she sat down in the chair.

She had her knees pushed together and her hands clasped on her lap, but she couldn't quiet the trembling. The woman's eyes looked wild, like a trapped animal. I waited, watched, hoping she'd talk, but she kept silent. She had a slight twitch in her right eye, and as hard as she tried—I assumed she was trying—her hands hadn't stopped shaking. I lowered my voice. "Rachel, you shouldn't have to be afraid. No one should have to live in fear. Why don't you untie me and let me help you?"

Her eyes scanned the room, as if she were trying to look anywhere but at me. I thought of the earlier visit Lori and Rachel had this week, the one where Stef dropped in to ask them about Lynlee and Danny. They must have had Violet hidden inside the house. Watching Rachel, I thought she looked like a frightened child. I recalled all Danny had told me about what Clyde had done to him. I remembered Lynlee saying that Clyde always had someone he used as a punching bag, usually one of the children.

"Lori must be Lynlee's and Danny's mother, I guess," I said to Rachel. "Were you living here when they left?"

At that, I appeared to have her interest, and she looked over at me and gave her head just the slightest shake.

"I talked to them yesterday. They told me what Clyde did to them, that he beat Danny and that he did other things, bad things to Lynlee."

I waited, thinking maybe she'd have something to say, but Rachel sat still except for her hands that continued to quiver.

"Lynlee says that Clyde always has someone he picks on, one person that he's mean to. Is that true?"

At that, Rachel turned her face from me. Despite her cleaning up the glass and sauerkraut, the place still smelled sour, and my stomach churned. I stared at her, watching for any reaction, and said, "It's terrible for a mother when she can't protect her own children, don't you think?"

This time, Rachel took a deep breath and turned even farther from me.

From the cellar room, another round of screams erupted, even louder than before. "Is she in trouble in there?" I shouted. "I could help."

No answer. I called out again, offering aid. The girl needed a doctor, a hospital. Something was wrong.

"Rachel, come here!" Lori shouted.

As obedient as a dutiful child, Rachel shot up out of the chair. This time, she sprinted around the shelves, toward the room. I dropped my head and wondered what I was doing wrong, why I couldn't engage her. I had no options. They'd taken my phone and my gun. Tied to the chair, I could barely move. My heart raced, and fear magnified the headache until it wouldn't be quieted. Minutes passed, Violet's screams nonstop, until all went quiet again. I scouted around the cellar, looking for something, anything I could use, and found nothing. I thought of my mother in the hospital. I wondered if death would frighten me as much if Mother and I had made our peace. It felt as if I had left so many important things undone. Unsaid. I thought of Max and wished I'd told him how I felt. I considered my sisters Lily and Delilah, my other siblings, many I might never know. I wondered what our mothers would tell them about my death. Most likely that it was a result of my bad choices, of not staying true to the teachings of Elijah's People. I could almost hear Mother Naomi cautioning them: "The secular world is dangerous. Devils stalk the night. Learn from your sister Clara's dire mistakes."

Rachel shuffled back and sat on the chair.

"What's going on in there?" I asked. "Is the girl all right?"

My companion didn't answer again, simply stared down at her hands on her lap. I noticed that the shaking had settled, but she tore at a fingernail. She had little to grab onto, since all ten had been gnawed to the quick.

"I could help Violet if you untie me. Rachel, you don't want her to die, do you?"

Nothing. No change in expression. No indication that she even heard me. I had to find a way in. I needed to get to her somehow. "I am sorry that you're not more appreciated by Lori and Clyde. Danny and Lynlee told me how cruel Clyde can be. Who does he beat now? Which one of the children?"

At that, Rachel stirred in her chair, the metal legs squeaking as she moved. When she glanced at me, the wildness was back, the look of being in danger. "Or is it you? Does he beat you?"

Her eyes dropped, and the trembling in her hands returned. *Maybe it is her,* I thought. *Otherwise she wouldn't have had such a reaction. She wouldn't have…*

"Not me." A guttural, low voice, barely above silence.

Why did she react as she did, then? I reconsidered and asked, "Clyde beats one of *your* children, doesn't he? The one he picks on is one of the children you've had with him?"

Nothing. A blank look. I had to be wrong. But then I knew, as a single tear trailed down the side of her face, that I was right.

"Which one of your children, Rachel? Tell me."

The woman shook her head. I wondered how many times she'd watched Clyde attack, torture her child and done nothing. I considered how agonizing that must have been for her. I felt angry at her and sorry for her at the same time. I recalled again that she didn't want her children to stay with Clyde's parents. She didn't trust them. A line of abusers, violence passed down through generations, most likely. My voice little more than a whisper, I said, "Rachel. I can help."

She shot me a suspicious glance, but for the first time appeared interested.

"If you help me, I have the power to put Clyde in jail. Put Lori away, too. Together, we can stop them from ever hurting your child, or any child, ever again."

She searched the room, as if checking to see if anyone else heard us. She stood up, took two steps toward me. I knew I had her. "My hands. Untie my hands." Rachel bent down behind me, and I leaned forward as she reached for the bindings on my wrists. I felt her soft touch as she began—

At that moment, a cry filled the cellar, a shriek of such pain that I had no doubt Violet and her baby were in grave danger.

"Come here quick, Rachel!" Lori shouted. "I need help."

In an instant, Rachel turned away from me, never looked back and ran, and again I was alone.

I tried to still my ragged breathing. I hadn't realized it, but in those moments when I thought she might free me, I'd been gasping for air, as if the hope mixed with fear lodged in my throat might choke me. I pulled at the binding on my wrists. Still tight. Again, I searched and tried to find something to use to free myself. Nothing. I waited, thinking any minute Rachel would return. I knew I had her. I knew she was ready to…

And then I heard it: the clomping of heavy boots coming down the staircase.

CHAPTER FORTY-TWO

Max tapped the horn as he slowed down and Stef fell in behind him. He drove toward the north edge of Alber, then took a right before he reached the trailer park. Fifteen minutes later, they were on one of the main roads heading north. The drive didn't take as long as Max would have thought. He saw the turn ahead, veered onto a side road and then turned onto a long gravel driveway. They pulled up to a cottage-like place with flower beds filled with yellow tulips and purple crocus and a stable at the side. Ash Crawford had on an old pair of jeans and a plaid shirt, and he was brushing down a good-looking chestnut with a flaxen mane. When they pulled in, Crawford gave them a suspicious glance and put down the brush.

"What're you doing here?" he asked, when Max and Stef climbed out of their squads.

"We're looking for Chief Jefferies. Has she been here?" Stef asked.

Crawford scowled. "Now, why would she be here? We're not exactly good friends."

"Come on, Ash, answer the question," Max said. "Clara's not answering calls, and she mentioned coming out here to talk to you."

Max had been thinking in the car, wondering, what if Clara was right? What if Crawford was behind it all? His suspicions took further root when he noticed a .38 in a holster around Crawford's waist. "You always brush your horse down wearing a sidearm?"

"Old habits, like old cowboys, die hard," Crawford said. "Chief Jefferies isn't here. Haven't seen her. You two go back where you came from. Leave me alone. She'll turn up."

Max suddenly started regretting that he hadn't listened to Clara. Why was Crawford trying to shuffle them off so quickly? What did he have to hide? "Mind if we look around?"

"You got a warrant?" Ash's voice had climbed an octave and grown rough around the edges.

Max took a deep breath. "No, but why would you ask for one, Ash? What's going on here?"

Ash's frown curved farther down. "Don't want you here is all, any of you. So leave."

"How long would it take to show us around?" Max asked. Stef had sidled up next to him, and she was giving Crawford a suspicious look. Max figured her instincts were clicking in, too.

"You've got no right to be here. And I don't want you disturbing my wife. So, unless you've got a warrant signed by a judge—"

Max put his hand on his gun, ready to draw if he had to, when he heard the cabin door swing open. Crawford scowled at him and shook his head. "Now see what you've done."

A tiny, slightly built woman with pure white hair walked out onto the porch. In a pair of blue jeans and a T-shirt, tennis shoes, she looked to be in her early sixties. When she saw Max and Stef, she appeared surprised. "I thought I heard a car, Ash. Who's come to visit?"

Crawford shook his head. "Go inside, Justine."

"No," she said. "Something's going on here. What is it?"

"We're looking for Police Chief Jefferies, ma'am. She said she was coming here," Max said. "Have you seen her?"

"No. No one's been here." She gave her husband a hard look. "Ash, what aren't you telling me? What's going on here?"

At that, Crawford glared at Max, as he said, "Let's just let these folks look around, Justine. Then they can be on their way and I'll explain."

"Look around?" she asked.

"Take the female officer inside, Justine. Give her a little tour of the house."

Ash's wife appeared uncertain, but she did as he'd asked. Once they walked inside, Stef scanned the place. The cabin was immaculate. It looked like a fairy-tale cottage with crocheted doilies on the backs of overstuffed chairs, a knickknack cabinet beside the kitchen table. "I don't know why you'd think Chief Jefferies would be here," Justine said. "But you're welcome to look anywhere you want."

Meanwhile, outside, Crawford walked Max into the barn. "I can't believe you came out here like this, Max. Barging in at my home, when I'm here with my wife? This doesn't seem like you."

Max gave the older man a sharp glance and shook his head. "Ash, something's bothering the chief about you, and I'm beginning to get the same vibes. You need to be upfront with us."

Crawford let out a short huff in response, shook his head and walked back outside without any more comment. Max glanced around but saw nothing tied to Clara, nothing that looked out of place.

When Justine and Stef returned, Max and Ash waited. "Anything inside?" Max asked.

"Nope. Chief's not there."

"Told you she wasn't here," Ash said. "Now leave and don't come back. You had no right to come here."

Max gave Crawford a stern look. "You know what, Ash? Chief Jefferies and I are going to figure out what you're hiding. What you aren't telling us about that girl's bones."

From the porch, Justine called out, "You found bones?"

Ash Crawford twisted toward his wife and glowered. "Not now, Justine. Don't be talking to them. They don't know—"

"We did." Max ignored the husband and gave Crawford's wife a sidelong glance. "A teenage girl. Pregnant. Buried on the side of the mountain. Do you know anything about this?"

Justine flushed angry, and Max thought that the woman appeared unsure whether she wanted to slap her husband or embrace him. As if she couldn't make up her mind what to do with him. "Oh, Lord, Ash, did you find our girl and not tell me?"

Max turned to Ash, an indictment in his eyes. In that moment, all doubt was gone. He knew. "Chief Jefferies was right all along, wasn't she, Ash? You do know something about that girl. Maybe that cop in Nevada is right, and you're behind it all."

"Have you lost your mind?" Crawford's face was twisted by anger as he jerked his head at Max. "Damn it, man. Don't you understand? I didn't want to rile her up."

Justine rushed down from the porch. Her husband draped his arms around her shoulders and pulled her close. "You found bones, Ash?" she cried. "How could you not tell me?"

Her husband's voice crackled with the pain of a thousand disappointments. "Because we've been through this too many times, Justine, and it's never been her. And this time, too, it probably isn't. And every time we go through it, both of us, a little bit of us dies."

Tears filled the old woman's eyes. Whatever they were talking about, whoever it was who'd disappeared, the agony lived deep in her heart. "Oh, Ash. Lord Almighty, I told you never to lie to me. You promised, no matter what, you'd tell me the truth."

"I didn't lie. I was just waiting to let you know this time, to save that little bit of you I didn't want to lose."

At that, her head fell against his chest.

"Who are you two talking about? Who is *your girl,* Mrs. Crawford? Tell me," Max said.

Stef hovered behind, watching the old woman melt into her husband's arms. "Our granddaughter, Amy," Crawford explained, tears welling in his eyes. "She disappeared out of Salt Lake four years ago. Left with a boy. They were on the road. We don't know where. We'd heard that they joined a fundamentalist Mormon sect that practiced polygamy. About three years ago, a friend saw her in St. George and Amy was with child. We were hopeful that she was well and her life was working out."

"What changed?" Stef asked.

"Not long after that, her boyfriend turned up dead, body found along the side of a road," Crawford explained, his voice thick with emotion. "No sign of our girl. We've been looking for her and fearing the worst ever since. I retired to search for her."

Max was stunned. "I don't remember seeing anything like this on NCIC. Why didn't you report her missing?"

Anger replaced the sadness on Crawford's face. "They wouldn't take a missing person report because our granddaughter ran away of her own accord. I tried pulling rank, pushing it through, but got turned away. No reason for alarm, the feds told us. No reason to look for her. They kept saying she'd come back home. They convinced our daughter and son-in-law, but Justine and me don't believe it. And none of us have seen anything of her. No word."

"Does she look like the sketch?" Max asked.

"A sketch?" Justine asked.

"Yeah. She does, but it's hard to tell," Crawford said, holding his wife's eyes in his own, as if he talked only to her. "I tried the computer program to match up the skull to a picture of her, and they were close, real close. So I gave Doc Wiley my DNA to check. I asked him not to tell anyone. I didn't want anyone else to know. Someone always leaks these things, and I promised her parents I wouldn't take it public. They think if we do and she sees it, she'll never come home. And I wanted to spare Justine the heartache, if it turns out not to be our granddaughter."

"You should have told us," Max said, his anger building. "Clara sensed something was off. She diverted a lot of energy looking at you instead of for whoever is responsible. That was irresponsible, Ash. You know better."

Rather than apologize, Crawford set his jaw and shook his head. "I had to do what's best for my family. We can't go through this over and over again. It nearly killed Justine with that girl in Nevada."

Max heaved a sigh. As sorry as he felt for the Crawfords, he wanted to shout at the man for wasting their time.

"If the chief's not here, she's…" Max's voice trailed off. He fought back a building dread as he considered how long it had been since anyone had heard from Clara.

CHAPTER FORTY-THREE

"What's wrong with her?" Clyde shouted. "Damn it, Lori, you're going to kill this girl, too."

I heard a lot of commotion inside the cellar room, voices, shouting; the girl, Violet, screamed more often, only a minute or two apart, and the pain, she must have been in tremendous pain.

"We shouldn't have rushed it with the medicine, Clyde. I think the baby's breech. It wasn't ready yet, turned the right way in the womb to be born," Lori shouted back. "But I'm not a doctor. I'm a nursing assistant. All they trained me for was to hand out pills and serve meals, tote bedpans. To help the midwife."

"What do you do at the home when girls have babies that come breech?" he demanded.

"They call a doctor. We should take Violet to the hospital, Clyde. Get the baby out. Save it, so you can sell it to those people. We can't have another dead one."

A dead mother? A dead baby? Again I thought of the girl's bones found on the mountainside. I had to strain to hear his reply. He dropped his voice low and hissed: "You know there's no way in hell we can take this girl to a hospital."

This time Rachel spoke, her voice timid: "What are we going to do?"

Listening to their voices, I could almost picture the scene unfolding in the room. I would have been willing to bet a month's wages that Clyde stomped over to Rachel and stared down at her. "We're going to let nature take its course. Nothing more."

The only translation was that he intended to let Violet and her baby die, just as they had the girl and her baby whose bones were spread out on the autopsy table at the morgue. My heart hurt, and I closed my eyes picturing the grave, knowing that could be Violet, and I was powerless to stop it.

At that, Clyde marched out of the room, and I heard his heavy boots again on the stairs. Moments passed, ones punctuated by more screams. I waited for Rachel to return. My only hope was that she'd finish what she'd begun and untie me. Then, Violet's cries for help waned. She was losing strength. The baby wasn't coming, and she no longer had the energy to fight. I rustled in the chair, tugged as I had since I'd awoken with the bindings on my wrists, but whoever had tied me hadn't made any mistakes.

That rope wasn't budging.

In the distance the girl softly sobbed, as if she'd lost all hope. And in the cellar, behind the shelves, I felt the same despair; perhaps nothing could save us. At that moment, when I had nearly given up, Rachel rushed toward me. She appeared frightened and worried. In my ear she whispered, "If I help you, can you protect me and my children?"

"Yes." That didn't seem to be enough. I wondered what to tell her, what to say. "My friend, Hannah Jessop, do you know Hannah?"

Rachel shook her head.

"She runs a shelter in Alber. Women and their children live there to be safe from their husbands, or some just because they have nowhere else to go."

"Hannah Jessop?" She whispered the name with a sense of wonder, as if surprised that there could be such a woman.

"Hannah will take you in. And I'll put Clyde and Lori in prison, so they can't hurt you. So they can't hurt your children."

At that, Rachel leaned behind me and tugged at the rope restraining my hands. The knots tight, she fumbled, but the bindings loosened and gave way. Once the rope fell to the floor, she knelt to work on the one around my ankles. My hands numb, I turned the rope around my waist until the knots were on my lap. I had one undone and one to go when Lori peered around the shelves. Her face flared red with rage when she saw that I was nearly free.

"What the hell are you doing?" she shouted.

Rachel shot straight up and focused on Lori, terrified.

I kept working on the rope around my waist, but it wasn't giving.

"Tie up her hands," Lori shouted to Rachel. "Now, before Clyde finds out. Or you'll have hell to pay."

Frightened, Rachel stood frozen, as if unable to move. In the room, Violet had gone quiet, and I wondered whether, if I did get free, it would be too late to save her. I kept pulling at that last knot, but then Lori rushed at me. I grabbed her arms. Still tied to the chair, I wrestled with her, until she pulled a hand free and came at me with her fist. I ducked, but she punched me on the side of my face. My head spun, and I tasted something metallic. Blood. I yanked on the rope, but I was still trapped.

"Help me," I pleaded. "Rachel, please, help me!"

"Clyde will kill you for this, Rachel," Lori muttered as she grabbed the rope that had been around my ankles. "You're a dead woman."

Still not a sound out of Violet's room.

Lori seized my right arm while I tried to fight her off with my left. She jerked it behind me and cinched the rope. I thrashed at her with my other hand, but I couldn't catch her. One hand tied, she grabbed for my free hand. I kept swinging at her, grasping at whatever part of her I could reach. In the chaos, I'd lost track of Rachel, but suddenly she stood over us, holding a gallon-size jar of green beans. I ducked and braced for the blow.

The jar came down hard on Lori's head with a thud.

CHAPTER FORTY-FOUR

Stef called headquarters. No one had heard from the chief. Kellie had left multiple messages asking Clara to call in, without an answer. "Do you think something's wrong?" she asked Max over the phone. "Should I let Mullins and the others know?"

"No. It's probably fine. But Stef and I are on the way to Clyde Benson's place to check on her," Max said. "The chief told Stef she was going there. She probably just got tied up with the women, maybe taking a statement. It has something to do with an old case, I guess."

This time, Stef had taken the lead. Since she'd been to Clyde's place before, she knew the route. Back on the highway, they picked up speed and Stef came on the radio. "It was a pretty rough case—child abuse. The pictures were pretty bad."

Max wondered why Clara hadn't told him she was investigating Clyde Benson. They both bought their gas at his station, had their cars repaired there. Max thought that she would have brought it up. But there'd been so much going on, maybe it wasn't surprising that she was distracted. "So Clyde Benson, the one who owns the station, abused one of his kids?"

"Maybe multiple kids, and bad," Stef said over the radio. "He's a violent guy, Chief Deputy Anderson."

Max felt slightly uneasy. "And the chief went out there alone?"

"To see the wives. The chief wasn't worried because Clyde's at the body shop, working, pumping gas. She wanted to talk to the wives, woman to woman, see if they'd open up."

"That makes sense, I guess," Max mused. "But I wish she'd taken someone with her. It's not always the best idea…"

On the highway ahead, he saw the sign for Benson's Body Shop with the missing "B." Something looked odd about it. Not long after five, the afternoon was transitioning to evening. This was the time when Clyde was usually the busiest, pumping gas for the after-work crowd before he headed home himself. The repair shop should have been open, but all Max saw were the abandoned clunkers that had been there for years parked in the weeds.

"Stef, do you see Clyde Benson's truck in the parking lot? He's still there, right?"

Silence for just a moment, then she said, the edges of her voice frayed with worry: "The truck's not there. It's gone. And the 'OPEN' sign is turned off."

"Shit. Stef, drive faster. Something's wrong."

CHAPTER FORTY-FIVE

"Where's my phone and my gun?" I massaged my wrists, and my feet and legs ached from the rope, but I was finally free of the chair. I winced when I touched the lump on the back of my head. From the size of it, it was no wonder that I'd blacked out.

"Lori gave them to Clyde," Rachel said. "I'm sorry."

I shook my head. "It's okay. Any idea where he put them?"

"He's got the gun in his belt."

The last part of that sentence made my stomach churn again. I hadn't noticed the gun when I saw Clyde, but that made sense. While we whispered, Rachel and I tied Lori's wrists and ankles. Unconscious, she was breathing well, and we had no way of telling when she'd come out of it. "We need a gag."

"I'll get it." Rachel ran off and returned a moment later with a baby's onesie.

As I tied it around Lori's mouth, I asked, "How's the girl?"

Rachel shrugged, unsure. "Asleep?"

We dragged Lori farther behind the shelves, where I hoped Clyde wouldn't see her. Then we walked warily around the shelves toward the room where the screaming had come from. I stationed Rachel at the door, to watch for Clyde. As Rachel had said, the girl appeared to be sleeping. Her skin was pale, tinged with gray. The liquid in the IV bag kept dripping. I thought about the Pitocin. That had to be it. I clamped the tube and unplugged it from the bag, then put my fingers on the pulse point in her neck.

"Is she dead?" Rachel asked. She'd walked into the room and stood inside the door, still looking out.

"Not yet, but she needs help. Quick. We need a phone." Violet's heartbeat felt thready and weak.

"We have one in the kitchen."

"Clyde doesn't know what's going on yet, that you're helping me. Before he figures it out, you could sneak up there and make a call to nine-one-one?"

"Me?"

"Please, Rachel. This girl needs medical attention, and they'll send backup. They'll help us with Clyde."

All the color drained from Rachel's face as she shook her head. "He'll catch me." Her hands had that slight shake again, and she didn't try to hide how afraid she was of her own husband. I thought back to a time in my life when the sight of my husband put every nerve in my body on edge.

Then we heard Clyde's boots slapping hard on the aged wooden steps. I pointed at the armoire and mouthed, "Hide."

Rachel slipped quietly over and stood against the wall, behind the armoire's open door. It covered everything but her feet. I searched the room, looking for something to use as a weapon. All I could find was a hypodermic needle, the one that Lori must have used to inject the Pitocin into the IV cartridge. I grabbed it out of the garbage and slipped over and hid next to the open door. *Clomp. Clomp.* He came closer. My heart pounded with each footfall.

"Lori, is that baby born yet?" he called out as he drew near. "I just got off the phone with the couple buying it. They'll be here in the morn—"

One thick brown boot entered the room, then the other. Clyde stared at Violet in the bed, then glanced around the room. He must have seen Rachel's boots because he took a sharp turn toward the armoire. "Rachel, you back there? Where's Lori?"

Distracted, he didn't see me when I rushed out, the needle in my hand, my thumb on the flat end. I had to jump up to plunge the needle into his neck. I hit him on the side, and the thick muscle resisted as I stuck it in. I knew it wouldn't bring him down, only act as a distraction.

He let out a shriek and brought his hand up to the needle and tore it out, looked at it as if surprised. Rachel peeked out from around the armoire door, while I grabbed at his belt, pulled on his pants, looking for my gun. In a single motion, he swung his massive arm toward me and punched me hard across my already throbbing jaw. I fell flat on my back, blood gushing from a split lip. He came at me in a rage. When he got close enough, I snapped my legs up and kicked him smack in his groin. Clyde clutched himself, screamed and cursed. I barreled toward him and knocked him as hard as I could with my shoulder. As he fell, something black skidded out from underneath him.

My Colt Pocketlite .380.

It slid across the tile floor and came to rest at Rachel's feet. Her face blank, she picked it up.

"Give it to me," I shouted, rushing toward her, but Rachel held the gun not on Clyde but with the barrel pointing at me, aimed at my heart. "No, Rachel, no. Give me the gun."

"Yeah, give it to her! Give her a bullet right through that damn brain of hers." Clyde scrambled back onto his feet, and he wore a grin that spread so wide I saw the empty gaps left by his missing molars. "Shoot her, Rachel. Wife of mine, you do as I tell you, shoot her!"

Rachel stared at me down the gun's barrel, and I could almost hear the debate going on inside her head. Should she shoot me and save herself with Clyde? She hated him, that I knew. I just had to remind her. "He'll beat your babies, abuse them, Rachel. He won't stop unless you stop him. You're their mother. You need to protect your children."

"Rachel's my wife. Bound to obey me by the prophet himself. She wouldn't…" He turned toward her, put his hand out. "Give me the gun, Rachel. You know the teachings: you must do as I say."

He edged closer to her, that hand ready to take what he wanted.

"He's going to grab the gun," I shouted. "Rachel, don't let him!"

She swiveled away from me, and pointed the barrel at Clyde, about halfway up his chest to the spot his heart would have been, if he'd been born with one. The fierceness in her words surprised me when she murmured out of nearly closed lips, "Step back, husband. No closer."

"Why you— Put that damn gun in my hand," he ordered, his face flushed with anger, a sneer so evil it could have represented every seed of rage planted in his soul throughout his miserable life. "You are not to disobey your husband, Rachel. You are to do as you are told and never question."

"Keep the gun on him, Rachel. Don't let him fool you. He won't change. He'll abuse you, your children. For as long as you live, he'll take advantage of you, dishonor you."

"Mouth shut!" Clyde shouted at me. He took a step toward her. "Rachel, give me the damn gun!"

I didn't see her finger compress the trigger, but later I thought I saw the bullet leave the barrel and enter Clyde Benson's forehead, the skin tearing open, the membrane parting, cratering through the skull into the brain. Shot one hit him square between the eyes. Shot two went into his open mouth and came out the back of his neck, sending brain and blood spatter across the room. I felt it hit my face, a shower of warm red liquid. Clyde fell with shot three, crumpled in a pile of dying bones, muscles, tendons, and organs. He'd stopped breathing before he hit the ground.

For a moment, we froze. Rachel had a look of surprise, of not understanding quite what she had done. I couldn't wait for her to put it all together. Violet needed help. Rachel didn't fight me when I took the gun from her. "Run upstairs and call nine-one-one. Tell them where we are and that we need an ambulance and backup, a crime scene unit. Tell them I'm here. And tell them to rush!"

I ran over to the bed where the girl lay still, and I began untying the bindings on her arms then her legs. I glanced over at Rachel. Her face drained of blood, looking as if she were in shock, she hadn't moved.

"Now, Rachel! Upstairs! Call for help!" I shouted as I searched for a pulse and found a reedy one on the girl's wrist. "Tell them we need an ambulance, now! This girl still has a chance. She's still breathing."

That somehow hit home, and Rachel ran. I heard her boots pounding up the staircase.

Violet's hand felt cold, too cold. I put my palm on her abdomen, and I felt a flutter. I couldn't think of what to do, what I should do, if there were anything that I might be able to do to save the girl and her child.

"Please, hang on!"

Later, I would try to make sense of it all. It seemed as if she'd gone into a trance and labor had paused, and then restarted, for suddenly she let loose a harrowing scream, a cry that God must have heard in the Heavens. My mother would have described such a scream as one that would raise the dead.

Perhaps it did, for the girl's eyes shot open, and she stared at me. Her irises were such an unusual color, nearly purple, and I suddenly realized why she'd said, "They call me Violet."

Something else: she looked familiar. "What's your real name?"

"Eden," she whispered.

"You're Eden Young."

"How did you…" she started to ask, but then she grabbed the side rails and shouted: "It's coming. My baby is coming!"

"Okay. It's okay," I fought hard not to sound as panicked as I felt. "We're calling an ambulance. I'm Clara, and until it gets here, I'll help you. We're going to get through this together."

"That terrible man and Lori, will they…"

"They can't hurt you. Just stay calm." I considered the location of the house, the distance the paramedics had to drive. I would have given a year's wages for one of the medical helicopters we had in Dallas, the ones that swooped in and ferried the injured to hospitals. Not here. Not rural Utah. Not on my beat. I had to handle this. I brought her legs up and parted them, and I saw flesh. I wondered if Lori was right, if the baby was coming breech. If that was the case, I had no training to help her, no idea of what to do.

"The ambulance is on its way," Rachel said, when she ran in. "And two cars just pulled in, one sheriff's department and the other a police car."

"Go get them," I said. "Bring them down here. They can—"

"Oh, oh God, oh." Eden released another long, deep scream.

"Tell them to hurry," I shouted. "And get me clean towels. Boil some water."

Rachel ran from the room, and I turned to Eden. "I'll be right back!"

She grunted, her abdomen cramping down hard. "No! No! Don't leave!"

"I need clean hands."

I washed Clyde's blood off my face, off my hands using a bar of soap in the laundry tub, then raced back, all the while trying to remember the one-day childbirth class I'd had more than a decade ago. I ran back into the room and found Eden holding onto the railings, grunting. There wouldn't be time to wait for an ambulance, and I wondered again about the baby's position, if Lori was right…

Max and Stef sprinted into the room.

"Did you call an—"

"An ambulance? Yes. But this baby's not waiting."

"What can we do?" Max asked.

"Max, meet Eden Young," I said.

Eden grunted, then gave him a weak smile.

"Well, I'll be..." he whispered.

"No time now," I warned him. "This baby is coming."

On the floor at the foot of the bed, Clyde's body blocked my way. I couldn't get in position to help her. I technically wasn't supposed to move him before the medical examiner and the crime scene folks arrived, but if I had to choose between sticking to the rules and saving Eden and her baby, there was no contest. "Get this body out of here," I said. "Then wash your hands, Max. Stef, there's a woman in the cellar at the back of the shelves. Go check on her. If she agrees to be quiet, you can take the gag out of her mouth, to make it easier for her to breathe. But leave her tied up until this is over."

Stef gave me a nod. "Got it, Chief."

Max and Stef yanked Clyde by his arms and pulled him out of the room. They abandoned him sprawled on the floor outside the door. Stef left to tend to Lori, and I heard Max at the utility tub washing his hands. When he walked back in, I turned to Eden, who was straining and pushing. "Eden, Max is going to help us."

She nodded, but said nothing, grunting, the contractions steady.

"Max, support Eden, give her your hand to hold." He did, and I tried to sound as in control as possible, ignoring the reality, that I had no idea what I was doing and feared I would do it all wrong. "Eden, steady breaths, relax, try to relax."

She nodded. "Can you see Josh?"

"Josh?"

"My baby."

Max looked over at me, sadness in his eyes. This wasn't the way a baby was supposed to come into the world: two amateurs and possibly lethal complications.

"Yes, he's coming. I can see him."

Rachel walked back in carrying a stack of clean towels. I took a couple and laid them under Eden's hips. She was crowning, and relief washed over me when I saw downy blond hair, more than peach fuzz—enough to understand that what I saw was the baby's head, just where it was supposed to be, traveling down the birth canal.

In safer territory, I urged, "Eden, push with the contractions, okay?"

She nodded. The poor kid looked exhausted. Just worn out. "Once the shoulders come out, I can help the baby," I said. "But you need to get it started."

"Owwwww!" A contraction, and Eden clenched her teeth and bore down. The baby slipped forward, its eyes and a tiny nose visible, a bit flat as if it had been smashed from being forced out into the world.

Moment by moment, the miracle of birth unfolded in that terrible room in the cellar of that horrible house where so much evil had lived. Once the baby's shoulders emerged, I did what I remembered the instructor describing, gently guiding this fragile and beautiful human being into the world. He had delicate hands with perfect fingers, eyes scrunched shut and nearly translucent ears. His lips looked like pink begonia petals. In the moments that followed, the baby glided out as I held my hands beneath him. His sturdy little legs bowed and his soft feet ended in ten tiny toes. Max glanced over at me, grinning, and I beamed back up at him. We'd both seen too much death, too much tragedy, but on this day, we were witnessing the miracle of a new life.

"You do have a boy, a beautiful baby boy," I said, and tears cascaded down Eden's cheeks. Max's eyes brimmed, and I felt my own grow watery. The bliss of that moment quickly passed.

"Why isn't he crying?" Eden asked, her voice hoarse with worry. "Is Josh okay?"

"Sometimes it takes a minute…" Frantic but trying not to show it, I wiped off the baby's face and gently rubbed his back. Seconds passed, an agonizing wait, and then his nose twitched, his mouth opened, and Eden's son clenched those miniature hands of his into fists and let loose a wail to announce his arrival into the world.

Eden cried harder, and Max shouted, "Yes!"

I didn't cut the cord, instead left that for the folks who knew how to do it the right way. When I looked up, Stef stood at the door.

"That woman, Lori, okay?" I asked.

"Yeah," she said. "I left her tied up, like you said."

"How far out is the ambulance?"

"Five minutes," she said. "They're under lights and sirens."

"Good." I used the boiled water which had cooled to warm to wet towels to wipe the child. Once I had him fairly clean, I slid over to Eden's bedside. In a moment I would remember the rest of my life, one I would replay whenever my job weighed on me and I wondered what good I had done, I placed little Josh where he belonged, in his mother's arms.

CHAPTER FORTY-SIX

Stef stayed with Eden and the baby while Max and I untied Lori, handcuffed her and hauled her upstairs. We deposited her on a wooden kitchen chair. I noticed my phone on a countertop, grabbed it and stuck it in my pocket. As the wail of sirens filled the air, Max fetched a digital recorder out of his squad. He returned with the EMTs following him. "She's in the cellar," I shouted.

"Got it!" one of them called back.

"Hey, put in a call to Doc Wiley for us. We need the ME. We have a body down there," I shouted.

Max said, "I already did. He's on his way."

Minutes later, Lieutenant Mueller loped toward the stairs to oversee his team. He waved at us as he darted past. When I saw him, I shouted: "We moved the body."

Mueller backed up, did a double take, irritated. "Why the heck would you—"

"So we could deliver a baby," Max said. "The chief didn't have a choice. The guy went down right at the foot of the bed."

Mueller grimaced and didn't look happy, but he didn't argue. His men followed him down the steps and then, to my surprise, Ash Crawford sauntered in right behind them. "I heard through a contact that you found one of the girls. I'm wondering—"

"It's not Amy," Max said, and I gave him a curious look. He shot me one in reply that I interpreted as: I'll explain later.

"Ah, well. I…" Crawford appeared different, more subdued than he'd been, and he turned as if ready to leave, but then, instead, I saw him head down the stairs.

I considered objecting but didn't bother. Crawford would know enough to stay out of the way of the crime scene team. If he didn't, Lieutenant Mueller would kick him out. At that moment, all I cared about was that Eden and her baby were well and that I had Lori and a long list of questions. After Max turned the recorder on, I recited Miranda, and then I started with, "How many?"

Max shot me a curious glance. He, of course, didn't know the extent of what I'd overheard in the cellar. Meanwhile, Lori tied her mouth up in a knot. I asked again: "How many girls have you kept here? How many babies have you taken and sold?"

When she didn't answer right away, Max, his eyes boring into her, pulled a chair up next to Lori's. He positioned it with the back toward the woman and straddled it to get right in her face. "We're going to find out. No question about that. What you need to do is talk to us, so we don't tell the district attorney that you were uncooperative."

Lori didn't look convinced.

"Okay, we're done," I announced. "Let's throw her in a cell and get the DA to draw up the indictments."

Max immediately understood my ploy and played his part. He shot me an exasperated glance, as if I were being unreasonable. "Chief Jefferies, give her a chance. Lori needs time to think it through."

"I don't have the patience. First charge: assaulting a police officer. I've got a knot on the back of my head from this waste of DNA, and I see no reason to bargain with her."

That wasn't entirely true. The best thing was to get her to talk and get a confession, so we weren't scouting around for clues and trying to figure out what had happened in this hellhole from scraps of information. But there was no reason to let her know that. The only way most folks talked when their necks were on the line was if they thought they would benefit. And then she said it.

"What do I get if I tell you everything?" Her attention shifted from Max to me, then back again. "I should get something out of it."

Max frowned, as if he were disappointed. "Not willing to help out just because it's the right thing to do, huh?"

Lori shook her head.

"Well, maybe the chief here would be willing to help me, and we could both talk to the DA for you, if there were extenuating circumstances," he suggested.

Appearing to think about that, Lori bit her lower lip. "Well, Clyde was… he was mean. And I was his wife, told by the prophet to do as Clyde wished, so what was I supposed to do? I had to help him, didn't I, or risk eternal damnation?"

Listening to her, I thought about how my ex-husband had threatened me just a night earlier, saying he'd ban me from Heaven. I considered how beautiful faith could be, but also how a tiny minority, those who falsely claimed to be religious, sometimes tragically misused it to manipulate others. It brought to mind the Bible verse about wolves in sheep's clothing.

Max looked at me. "Chief Jefferies, are you okay with talking to the DA about what Lori just said, letting him know that she was following her husband's orders? We're not making any promises that it will help her, but it might make a difference."

As doubtful as I was that Lori had assisted her husband in his awful crimes purely to gain entry into the hereafter, not for the money it brought them, I played my part and acted as if every word she uttered were gospel. But then again, even if it were true, it wouldn't have helped her. Not when she faced charges of kidnapping and murder.

I smiled at her. "Yes. I'm okay with explaining Lori's situation to the district attorney. I'll explain to him that the prophet's rules instruct a wife to obey her husband."

Lori looked pleased.

"Now tell us: How many?" I repeated.

She took in a couple of deep breaths and huffed them out, thinking, I guessed. "Well, it started about five years ago. There were a couple of girls in the beginning. We brought them here and delivered their babies, then Clyde sold the babies. He threatened the girls, said that if they ever told what we did he would kill them. He dropped the girls in Salt Lake. Told them to forget they ever had those babies. That was the first two."

"And after that?" Max prodded.

"Three more. This one downstairs and the girl you found up on the mountain. We didn't kill her, though. She died trying to have the baby."

"Did you administer the Pitocin?" I asked. If she admitted that she'd drugged the girl, gave her an overdose of the drug that killed her, it would establish guilt. Lori may not think she was a killer, but the law said that she was.

"Yeah, I did, but—"

"I see," I said. "And you mentioned one more?"

"A girl about, well, a month ago, a little more. Another girl from one of the polygamous towns named Samantha. She and Eden were really good friends."

"What happened to her?" I asked.

"I brought her here like the others, and we delivered the baby. After what happened with that other girl, that we had to bury her, Clyde didn't want any bodies to be found. And he didn't want to let her go. He worried those first two girls would tell, and we'd get in trouble."

I felt my stomach cramping. The headache that had eased up came raging back, and I closed my eyes for a moment as Max asked, "Lori, what happened to Samantha?"

"I'm not sure."

I opened my eyes, leaned toward her. "If you want us to talk to the DA for you, you need to tell us everything you know."

Lori screwed her mouth into a nub, thinking. "Well, Clyde got rid of her."

"How?" Max questioned.

"He put her in an oil drum and carted her away." She said it as if it were the most normal thing for her husband to have done.

I thought again about the jugs of lye, the drain cleaner, in the shed. If Clyde Benson wasn't already dead, at that moment, I would have taken my gun and…

I guessed that Max realized by looking at me that it wasn't wise to let me ask the next question. It wouldn't have been the kind that kept Lori talking. I must have appeared ready to attack. And we wanted her to talk. I looked down at the table and the red light beaming on the recorder. No way was I letting any of this slip through our fingers. I wanted a jury to hear every word.

Max talked to the woman for a while, and I calmed down. I had one more question I had to ask. I needed to understand how my two cases had intersected. How had the girls ended up in that cellar room? "Lori, how did you and Clyde find the girls?"

The woman's lips curled up at the edges, as if proud. "I brought them home from work."

"Home from work?" I repeated.

The woman smiled, and I looked at her scrubs and read her name tag again: Miss Lori.

"I work as an aide at a shelter for unwed girls. Runaways and such. The man who owns it finds the girls at bus depots. Their parents drop them there when they get in trouble. At the home, they deliver the babies, tell the girls they put them up for adoption. Really, they auction them off. I told Clyde about it, and right away he said, 'Lori, we could do that, too.'"

I thought of what Sam Young had said, that Eden had run away. "How did this man you're talking about find Eden?"

"Like the others," Lori said, staring at me as if I were trying her patience. "Her dad took her to the bus depot and left her there. He didn't want her anymore."

"And you just brought them home with you?" Max asked.

"Yeah. Kind of," she said, turning her head to the side and squinting at me. "I look for the ones who want to keep their babies, and I offer to help them escape. Instead, I bring them here to the house and we make the money."

"What's the name of the home?" Max asked. Lori said it didn't have a name, but she gave him an address.

"This is where you got the Pitocin from, isn't it?" he asked her, and she nodded. Max turned to me and said, "I got this address this afternoon off the response to one of the subpoenas."

Max looked upset, and I understood why; he'd been so close and hadn't realized it. He pulled out his phone and shot me a pained glance. "Keep tabs on her. I'll be right back."

Max walked over to the corner, and I heard him talk to his boss, telling him what we'd just heard. "How about contacting the sheriff's department in that county? They need to look into this unwed mothers' home. Start an investigation into the place, find out what's going on over there." For a moment, he was quiet, listening. "Thanks, Sheriff. Yeah, we'll have her at the jail shortly. I'll book her myself."

As much as I wanted to, I couldn't haul Lori off to jail. This case, none of it, was in Alber proper, my territory. It was in the county, and Max had jurisdiction. As soon as Max turned back around to us, I asked, "You want to escort Lori downtown for more questions and to talk to the DA? I can stay here and help with the CSU and wait for Doc Wiley."

"Sure. I'll do that," he said. "But let's put her in my squad. I need to tell you something, explain what's up with our ex-US marshal."

I'd nearly forgotten.

We stood outside the squad car, where no one could hear, and Max laid out what they'd learned at Crawford's cabin from Ash and his wife, Justine. I listened, and I thought about Lori's list of victims, the girls they'd lured to the farm. "What's his grand-daughter's name?"

"Amy," Max said.

I popped the squad's back door open and said, "Lori, one more thing, were any of the girls named Amy?"

Lori looked like she didn't want to answer, and I thought she was going to shake her head, then she shrugged like she realized it probably no longer did any good to lie. "That girl you found up on the mountain, the one who died in childbirth. That was her name."

"Where did the man find her?" I asked.

"She was different. Her man had been in some kind of trouble, and after he got killed, she was living on the streets."

There were so many things I wanted to say to her, but while they would have given me pleasure, I couldn't mess up the case. So I made it a point to simply nod at her. Thinking about the one last mystery, the remaining girl who'd disappeared from the area, I asked: "What about Carrie Sue Carter? Is that name familiar?"

This time, Lori appeared genuinely puzzled. "I don't think so. I've never heard that name before."

I said nothing else, but I felt an overwhelming sense of relief. Maybe there was a chance Carrie Sue was still alive somewhere. Maybe she'd truly run away and started a new life. I said nothing more. I simply slammed the car door and turned away from Lori, hoping I'd never see her again.

As Max drove away, the EMTs emerged with Eden on a gurney, holding her baby. They'd cleaned them both up and cut the cord. Ash Crawford, that cowboy hat of his on his head, walked beside them, holding Eden's hand. Maybe, missing his granddaughter, she reminded him of her. When we'd looked at the sketch, the girls looked similar in many ways. I thought about Amy, and how Ash had to be told, then I remembered that Max had said Ash had given a DNA sample to Doc Wiley, and I decided that it made more sense to wait until we were sure. While I was thinking it through, the EMTs loaded Eden into the ambulance.

"How is she?" I called out.

One of the women, a paramedic, waved at me. "Great, because of you. Baby looks good, too."

"I'm going to ride in with them, come back later for my truck," Crawford called out. "Keep her company until you get her parents to the hospital."

I waved at him: "That's great, Ash. Sure. Thank you."

Eden's parents. I thought of the Youngs and how the girl's father had lied to us. Still, maybe there would be a chance that they'd do the right thing. At least this time I had good news to deliver.

As soon as the ambulance pulled away, I called the station. "Kellie, I have a phone number on file for a Sam Young."

Kellie rattled it off and I punched in the call. It rang twice before Eden's father answered. "Mr. Young, it's Chief Jefferies. We've found Eden."

I'd hoped for shouts of joy, at least an inkling of happiness in his voice. Instead, he cleared his throat and then in a monotone asked, "Is she all right?"

"I think so. It turns out that she *was* pregnant. I delivered your grandchild this afternoon."

Silence. *He knew she was pregnant*, I thought. *He'd known all along.*

When he remained quiet, I said, "Eden and the baby, a little boy she named Josh, are in an ambulance on their way to the hospital in Pine City. You and your wives can meet them there. They should arrive in twenty minutes."

Again, he didn't respond. "Mr. Young? Did you hear me?"

"Yes." He hesitated, then said, "I'm glad Eden is okay, and that the baby is all right. But we won't be visiting her. And she's not welcome at the house."

"Mr. Young—"

"I'll tell my wives that you found Eden. They will be relieved. But Eden isn't to come home. We can't have her and the child around our other children, to lead them astray. We follow our prophet's teachings, and Eden is one of the fallen girls now."

Furious, I didn't hold back. "Are you going to tell your wives that they have a grandchild? Don't they deserve to know and to decide for themselves if they want to see Eden and meet their grandson?"

The call went dead. Sam Young had hung up. I stared at my phone's blank screen. I pictured that young girl, thought about how she'd nearly died, and her beautiful baby boy. How sad, how tragic that anyone would think of them as less, simply because of religious dictates. How could a loving God want that for his children? I didn't believe it.

It'd been a long week, but both the cases we'd been working were wrapping up. With Clyde dead, he'd have no trial. All we had was Lori to contend with, and then I remembered Rachel. Where was she? I'd been so busy with Lori's interrogation and the crime scene team that I'd lost track of her. I looked around upstairs, then went down in the cellar. I walked behind the shelves, then backtracked into the room with the bed. The armoire door was open. I looked down and saw Rachel's work boots. Plodding toward her, I thought about what could have happened to me, to Eden and the baby, if Rachel hadn't sided with us, if she hadn't killed Clyde. I closed the armoire, and there she stood, her hands over her face, wet from tears. "Are they going to take me away now?"

I sighed. So much tragedy. Such sadness. And for what? Money. Greed. It felt so senseless. "Rachel, no one is going to take you away. I promise."

After Rachel and I both gave statements, walked through what had happened with Lieutenant Mueller, Doc and the others, I looked at her and said, "Come with me. We're going to get your children."

At that, we began to walk out. But before we left, I asked her to wait for me outside. I stopped to talk to Doc alone. "Is the DNA in? Is the girl from the mountain Ash Crawford's granddaughter?"

Doc frowned, and I knew this was news he hated to deliver. He didn't say a word, just nodded.

"Have you told him?"

"I didn't have time. I just found out before the call came in to come here, to the scene."

I considered what Ash and his wife, his family, had been through. "I'll tell him, Doc."

"No, Clara, I will," Doc said. "Hate to do it, but I'm the one who did the DNA match. And that's my job. I'll have the report to refer to if he has questions."

I considered arguing with him, but then decided Ash might take it better coming from Doc. My relationship with the ex-marshal hadn't been particularly warm. Maybe we could get past that, but it might take time. "I think you'll find him at the hospital with Eden Young. He rode out with her in the ambulance."

"Got it," Doc said.

"Since you'll be there…" I went on to tell him about Eden's father, that her parents wouldn't be coming to the hospital to claim her. More bad news to deliver. I would have done it myself, but I had Rachel and her kids to sort out. I needed to check them into the shelter.

Doc scowled and looked fighting mad. "Damn shame. Makes me sick that the girl's parents would act like that. But don't worry. I'll break it as gently as possible to Eden."

"Thanks. I know you will."

"Oh, one more thing," he said.

I'd already turned to leave, so I glanced back at him. "Your mother was released this afternoon. Your brother Aaron picked her up."

I shouldn't have asked. I mean, I had no reason to, and I knew the answer, but for some reason, I felt compelled: "Doc, did she ever ask about me? Does she know that I was there?"

Doc shook his head. "I'm sorry, Clara. No."

CHAPTER FORTY-SEVEN

It turned out that there were no rooms available at the shelter, so I packed my bags and moved out of mine to make space for Rachel and the Benson kids. I spent the night on a cot in Hannah's room. As tired as I was, I didn't sleep. Every time I closed my eyes, I saw that damp cellar, where for what felt like an eternity, I'd thought I would die. By morning, I'd decided that I'd made some serious mistakes in life. The primary one: I'd left too much unsaid, and I had regrets. None of us know if we'll have tomorrow, and todays pass quickly. Gradually, I decided that life had given me a second chance, and I wouldn't waste it.

A message waited for me when I walked into the police station: DA Hatfield had worked a plea deal with Lori Benson. She'd be spending her life in prison. After all she'd done, it seemed more than fitting. That settled, I cleaned up my paperwork, then told Kellie that I had personal business to attend to. After a stop at an office building on Main Street where I signed a stack of papers, I drove to see my mothers in their trailer under Samuel's Peak.

On the way, I called Max at his office. He started out by telling me that Ash and Justine Crawford would be picking up their granddaughter's bones, and those of Samantha. The crime scene folks had found what little remained of her in an oil drum in the woods. "We contacted Samantha's parents from the information she gave the home, but they refused to claim her. Ash is going to bury the girls together in the church cemetery. He wants them in hallowed ground."

It broke my heart thinking of the two girls and their open grave. "That's kind of him," I said. "Did you ask him about Eden and Josh?"

"They're moving in with him and Justine. They're going to give Eden a job on the ranch, tending the horses, help her finish her schooling. Ash said to tell you Josh is doing well. You know, Clara, I think this might work out. There's a chance they'll form a family."

"I hope so. I think all four of them need each other." Then I got to the reason for the call. "Max, are you and Brooke busy tonight?"

"What do you have in mind?"

"We never had our dinner this week."

"Pizza?"

"I was thinking of something a bit fancier. Something to fit the occasion."

Max sounded confused. "What occasion? Oh, gee, did I forget your birthday?"

"No." I laughed. "I thought maybe that little place on the edge of town, the steak place? It's quiet, and we won't be interrupted when we explain things to Brooke."

Max was silent for a moment, then his voice became soft, urging. "Clara, you need to tell me what this is about. I don't want to guess."

I slowed down at the entrance to the trailer park to let a tow truck hauling a broken-down pickup pull out. "I'm sorry I dragged my feet. I realize now that you've been right all along. We need to stop hiding."

"You're sure?" I heard doubt in his voice.

"I am. And the first person we need to tell that we're dating is Brooke."

Max sighed. I don't know if he sounded happy, maybe more relieved. "I wasn't sure I'd ever hear you say those words."

We made plans for later that evening and hung up as I parked outside the run-down double-wide where my three mothers and a good number of my siblings and half-siblings lived. Two tractors worked in the cornfield behind the trailer, getting it ready for the spring planting. I passed the outhouse, sprinted up the cement steps and pounded on the rickety storm door. In the distance, I saw Delilah and Lily playing with a pack of the youngest children. They waved at me, and I waved back. My heart drummed hard in my chest. Nerves. Mother Naomi opened the door. She looked alarmed to see me.

"Clara, does your mother know you're coming? No one told us that—"

"No. No one knows. But get Mother and Mother Sariah. We have something to discuss. I'll be in the kitchen."

I should have realized that it would take time to bring Mother. I wondered if I should be doing this, but I had fences to mend that couldn't wait. What if Mother died? What if I did? One or the other of us would be left with regrets. I didn't plan to spend the rest of my life without a family. I thought about what Doc had said, that Mother shouldn't be upset, but life always has ups and downs. She couldn't live cushioned by bubble wrap, nothing ever touching her. To be alive is to endure pain along with the joy. And I knew my mother. She'd had a rough road, but I knew not to underestimate her strength.

Mother Sariah wheeled her in. Mother appeared shriveled in her chair and she kept her head down, as if embarrassed. I saw that the right side of her mouth drooped just a touch from the stroke. Her hand was clasped around a tennis ball, I assumed to keep it from clenching into a fist.

They pushed her to the table, got her settled, and took their own chairs.

Mother held up her good hand, pointed it at me, and her mouth struggled, attempting to form words. Spittle drooled down her chin, and Mother Naomi wiped it away, as Mother pointed from me to the door. I understood what she wanted, but I stayed.

"Why are you here?" Mother Naomi asked.

"I have a proposition for all of you." At that, I pulled the paperwork out of my bag and placed it on the table. "A little while ago, I made an offer on a house in Alber. The real estate agent contacted the buyers, and they've agreed to accept it."

Mother shook her head. That good hand of hers went up again, and she struggled, tried hard to form her lips the right way. "N-n-n." She pointed at the door again.

"I understand. You're saying, 'No.' You want me to leave. But you don't even know what you're objecting to yet." I put my hand over her paralyzed one, trying to calm her. "Mother, you need to hear me out."

"Listen to Clara, Ardeth," Mother Sariah urged. She appeared intrigued. "Please, let her talk."

Mother's good hand dropped onto her lap and she turned her head from me and toward the door, as if again trying to order me away. Her face swiveled back to me when I said, "Mother, the house I'm buying is our house, the home I grew up in."

Mother Naomi raised her hand to her chest, as if in shock, while Mother Sariah reached over and grabbed the papers from me. She paged through them. "Is this true? It's the right address. Look, Ardeth." Mother Sariah held the paperwork in front of my mother.

"Are you planning to live in it, Clara?" Mother Naomi asked, staring at me as if trying to decipher my intentions.

"I'll be moving into the room over the garage, refurbishing it and putting in a small kitchen."

My three mothers glanced from one to the other. Then Mother Naomi asked the question I felt certain they were all thinking: "Who will live in the main house?"

"I'm hoping all of you will," I said. "And that you'll bring the children. If you need more room, you can put the trailer where it used to be in the backyard."

They looked from one to the other, as if unable to truly understand. "We can't afford..." Mother Sariah started.

"Rent-free. The only catch is that I will be in the garage apartment," I said, watching for clues in their faces. "I can't afford to pay the mortgage and rent an apartment for myself. So the house and I are a package deal."

Mother Sariah looked stunned, but Mother Naomi had a grin on her face. "Praise the Lord," she screamed. "We are saved!"

Meanwhile, Mother, who has never been an easy woman, bowed her head and shook it, every ounce of determination she'd retained evident.

I'd expected as much. I knew this wouldn't be easy, that she wouldn't come willingly. I was prepared to wait her out. Not wanting an argument, I stood. "Mother, I am staying in Alber. This is my home. This is where my job is. It's where my heart is. With all of you. You are my family." I paused, wondering if I should say more, then decided I had to. Like Max telling Brooke, it was better coming from me. "And with Max Anderson. We're dating. I haven't told him yet, but I love him. And I'm hoping he loves me."

Mother Sariah stood and grabbed me, hugged me, and whispered in my ear, "Oh, Clara, I am so happy for you."

"This is a godsend, a new start for us all," Mother Naomi said. "We will praise the Lord for our good fortune, Ardeth. He is good to us."

Meanwhile my mother saw it very differently. She kept her head bowed, and slowly shook it back and forth. There was no mistaking her message. She would have none of it. At that, Sariah let go of me and took a step away.

"Oh, Ardeth, please," she said. "Don't do this to Clara, to us."

Mother Naomi began to cry and ran from the room. Even in Mother's fragile condition, she ruled that house. She remained the head of the family.

My head still ached from the blows I'd taken at the Benson place, my face was bruised and I had a butterfly bandage holding together the cut in my lip. At that moment, I didn't have it in me to argue. So, I said the last of what I'd come to say: "The family selling the house has already moved out. I will take occupancy in one month. At that time, I will move into the garage apartment. Any or all of you are welcome. If none of you decide to join me, I understand. But I'm not renting the house out, Mother. That big house will be empty. Waiting for all of you."

At that, I turned and walked out the door, not giving any of them time to answer.

From the trailer, I drove back to the station. I shuffled in the back door and found Kellie sitting on the corner of Bill Conroy's desk, laughing. I probably should have acted annoyed, but I was too happy being alive, and besides, who was I to tell anyone whom to fall in love with? At least she'd come in dressed appropriately, in a skirt and sweater.

"Messages? Mail?" I asked.

Kellie jumped up, looking as if she'd been caught. "Yes, Chief. I'll get them."

Once I had them in my hand, I walked toward my office, but I turned back. "Conroy, are you on tonight?"

"I'm just here cleaning up paperwork. I don't really start for three more hours," he said. "Do you need anything special?"

"Find out how Gladys's son's team is doing. If they're winning. Leave me a note?"

Conroy broke into a grin. "You bet."

At my desk, I rifled through the messages. The pink envelope was the fourth one in the pile. I smelled the vanilla before I saw it. I reached down in my drawer and pulled out a pair of latex evidence gloves. Same handwriting. Postmarked two days earlier. I cut it open with a letter opener, pulled out the single sheet of paper and unfolded it.

I WARNED YOU. YOU DIDN'T LISTEN. NOW IT'S TOO LATE.

A LETTER FROM KATHRYN

I want to say a huge thank you to you for choosing to read *The Blessed Bones*. If you enjoyed it and want to keep up to date with upcoming books in the Clara Jefferies series, just sign up at the following link. Your email address will never be shared and you can unsubscribe at any time.

www.bookouture.com/kathryn-casey

Where did the idea for this book come from? Years ago, when I wrote for magazines, I interviewed a woman who was sold as a child. She talked about her struggle to find her biological mother, and how she'd been robbed of her family. She wondered what kind of life she would have had, how different it would have been, if the doctor who'd told her mother she died at birth hadn't sold her to a childless couple.

I've never forgotten my day with that woman. Her story touched my heart, and I will remember it always. Like Eden, her mother was an unwed teenager, one with few options, but one who wanted to keep her child. That's not always possible; not all of us make the same decisions, and no one decision is right for everyone, but I remember thinking during the interview how important it was for everyone's rights to be protected and for all of us to be heard and respected.

In closing, I hope you loved *The Blessed Bones*. If you did, I would be grateful if you would write a review. I'd appreciate hearing what you think, and it makes such a difference helping readers discover my books. I truly enjoy hearing from readers, and you can get in touch on my Facebook page, through Twitter, Goodreads, email or my website.

Thank you again, and happy reading,
Kathryn

kc@kathryncasey.com

kathryn.casey.509

@KathrynCasey

www.kathryncasey.com

ACKNOWLEDGMENTS

There are always so many to thank when I finish a book. Regarding *The Blessed Bones*, I'm very grateful for the assistance of the following people:

Texas Ranger Lt. Wende Wakeman for sharing her expertise.

Retired prosecutor Edward Porter for his support and advice.

My literary agent, Anne-Lise Spitzer.

My reader: Sue Behnke.

All the wonderful people at Bookouture: my editor, Jennifer Hunt, who has taken such great interest in the Clara Jefferies series. She's been there from the beginning. Also: Alexandra Holmes, Fraser Crichton, Jenny Page, Lucy Dauman, Alex Crow, Sarah Hardy and Jenny Geras.

As always, I thank my husband and my entire family for their constant support. I love all of you. This book is dedicated to my three brothers and their wives. I don't get to see them as often as I'd like, but I appreciate them more than I can say. Like Clara, I believe family is important.

Finally, I am very grateful to all of you who read my books. Without you, I wouldn't be able to do what I love. And a special note of appreciation to those of you who recommend my books to others. You make a world of difference.

You've just finished reading *The Blessed Bones*, the third book in the Clara Jefferies series. I've loved writing it, and I look forward to many books to follow.